The Grey House

CAT STARK

Also by Cat Stark

The Elven Prince (novel)
Enter the Maze (short story collection)

CAT STARK

The Grey House
A World of Contagion Trilogy

Cat Stark

ISBN: 0-578-53631-5
ISBN-13: 978-0-578-53631-6

DEDICATION

This Trilogy is dedicated to Travis Legge
Whose ambition sparked my own.

ACKNOWLEDGMENTS

This trilogy was originally finished in 2006. Thanks to those who helped me the first time around. There were many. Special thanks go to Corey Frang who helped me understand computer terminology from that era a little bit better. Tim Stotz for helping me come up with L337. jason ssg who encouraged me to understand that a vampire had to be more than a human with sharp teeth.

I finally decided it was time to publish this trilogy in 2016. It took a long time to get it ready. Thanks to the people that helped me this time around. Richard Pulfer, Katie Eickman and Kelly Fields, my friends and editors. Miranda McMahan and Caitlin Campbell my readers. And to Travis Legge, who created the World of Contagion and allowed me to use the setting for my imagination.

1

Natalia looked around the bar from her perch on the second floor. The bar, Lava, wasn't too large. There was room for about three hundred people in the two-level establishment. It was a long room, with a well-stocked bar on the wall opposite the door. Stools were lined up along the bar. A stage sat to the right, in front of floor to ceiling windows. There were tall tables with bar stools along the walls, but not many. The downstairs was meant for mingling. The upstairs was meant for people watching.

Lava's upstairs was not a full floor. The middle of the floor was cut out, with waist high railings along the edge. There were tall tables with bar stools along the railings to allow guests to observe friends and strangers downstairs. If intimacy was desired, comfortable couches were scattered around the wall. The upstairs was dimly lit and most of the light came from downstairs.

The bar was popular, and a good crowd had gathered. Natalia could duck behind people if she needed to and keep an eye on her target. She almost laughed at the word. He wasn't really her target, but she couldn't think of a better word. As the DJ flawlessly switched from one song to the next, Natalia took a sip of her soda and looked around again. From her seat, she could clearly see the front entrance. She sat on a couch on the second level and watched as people entered the bar.

"Hey. You don't look like you're having fun." Bethany sat down next to Natalia.

Natalia placed a smile on her face and tried not to be irritated at her best friend. Bethany didn't know Natalia's true reason for being here tonight, but that was all right. The ladies had been friends for fourteen years. After all this time, Bethany was still oblivious to the world around her, and

Natalia planned to keep it that way.

"I had a rough day, but I'm having fun. All I want to do is sit and people watch." She gave Bethany a real smile. "I warned you I wouldn't be much fun."

Bethany leaned back on the couch. "You haven't even danced. The songs are pretty good and there are a bunch of people dancing. Come on. One dance!"

Natalia laughed as Bethany's lighthearted attitude washed over her. "All right."

"Awesome!"

Natalia followed Bethany and headed downstairs. She wasn't looking to approach the vampire tonight, therefore it didn't matter too much if she missed seeing him. She wanted mostly to make sure he was the type of vampire she could approach. She had found him on social media and liked what he posted. He showed off artwork and quoted Buddha a great deal. She didn't think it was smart for a vampire to use social media, but for some reason, he did. It made him easier to find, but that wasn't always smart. A Slayer could find him as easily as she could.

As Bethany and Natalia found a good spot to dance, Natalia took a deep breath and let her worries go. She would be back in two nights to look for him without Bethany. It would be easier then.

 beginsegment ✸ ✸

Tony Lam looked like his profile picture. His short, dark hair was tousled, as if the wind had blown it around. His easy smile reached his eyes; a good sign. He was dressed in dark jeans and a plain green t-shirt. He walked around the bar, talking to people and seemed to know one or two. He engaged in conversation with the bartender and ordered a beer in a bottle. From her perch, Natalia watched him carefully and noticed that though he carried the drink around, he never drank from it.

She planned on staying in her spot upstairs for an hour or two, to simply watch him. She had a tablet in hand and occasionally took pictures and typed. She had a fake social media page and blog site up, in case anyone asked what she was doing. She would show curious onlookers her page and let them know she was trying her hand at blogging local events. All the while, she kept Tony Lam in sight, to see what he was up to.

At the end of her two hours, Natalia left the bar. She had watched him enough and he was starting to act as if he could feel her eyes on him. Satisfied, but not yet ready to approach, she knew she would be back. He liked coming to Lava when there was a DJ. The DJ was there Tuesdays and Thursdays. She would be back next week to watch him some more.

Natalia watched Tony Lam for three weeks before she felt ready to interact with him. It was late on a Thursday and he was carrying around a second drink. He had stepped into the bathroom a few minutes earlier with a nearly full drink. He came out with no bottle and ordered a second one. She was pretty sure he dumped out his beer in the bathroom sink. He never drank anything.

After he had his second drink in hand, she watched as he stepped outside. It was a warm San Francisco night. There was a patio out back, with tables and chairs. Natalia followed him out and walked right up to him. She tapped him on the shoulder and smiled.

"Hi. I think I've been following you on Instagram. You're @LonelyTony, right?"

He laughed. "Yeah." Tony smiled. "And who might you be?"

"Leslie Childers."

He smiled again. "An actual name. I like that. Most people tell me their Instagram name. My name is Tony Lam."

"I know. I found you on Facebook, too."

He smiled. "I hope you're not stalking me."

Her eyes grew big in fake surprise. "Oh goodness, no! I saw you here awhile back and then thought I saw you online."

Tony laughed. "No worries. Buy you a drink or something?"

"Um…" She wanted to turn the talk to something else and looked around to see if anyone else was close by. A noise in the distance caught her attention but faded too quickly. "Not really a drinker." She turned back to him. "You don't really seem to be either."

They stared at each other for a moment before he put his drink down. "This doesn't feel like a social call anymore."

The noise came again, and Natalia's breath caught. The patio was fenced off but faced an alley. The fence was shoulder high and was only there to keep people from wandering into the alley with a drink in hand. There were voices coming down the alley and she could now hear them.

"You're sure he's here?" The gruff voice chided.

"Yes. He checked in on Facebook." This voice was younger.

"I don't even understand what you said."

Natalia looked around fast, noticed they were alone on the patio and turned back to Tony. "Are you full?"

He stepped back. "What?"

She glared but kept her voice down. "Are you at full blood?"

Tony's eyes went wide.

"There are Slayers coming down that alley. Probably looking for you. Are you at full blood?"

He looked over her shoulder as the voices grew closer. "Yes."

She grabbed him around the neck. "Jump!"

It was a command, said softly but firmly into his ear. He did as told and jumped to the rooftop. Once there, Natalia let him go and peered over the edge. She had read that older vampires at full blood could jump rather high and run faster than the eye could see. She was impressed, and not only because it got them away from the approaching Slayers. She and Tony were only two stories up and she could see the men coming into the alley. Dean was in front, leading Zechariah. She breathed a sigh of relief and turned to Tony. She moved away from the edge and indicated he should do the same. When they were away from the edge, she realized he was appraising her.

"You know what I am."

"Yes, and I can offer you blood for getting us out of here."

"And why don't I just leave you here?"

"My name is actually Natalia. I have some questions I think you can answer. I've tracked you for some time, Mr. Lam and I'm willing to pay for the information I need."

"What are you?"

"Human." She said it without fear. Telling him what she was would give him nothing but advantages.

"And the people down below?"

"Slayers."

He cringed. "You know them?"

"I work with them on occasion, but the angels don't talk to me. I make my own decisions."

"How do I know I can trust you?"

"You don't, but I did warn you about the Slayers. I'm not trying to get you killed. I'm trying to get some information and I can help you get out of the city." Her hand strayed to her small silver beaded necklace, as she wondered if she would have to hypnotize him into helping her. She hoped she wouldn't. She preferred allies.

"Why out of the city?" He crossed his arms.

"They're hunting you and other old vampires. Not sure why, but I know they know who you are."

He sighed. "Let's go someplace safer. Looks like they're going around to the front. They might be able to sense me."

Her hand dropped from her necklace. "Where to?"

Tony picked Natalia up in his arms without a word and ran. Everything passed by in a blur, as if they were on a bullet train. After a few minutes of running and jumping, he stopped. When they stopped, he let her go and Natalia stepped away. She breathed deeply to allow her heart to calm down. The trip had left her a little lightheaded. As her breath slowed, she looked around and saw they were not in the same area, but still on a roof.

"Impressive."

"Thank you."

She leaned against the low wall around the edge of the roof. "You'll want blood."

He took a good look at the human. She was tense, and her arms were crossed. Tony guessed she didn't want to give him blood but would. "Let's take care of that after we understand what we both want."

"That sounds fair."

Tony leaned against the wall close to her. "How long have you been following me, really?"

"The Slayers have been looking for older vampires for a while. I think they've known about you for a year or more but didn't start tracking you until recently. I found out about you a couple months ago. I just didn't want to approach you too soon."

"Why me?"

"Well, Mr. Huang Lam, you've been in San Francisco for decades. Like I said, I think you can help me with information. I tracked you here about three weeks ago."

"I haven't heard my first name since the earthquake in '06." He shook his head. It was obvious she had done her homework. "I thought someone was watching me. I thought it might be Slayers."

"They may have been. They don't always tell me who they're watching."

"Don't trust you?"

"Not entirely." She didn't sound worried.

"Do they know you work with both Slayers and vampires?"

"No, and I'd like to keep it that way."

"Ok." He gave her a skeptical look. "What are you looking to find out?"

"I'm trying to find the vampires that are running this city. I heard there were a few vampires in this area that have been here since the city was founded. I wanted to talk to one who might be able to give me information on the newest problem. Do you happen to know who is trying to be in charge?"

Tony thought about it for a moment. "I don't have his last name, but there's a vampire named Christopher who seems to have taken control. He's been sending people out to try and get others to join him."

"Why won't you join him?"

"I don't like groups. Most vampires don't like being controlled by other vampires. I don't know how he's doing it. I have a feeling he's killing the older ones off and changing new ones, forcing them to live how he wants." He shook his head. "The thing is, Christopher seems to have left the area. Edwin is in control now."

"Is Edwin older?"

"No. Fairly young."

"I've heard rumors of another vampire in the area. An older one. A lot of Slayers think he's the one who's really in charge."

Tony frowned at her. "Who?"

"Vincent Grey."

Tony laughed. "Vincent isn't with them. He reached out to me; offered me safety and money if I joined his people."

"Why didn't you?"

"Told you: I don't like other vampires."

"What do you know about Vincent?"

"I don't have too much information. I know he owns a couple places in the area. I can tell you the names of his businesses, and you can find out more on your own."

"Ok, what are the names?"

"No, this is where we negotiate. What can you do for me?"

"Blood or money."

He frowned at her. "Don't play stupid. You've already proven you're not."

Natalia nodded her agreement. "Human has to try."

He laughed. "All right. Of course, I want your blood. Especially since you've already offered. As for money, I was changed when I was a railroad worker in the late 1800s. I learned to save. I need a place to go. Give me the contacts, and I'll give you the information."

She didn't even pause. "Where?"

"How far East can you get me?"

"I know a couple people in Washington, D.C., one in Boston."

"Friendly to my kind?"

"I wouldn't have listed them if they weren't."

"How soon can I leave?"

"You tell me the information I want, I'll send you a private message on Facebook, under the Leslie Childers profile with one contact."

"Why only one?"

"These people owe me favors. I give you their contact information, I lose those favors. You get one contact."

"I would have to choose between Boston and D.C. now?"

"Yes."

Tony thought about it for a moment, then nodded. "Blood first."

She nodded, took a deep breath and held out her arm, hoping he wouldn't demand blood from her neck. It was more dangerous if he took from her neck. Tony came closer, took her arm in his hands and bent to bite into her tender flesh. He bit her inner arm, near her elbow. She winced at the pain but didn't pull away as he drank a few swallows of her blood. When he pulled away, she covered her arm with a cloth handkerchief she pulled from her back pocket.

Tony licked his lips and smiled. "Vincent owns a restaurant called The Ocean's Edge and a nightclub called The Red Thread. Other businesses too, but I don't know them all."

She nodded and pulled her mobile device out of her front pocket

"Boston or D.C.?"

He thought about it for a moment. "Boston seems like a better idea."

She chuckled. "I think so, too." Natalia entered the information into her phone then went to Facebook and sent him the information. Natalia looked to Tony.

"Sent."

He grabbed his own mobile device out of his pocket and checked his messages. The information for her contact in Boston stared back at him. He nodded. "Thanks."

"You sure you don't need anything else?"

"I want to know more about you, but I don't think there's time for that."

"Even if there was, I wouldn't tell you much."

"Fair." He looked around. "You know where you are?"

"Yep."

"Good."

With that, he was gone. It surprised Natalia how fast he could disappear. She shook her head then looked around and found the entrance to the stairway. The door was locked, but that didn't stop her for very long. She knew how to pick locks, and this was a cheap one. She was on the street and on her way home shortly after Tony Lam left.

By the time she arrived home, Natalia already had a message from the contact she gave Tony. She told her contact Tony needed a safe place to go; she considered it a favor. The contact thanked her and told her she still had a favor or two left. After that, the message ended. If the contact information had been given in distress, the message would have been far different. Knowing Natalia had given the name freely, the contact was no longer worried and would invite Tony Lam into their home and help him get settled.

That taken care of, Natalia searched for Vincent's businesses online and found a lot more information than she thought possible. When she searched his name before, without the business names, she came up with too many results. The business names narrowed the results to one person. She found public records on his businesses in the area. She also found his current birth certificate and a photo ID. Vincent Grey's information stated he was in his 30s, but the photo was terrible. Still satisfied with the night's work, Natalia readied for bed. She had a meeting with Zechariah and the other Slayers early the next day.

2

Natalia settled into a wooden chair, wishing the library had better seats. The wooden seats had just enough cushion to look pretty, and that was all. She would be here for about an hour, if everyone else showed up in time. Zechariah liked meeting in public places, as that made it harder to target him and his group. Natalia preferred public places too, as it made it harder for Zechariah and the others to get too loud.

She came to the reserved room first, mostly to get the best seat. She liked to sit facing the door, with only the wall at her back. It made it harder for anyone to sneak up on her. She didn't trust the Slayers and had a feeling they didn't trust her either, due to her checkered past with them. It didn't matter. As soon as she could, she would find someone else to work with. Problem was, there weren't that many people she could turn to.

Most humans, like Bethany, were unaware of the creatures in the shadows. Natalia felt it best to keep Bethany and other humans unaware of the creatures. She learned herself, at too early an age, that monsters existed. Not all were non-humans like vampires or werewolves, either. Some of the worst monsters she'd met were humans. Still, the human ones could be held in jails, prisons and hospitals. No one could contain a werewolf in jail. Not for long anyway.

That's where the Slayers came in. They were sent by God to hold back the monsters. Most times, Slayers killed the monsters outright, even if there were humans around. Natalia didn't agree with that. She felt there was a better way. She found she could approach most vampires if she was careful. Sometimes, she could approach werewolves, but they were trickier. Too close to the full moon, their rage was just under the surface. She rubbed her shoulder as the memory of Charlie's betrayal came back to her.

Natalia found out the truth about the world when her mother started dating someone who appeared to be a vampire. While trying to find out more about vampires, she ran into a werewolf name Charlie, who helped her escape a Slayer. She rubbed her face in her hands as the memories threatened to take hold. She didn't want to remember right now. It wasn't a good time.

Natalia shoved her memories aside and turned her attention back to her tablet. The tablet was encrypted; only she knew how to open it. Even if someone did get it open, they wouldn't be able to read any of it. She had a B.S. in Computer Science, and a minor in Romance Languages. She currently worked for a game company part time, writing code for games. Using her skills, she had hacked her tablet and programmed it in a mixture of Latin, Romanian and French. She could read everything easily, but no one else could.

She typed some information into the tablet, then changed the screen to a blank note page when the door opened. She smiled to Dean as he walked in. "Didn't know if you'd be here today."

"Zechariah wants me here. Says you have information on one of the head vampires?"

"Sort of. I'll bring everyone up to date."

Dean smiled and sat down. He absentmindedly rubbed at his face, which was covered in acne. He was young and had joined with the Slayers when he was barely fourteen, even though he wasn't a Slayer. He couldn't hear the voices of the angels in his mind as the Slayers could, but he hoped to hear them one day.

Natalia thought of forming a group with people like Dean. People that had lost family to vampires in the area, but who didn't hear the voices. She felt they were more able to see that not all the vampires and creatures of the shadows had to die. Dean was still too close to the death of his family though. He was convinced that the angels would talk to him one day. Natalia almost hoped not. Slayers only saw black and white, good and evil. The world wasn't that simple.

She sighed and pulled her loose black hair into a ponytail as the door opened again. Zechariah and Judith walked through the door. The two settled into their seats and Zechariah started the meeting. Natalia listened and added her opinions when needed but didn't over share. They spoke of their loss of Huang Lam, annoyed that he had slipped through their fingers. Once they went through other vampires they were looking into, Zechariah turned to her.

"Natalie, did you find anything more on who is trying to run the vampires in San Francisco?"

She glared at him for not saying her name right. She didn't say anything as he seemed to do it to push her buttons. "Vincent Grey isn't the head of the vampires. A man named Edwin is. His group is the one killing the kids."

"Are you certain?"

"No, but I have an interview at one of Vincent's establishments this weekend. I'm going to get a job at The Ocean's Edge as a waitress to see if I can learn anything more. We might want to look at one of his other establishments, The Red Thread. They aren't hiring there, but you may want to have people watching that club."

She didn't want to give them that much information, but all she said they would be able to find if they looked online. Zechariah didn't use the internet too much, but Dean did. He searched online almost as much as she did.

"How safe is it to get a job there?" Dean asked with true worry in his voice.

"It's a five-star restaurant. There haven't been any killings or murders there." Sometimes, when a vampire or other creature owned a business, there seemed to be a lot more crime than one would expect at the establishment. Vincent Grey seemed to know how to stay safe.

"Don't you already have a job, though?"

She looked to the young man. "Dean someone needs to do this. I'm the best bet. They seem to prefer women as servers."

That wasn't true. She had stopped by the restaurant during the lunch rush to pick up an application and during the dinner rush to drop it off. Their wait staff seemed to be a good mix of all genders, but she wanted to be the one to approach Vincent. If he wasn't the one causing the problems in the area, she wanted to find a way to warn him of the danger of Slayers.

Some time ago, she found a few Slayer journals with passages about Vincent. He was almost 300 years old. After finding more about him online Natalia knew he was quite the looker. He also did his best to work with humans, not use them only as food. He didn't cause problems for humans, only Slayers.

"Natalie!"

She looked up. "What? Sorry."

Zechariah glared at her. "Let me know if you get a job there. We'll need to plan our next move."

"Of course."

He nodded and looked to the others. "All right. Any other business?"

The others mumbled and shook their heads. Zechariah nodded, waited for Judith and both left the room together. Dean looked to Natalia, who smiled and went back to looking at her tablet. He took the hint and left her alone. Natalia waited ten minutes, then left as well.

CB EO

"I don't think that's a good idea." Natalia spoke into her phone, trying not to clench her teeth.

"The Ocean's Edge is an easier target."

"Zechariah, I've been there six months, now. It's an establishment for humans. The police will get involved."

"They may anyway."

She closed her eyes, glad the Slayer couldn't see her reaction. She licked her lips, took a deep slow breath and tried again. "Let me see if I can get into The Red Thread. Please."

He was silent for a while with only the sound of his breathing coming through. Finally, "Fine. See if you can. God keep you well."

Zechariah hung up as did Natalia. She was nearly shaking as she turned off her phone. She needed to calm down and didn't want to deal with any more calls or texts from the Slayers. She paced her living room, trying to calm down. He wanted to set bombs at The Ocean's Edge. Natalia had been trying to convince him of how bad an idea that was for the past month. Today was the first time he had decided to listen to her plan to try to get into The Red Thread.

Natalia took deep, slow breaths and calmed down. She hoped working with Zechariah was temporary. She had to find another way, but didn't know where else to learn about Hellspawn.

Slayers were dangerous and unpredictable, as were vampires and werewolves. Natalia rubbed her shoulder as thoughts of Charlie came back. She shook her head and stopped pacing. Charlie had broken her trust; Zechariah had as well. Natalia wondered, not for the first time, if it was time to head out on her own to find her mother's killer. She didn't know what Zechariah might do to her in the future, but she still remembered the day he locked her in the spiked closet.

Natalia took a deep breath and tried to let the memories go. It was a long time ago, and she had other things to take care of. She needed to focus on how to get into The Red Thread, Vincent's night club. She had staked it out a few times and knew it was a membership only night club. She nodded to herself as she reached for the silver hypnosis necklace she always wore.

She twirled the beads and started to pace. She knew there was a doorman on street level. She would need to get past him. Once inside, she would find out more. It might take more than one trip to understand where she could go. A determined smile came to her lips. Natalia knew she could get into the place. It was only a matter of time.

3

Vincent was bored and was progressing beyond bored into highly annoyed. The Red Thread was <u>his</u> club. Yet, there was Edwin, waltzing into the room with his bodyguards as if he owned the place. He had five bodyguards shadowing him and another ten arrayed about the room. The bodyguards, were of all different walks of life. The younger vampire was like a plague in Vincent's club. Too many of Edwin's people felt they could act and dress as they pleased, even at a social affair. Most of the bodyguards, regardless of gender, were dressed in ripped jeans and dirty t-shirts.

At least Edwin was dressed better than usual. His black slacks were a good choice, but the yellow shirt made him look like a canary with flamingo legs. Edwin was the Captain of San Francisco, or rather, as he was very quick to remind everyone with a coy smile on his face, he was the Acting Captain. And <u>that</u> was what made the whole situation rather irritating.

For the past ten years Vincent Grey and his people had been traveling to various cities in the United States, trying to discern which city most needed their attention. For the most part, Vincent didn't interfere when vampires roamed a city. If they lived their lives peacefully with humans, nothing needed to be done. Every so often, he would find a city with vampires that desperately needed to be reined in, like San Francisco. The vampires who were in semi-control here were allowing atrocities to be committed and laughing about it, while the Slayers moved in, making it hard for those like him to be able to live. His people started coming here in stages for the past five years, assessing the situation and plotting.

San Francisco was currently one of two cities where there was a group of governing vampires. Most of the time, vampires didn't listen to other vampires. They preferred to roam cities unhindered by rules. Lorraine

Graves ruled New York City. She took over when too many vampires started killing too many humans. Lorraine took over to keep Slayers out and her and her people safe. She had been in charge for a few years and loved it. Her human family had been nobility, and now she was again.

Christopher Tyler, the original ruler of San Francisco, had lived in New York and liked the idea of people giving him tribute and bringing him tasty treats. He went to San Francisco and took over by changing people he could keep under his thumb and killing those he couldn't. Christopher had been an ensign in the navy before he was changed. Upon taking control of San Francisco, he called himself Captain and his underlings Lieutenants and Sergeants. Now, the vampires were even more out of control than they had been before Christopher took over. Vincent couldn't accept the situation.

A few months ago, Vincent tried to take over. He and a few of his men went to Christopher's home to confront him and kill him, only to find that the vampire had left on a quest the night before. The man was always off trying to find artifacts that would make him invincible. Usually the Captain left someone with some intelligence in charge. This time, he chose Edwin, because Edwin was his favorite. They shared the same sick tastes. Both sought out children for their victims.

The young vampire laughed in Vincent's face when he realized that the older vampire wanted to take over. Edwin then continued to laugh as his second in command read the list of twenty or so vampires Christopher named as successors should anything happen to Edwin. Vincent could not kill Edwin and take control of the city, not until Christopher returned, and Edwin loved that fact.

Since that night, Christopher's list of successors grew shorter as many of them found untimely deaths. Accidental deaths, or Slayer induced deaths that seemed a little too convenient. Not all of Christopher's named heirs were meeting their deaths. The smart ones were making sure Edwin understood who they followed and wanted to protect.

Due to the shift of power, Vincent revised his plan and told his friends to scatter until they were needed. He kept a small amount of people in San Francisco and around the Bay Area to make sure he was kept safe. As his lands were not in the city, only his businesses, Vincent did not have to worry about Edwin trying to kill him. Also, Edwin took a certain amount of pleasure in sparing verbally with Vincent about their mutual hatred of each other. The younger vampire brought up the attempt on Christopher's life almost every time Vincent was in earshot. He thought it was funny that Vincent could not take over the city.

Some of Christopher's, and now Edwin's, followers wondered why Vincent wasn't either banished or killed. Edwin stated that since he knew where he stood with Vincent, it was best to keep him around where he could be watched and controlled. As long as Vincent had businesses in the city, he had to listen to the Acting Captain. What better way to make sure the vampire didn't kill him? Consequently, Edwin allowed Vincent to stay.

Vincent's thoughts were brought back to the party when he saw one of Edwin's bodyguards bringing a young girl into the private room. He bared his teeth, growled and grabbed a goblet from a passing waiter. Vincent didn't like Edwin due to Edwin's dangerous policy on humans. He allowed his people to kill and feed from humans regardless of their age. He didn't care how often his followers killed, and Edwin often demanded young sacrifices as gifts. It made Vincent and his people sick.

Vincent sipped from the goblet of blood, wishing it were fresh. Fresh blood would take the edge off his anger at Edwin. The blood used for his parties were taken from willing humans and stored in a small refrigerator in his office. The vampires who drank the stored blood couldn't receive sustenance from it, but they could still enjoy the taste. It helped relieve the fact that there were no human guests allowed in this part of the club for feeding purposes. His rules. Vincent wanted to keep his fellow vampires from killing anyone in the club. It was bad for business. Half the wait staff was human, but they were off limits. Joseph taught them how to stop vampires and other monsters before letting them work in the private room.

The Red Thread was a membership-only club for humans who had a taste for the unique. There were very few humans who knew that the people dressed as monsters were real. Most never found out unless they were chosen as victims. Vincent had hired five vampires to make sure the monsters did not make snacks out of his paying members.

There were also three bouncers in the club who were to follow Vincent's rules or die. A human, stationed at the street level door, only let members in. A vampire at the bottom of the steps inside, only let members on the guest list pass. Occasionally, humans and other uninvited guests were able to get past the first two bouncers, but then they would meet Jordan. He sat at the top of the steps and sniffed out the liars and the humans.

Jordan liked humanity and lies; they tasted good according to him, which meant the young girl being led to Edwin was probably a vampire. Perhaps even against her will. Vincent shook his head as the young girl and the bodyguard disappeared into the corner room. Edwin was probably already there. If the Acting Captain asked for more parties here, the rules of the private room would have to be changed: no humans, no uninvited guests, and no one under the age of eighteen. No exceptions.

Vincent shook his head and looked to the door again as a woman in a deep blue velvet dress stepped through the door. He spared her a brief glance, then went back to his previous thoughts. He felt that if he could find out more about Edwin's human identity, then he might be able to maneuver the younger vampire into a more vulnerable position.

Unfortunately, short of obtaining the vampire's fingerprints, there was no way to find out who he was. That did not stop the rumors though; none of them were pleasant.

Edwin may or may not have had young daughters. Some said the girls were twins, some said they were not. Some rumors stated he also had sons but killed them and left them to rot with their mother in the basement. Other stories stated Edwin was a nudist and he taught his daughters to be the same way; that they wandered around their farmhouse with no clothing, doing anything that Edwin asked of them.

Vincent tried to find the truth to the rumors but could find no concrete evidence of the man's true beginnings. He hated to acknowledge that he believed the rumors about Edwin training his daughters to be his sex slaves. Having witnessed some of the vampire's less heinous acts, Vincent had to admit it was possible.

A tall thin vampire with a shaved head stepped in front of him and tried to get his attention. It took a minute for Joseph to catch Vincent's eye.

"What is it?"

"We have an intruder." Joseph spoke quietly and directed Vincent's attention to the woman in the blue velvet dress. She was speaking to Morgan, or rather; she was ignoring Morgan, who was trying to talk to her.

"Who is she?" Vincent was mildly curious about the olive-skinned woman in the blue dress. Her beautiful black hair was mostly tied back in a French twist, with a few loose strands framing her face. He could not see her eyes, but he assumed they would be dark.

"Human."

Vincent nearly choked on the blood he was sipping. "What? How?"

"Unsure. Jordan doesn't remember letting her in." Joseph pulled out his handkerchief and started blotting at Vincent's fine Italian suit. "You should be more careful sir, you're wearing a white shirt."

Vincent frowned, looked down and waved his friend's hand away. "Blood stains never show up on my black suit. Send Anthony to Morgan and anyone else she speaks to. I want to know more about her."

Joseph refolded his handkerchief to hide the stains and put it back in his breast pocket. "As you wish, sir."

Vincent placed his empty goblet on a passing tray, and he watched his First Lieutenant, Anthony. He saw Joseph approach Anthony and whisper. Vincent nodded when Anthony looked to his boss for confirmation. Knowing well that Anthony could take care of himself, Vincent let his eyes travel around the room. He growled softly when he realized that Edwin was coming his way, a coy smile on his face.

"Vincent. How are you? Lovely party."

Vincent narrowed his eyes at the sardonic voice and gave the vampire a less than friendly look. "Edwin."

The two men looked at each other across the small space. Edwin enjoyed the fact that Vincent tried not to look too angry at his presence. The silence stretched between them until Edwin broke into a greater smile. "You should lighten up a bit, Vincent. You look...tense."

"Only due to the present company."

Edwin licked his lips, showing off his fangs as he smiled. "I know you hate that I'm in charge. It must kill you that you can't take control of San Francisco until Christopher comes back."

Vincent started tapping his fingers against his thigh, trying to control his emotions. Edwin enjoyed egging him on too much, and there was nothing Vincent could do about it, yet.

Edwin's eyes slipped down to Vincent's tapping fingers and the smile grew larger. He enjoyed being in the controlling position. He caught the larger man's gaze and decided to take it a step further. "If Christopher were still here, I'm sure you would find a way to kill him. Who knows, maybe you'll manage to kill me off."

Vincent's jaw twitched, and Edwin watched as his whole body tried not to move, causing the Acting Captain to lick his lips again.

"But then you'd have to kill all the rest of them off. Do you know how many of us you would have to kill before you would actually be in charge?"

Vincent, seeing a way out of this situation, let the smallest smile touch his pursed lips. "There were about 20 when Christopher left, but it seems the list has grown smaller in the past few months. Your competition seems to have a lot of ill luck. Christopher won't be happy if he learns you had anything to do with that."

Edwin's attitude fell just a touch as he was challenged. He took a moment, then looked his potential executioner up and down, allowing a smile to show again in his eyes. "It really is a shame we don't share more interests. I have a feeling we would have a lot of fun if we were more like minded."

Vincent narrowed his eyes again. "We have a lot of similar interests. We will never share the one that makes me want you out of power."

"Oh, come now, Vincent, you can't tell me you've never used a child for your pleasure."

The larger, older vampire gave a low growl of disgust and showed off his own fangs. There was death in his eyes. "I will admit that in times of war, I have taken a child for its blood with great relish, but I have never and will never take a child for pleasure."

Edwin's voice was full of joy. "But to take a girl when she still has all that innocence, or to train a girl to do exactly what you want and to make sure she knows how loved she is, what a joy. A girl needs a man to show her what love really means."

Vincent stared Edwin down, hands in fists at his side. "How would you train a girl, Edwin? Most of them know older men are not supposed to touch them."

Edwin shuddered a little as memories of his past as a human surfaced for a moment. "Well," he laughed a little, "telling you that might reveal too many secrets. You'll have to do better than that, Vincent."

Vincent, tired of these talks, shook off his abhorrence of the vile man that stood before him. He wanted an end to this conversation. "What do you want, Edwin?"

He smiled a sinister smile. "A girl was brought to me. I'm done with her." He raised his hand and one of Edwin's bodyguards moved to them, pushing a girl in front of him. "She wants a membership here. Told her I could get you to take care of that for me. Be a good boy and take care of her for your Acting Captain, Vinny."

Edwin did not wait for a response but left the girl and took his bodyguard. Vincent watched them leave, a little baffled that Edwin seemed to relish the fact that he was not the actual Captain. He shook his head then realized: if Christopher was alive, no one could kill Edwin for the title, unless they were next in line. The next in line was doing everything she could to ingratiate herself with Edwin. The rest of them were watching their backs or getting killed systematically. Until Christopher returned and took his title back, Vincent would have to leave Edwin alone.

The Acting Captain off his mind for the moment, Vincent turned his attention to the young girl before him. He stared at the girl for a moment or two, assessing her as she looked at him expectantly. At barely five feet tall, she was more than a foot shorter than he. She had to strain to look at him. He let her stare a good minute before deciding on the best course of action. He didn't care if Edwin wanted to drink their blood. Young blood tasted better, if only because the victim's fear was more acute. It was what Edwin did to them when he was done drinking their blood that angered Vincent. The police noticed when young ones were harmed. Edwin didn't seem to realize it was better to drink once and turn them loose. He sighed, shook his head and looked her in the eyes. "What's your name?"

She pointed after Edwin. "He said my name was now Edwina."

"Really. Did you know you were the third?" When she shook her head, he continued. "Do you want to know what happened to the first two?"

The expectant look slowly withdrew and was replaced by worried curiosity. He watched her transform from a young woman to the child she really was. He noticed a small shudder as she really started looking around. There were all sorts of strange shapes in this room, and some did not look at all human. She opened her mouth to say something, but Vincent interrupted her.

"Did they change you, Edwina?" He knew the answer to this one but wanted to know how much the young vampire understood of her new world.

"Change?" Confusion marked her face. "I don't..."

"Did someone bite your neck, or some other part of your body, making you," he couldn't say 'die', "fall asleep? And when you woke, was their arm in your mouth and were you drinking their blood?"

Her eyes brightened in recognition. "Yeah! He bit my neck, then said I would enjoy my life better."

Vincent reached out, moved her hair out of the way and saw the new bite mark scar, which was surrounded by almost dried blood. He wiped part of it away with this thumb, as if making sure it was real. Vincent let his hand fall away and stared down at her again. She was vampire. Edwin was done with her and expected him to take care of her. The Acting Captain knew well what Vincent did with child vampires. He looked around the room again, found Edwin, who was looking in his direction. Edwin gave him a satisfied smile, raised a goblet and toasted him from across the room.

Vincent's jaw twitched, but a hand on his shoulder stopped his movements. He turned to regard the man now holding him back and smiled. His bodyguard and long-time friend always had such impeccable timing.

"Joseph, please take care of 'Edwina'. She is one of us now and you know how I feel about that."

Joseph took Edwina by the arm and led her away, her demise already mapped out in his mind. Vincent watched the odd pair leave, then turned his back, looking for Anthony.

Anthony was standing by a new vampire. Vincent searched for her name and remembered when he heard her laugh. Kari. He liked her well enough but was not sure where her loyalties lie. Anthony turned from her, saw Vincent watching and came toward him. Before he arrived, Vincent flagged down a waiter and asked for two glasses of his private stock. The waiter, a long-time employee, bowed and went off to do as he was told.

Anthony arrived before the waiter returned, so Vincent made small talk. When two champagne glasses with thick red fluid were presented to him, Vincent smiled. He thanked the man and slipped him three twenties. Vincent believed strongly in rewarding loyalty.

Anthony smirked at the gesture, clinking glasses with his leader. "You pay them more than anyone else. Why tip them for wine?"

"It's not wine." Vincent stated between sips. The warm liquid held no sustenance; the taste was all he wanted.

Anthony took a small sip. A look of real surprise crossed his face. The liquid was still warm. "How?"

"I get what I pay for." A mischievous smile floated across his face, then faded. "What have you learned?"

"I watched as she spoke to ten individuals, yet only half remember talking to her. Interestingly enough, the ones claiming amnesia are some of the most flirtatious of your guests."

Vincent raised an inquisitive eyebrow.

"The others stated she asked them questions of the city, like a tourist would ask. I considered talking to her myself, but I wanted you to witness it, in case I forget."

"What is she doing when she talks to them?"

"They greet her, she speaks, they answer back. She then starts playing with her necklace, talking nonstop. She generally walks away in the middle of a sentence and then after a second or two, the person shakes their head and walks away or starts talking to someone else."

Vincent held the goblet up to the light as if he were admiring the color of a fine wine. He understood what she was doing but wondered why Anthony did not catch on. He had known Anthony for a long time, as they shared the same sire, and he respected him deeply. He was surprised by Anthony's ignorance, and he decided to test him.

"Go speak with her. See if you can get anything out of her. Bring her to me when you're done."

Anthony drained the blood in his glass. He shuddered with pleasure, and dropped the glass.

Vincent caught it before it shattered. "Careful."

Anthony composed himself and looked slightly embarrassed. "I forgot myself. I'm not used to his presence in your club."

Vincent drained his own glass and closed his eyes with pleasure. He sighed, opened his eyes and placed the glasses on a passing tray. He turned to Anthony. "Wait five minutes then go talk to the lady. I'm going to the security office to observe."

؃ ؄

Natalia watched as the man she assumed to be Vincent Grey walked toward the back hallway and places beyond. The man he had been talking to was slowly making his way toward her. She had watched them talk and was worried that Vincent's man had figured her out. Since he was making his way toward her, she would take care of it. Vincent Grey she would take care of later.

The large vampire entranced her. She had read a little about him in the Slayer journals and knew he was of Viking descent. He was tall, broad shouldered with blond hair, and light blue eyes. He walked with the grace and dignity befitting a leader. She knew the situation of the vampires in San Francisco and knew that although Vincent was not the leader, most of the older vampires looked to him for guidance.

Her heart pounded in her chest as he passed from view. She hated herself for being drawn to someone who should be her enemy but could do nothing about it. She noticed him the moment she walked through the door and in one way or another, kept him in her sights while trying to deter the questions of the other, less intriguing party quests. She wanted to follow him but knew that was out of the question. She had a job to do and wondered if Vincent's man would be the right patsy. She caught his eye as he continued to advance toward her.

"Madam, may I have a word with you?" Anthony gave her a small nod.

"As long as you tell me your name." Natalia regarded the man, sizing him up. He was not that much taller than she, and not that much wider either. He had darker skin than her, revealing a history of mixed ancestry. It made his green eyes stand out beautifully. His deep auburn hair was swept back, showing his high forehead. He wore a black suit with a gray shirt, and gray handkerchief. He was rather handsome.

"Anthony. Can we talk now?" He had been trying to find a less abrupt way of approaching her, but the Incubus had been striding towards her, a hungry look on his face. There were too many reasons to keep humans out. Which was why, even with the taste of fresh human blood on his lips, Anthony didn't understand the human waitstaff.

"To what do I owe the pleasure? Did Vincent send you to throw me out?"

Her directness surprised Anthony into looking at her. He had been leading her toward a less crowded corner, not really paying attention to her. Not having a retort, he settled for the inane. "I gave my name, what's yours?"

Natalia stood looking at him, then started twirling her necklace. "I'll give you more courtesy than you gave me. My name is Natalia Mirela Liliana Dveski. My first name comes from my mother's mother. It means 'born on Christmas Day'. Mirela Liliana was the name of my mother's grandmother. Mirela means 'to admire'." Her voice was slowing down; becoming melodious. Anthony was caught in the reflection of the dancing silver beads. As he was not yet hers, she continued. "Liliana is pure simplicity. The meaning there will not be a surprise. Can you guess? It means lily. Put them all together and you see that my name means: 'To admire the lily born on Christmas Day.' Do you think that is a fitting name? Am I a lily to be admired?"

Anthony's eyes closed slowly as she spoke. He swayed a little but steadied when she asked her questions. "Yes. A lily. I must find one for you. But there are none as beautiful as you. I apologize-"

"Hush." Natalia had heard this type of rambling before and had no desire to hear it again. Especially when she could hear something more interesting. Vincent had made her job a lot easier. Needing to ensure Anthony was under her control, she held out her hand. It was empty, but she mimed holding a glass. "Take my glass. I'm tired of holding it."

Anthony reached out, took the phantom glass and placed it on a passing tray. Natalia was almost convinced. He was either hypnotized or faking it rather well. Either way, she could probably get the information she needed. She smiled and took Anthony by the arm. She had selected an out of the way corner earlier that would do just fine for an interrogation room.

4

Vincent watched as the mysterious woman led Anthony away. From the security office, he could see the whole club. He followed them as they walked from one screen to another. His blood boiled as she took the bait. There was one section of the private room that was set up to be out of the way. There were hidden cameras everywhere, but that corner had cameras and microphones.

Vincent loved technology. He had watched its rise and invested everything he had in it. He was the money behind a lot of new inventions. And he used it. His restaurant, two clubs, his office in San Francisco and his house in Marin County were all rigged with hidden cameras and microphones. One of his businesses, L337, was a wireless Internet club for all ages. Access was cheap, and customers stayed all night, playing games, finding information, or connecting with friends through social networking sites, spending their money on snacks and sodas.

Then there were the cameras. His favorites were the ones he could hide in the palm of his hand. Or, as with the hidden corner, behind small mirrors, in pictures, in plants and in various other areas. Every angle was covered, and each one was now displayed on its own screen in front of him. Vincent smiled with satisfaction as Anthony was instructed to sit down. He turned the sound up and sat back to watch the show.

The woman placed a hand on Anthony's knee and leaned in as if to kiss his ear. A frown crossed Vincent's brow. What was her game? She stayed in that position and then Anthony turned his head toward her ear. His lips were moving, but Vincent couldn't hear anything. He turned the sound up fruitlessly, bringing in more surrounding noise. Realizing he had been outsmarted, he calmly turned the sound down, punched up other camera views and vacated the chair. Mierka, one of his other bodyguards, smirked as she took the seat and went back to guarding the club.

Slowly, deliberately, Vincent walked out of the office, down the hallway and out into the main room. Scanning the crowd, he found the quickest route through the guests to the private corner. Anthony and his mystery woman were still speaking softly. He stood unnoticed for two minutes. Vincent was not a happy man. He wanted to pull Anthony away from her, but he knew from experience that to rip a hypnotized person away from the hypnotist was a dangerous idea. Instead, he cleared his throat. Twice.

CS   ♉

Natalia saw him approaching in the mirror, but found it amusing to wait and see what he would do. While he stood watching, she told Anthony to forget everything they talked about. When Vincent cleared his throat the first time, she told Anthony not to move. The second time he cleared his throat she slowly removed her hand from Anthony's knee, running her fingers up his leg. She backed her head away, and then languidly stood before Vincent. His arms were crossed, and he looked displeased.

They stood regarding each other for a full minute not saying a word, sizing each other up. Vincent, at six feet two, towered over most women. Natalia was nearly as tall as he, with her heels on. She noticed as his eyes narrowed a touch when she took a step forward.

"Do we stand regarding each other all night," her warm fingers brushed his chilled right hand, "or do we pretend to be civilized and introduce ourselves?"

His eyes never left hers as he caught her hand, brought it to his lips, and planted a light kiss upon her long, living fingers. "Vincent Grey, but I have a feeling you knew that already."

"Natalia Mirela Liliana Dveski." She did not pull her hand away and he did not let go.

"Before we proceed, let Anthony go." He didn't even try and look away from her gorgeous dark eyes.

"But he was so informative." She pulled her hand away finally, took two steps to his right, faced him, and started playing with her necklace. A mischievous glimmer entered her eyes, though her voice was harsh. "And I'm not done with him."

He knew she was trying to hypnotize him and wondered if she really knew whom she was dealing with. He let his eyes stray to her neck and watched her fingers nimbly twirl the silver beads. He wondered how her neck would feel against his lips and what the beads were treated with. They sparkled more than silver should. Vincent brought his blue eyes back to hers, narrowed them, and growled.

Natalia's fingers stopped, and her eyes grew wide, but with surprise not fear. Vincent moved faster than she had ever seen, and she felt her back slam into the wall behind her. She was only moved two feet and wasn't hurt. Vincent was pressed hard against her. One hand was around her throat. She could still breathe, so he wasn't trying to kill her.

"Let me go." Her voice was almost melodious, but something crumbled within her.

"You're not in a position to demand anything, madam." His face was inches from hers; his cool breath caressed her cheek. In other circumstances, it would be pleasant.

"Anthony is still mine. You kill me, you'll never have him back." She was having a hard time concentrating. The wall she had built up since Charlie was slowly dissolving. She had not been with a man since the wolf, and her body was reacting.

"There are many creatures here that would take pleasure in torturing you. There is one that would simply take possession of your body, invade your mind, find the right words and let him go."

Vincent felt the laugh in her chest before it bubbled and broke to the surface. "I can't be possessed. And torture?" She laughed again and looked at Anthony. "You have more to lose if you torture me. I will not be broken."

It was Vincent's turn to laugh. "Humans always say that, until they meet Torin. Would you like to meet Torin?"

"Depends. What type of creature is he?"

"Incubus." He breathed the name into her ear, slowly letting the word penetrate.

She remembered reading about these creatures. The incubus was the male version of the succubus. Both were said to draw power from humans by sleeping with them. Natalia was not worried. She felt she still had control of the situation. She moved to reposition her legs. She put most of her weight on her left leg and made sure the right was between his legs. This shifting caused her whole body to move, and Vincent moved his hand with her. He wasn't hypnotized, but he was still under her control. Natalia had calculated well, Anthony was important to him, and Vincent would not kill her before she let him go.

Natalia wondered, though, if he was trying to control her with his body. He could not kill her, but he could play her. He had started caressing her jawline with the thumb of the hand around her throat. He growled seductively into her ear, sending shivers down her spine. Hungry to play, she brought her hand to his face. She caressed his cheek and neck with the back of her hand, then ran her fingers down his chest to the line of his pants. Her hand strayed, for a brief moment, to the top of the zipper, then moved around his pelvis to his cheek and stopped at the top of his leg. Her fingernails dug into his flesh, causing him to step even closer.

"It would seem, sir, that you would prefer to have me, rather than lose me to an Incubus."

Vincent heard the desire in her voice but knew she could be faking it. They were playing each other, using their bodies to try and gain control. Vincent was having fun, but he was also fascinated. This woman was not afraid. She should be, even if she did have Anthony under her control. Either she had no idea what she was doing, and was therefore a child playing adult games, or she knew, and liked it. He found himself hoping she knew what she was doing. He preferred smart, beautiful women. He decided to try one more tactic to win control.

The hand around her throat moved out of the way. Vincent leaned in close and brushed his lips against the pulsating vein. He could almost smell her blood as it flowed under her skin. He opened his mouth and bared his fangs. He pressed the sharp points against her skin, denting her flesh, but not penetrating. She let out a strangled sigh, and he was sure he had her.

Natalia finally felt fear, and her desires shut down. She had been trying to prepare for this moment mentally, but it still brought memories of her mother's death. She gripped Vincent's leg harder as she entwined her other hand in his hair. She tried to pull his head away, being careful not to act panicked. Reminding herself she still had the upper hand, she squeezed her eyes shut and clamped down on her fear. She was breathing hard and her heart was still pounding, but her fear passed. She pulled harder on his hair, and he growled with pleasure.

"Vincent?" She purred.

He made an affirmative noise against her throat; nipping her skin with his front teeth, as he thought of the many things he wanted to do to her sinuous body.

"Do vampires feel pain?"

He drew his head back, looking her in the face. It felt wonderful to play with her, but the question seemed too calculated and out of place. "What?"

She was still holding onto him and used him to steady herself as she slammed her knee up between his legs.

Vincent should have known. He staggered back, trying not to fall. He felt his ass hit the far wall, five feet away and steadied himself. He looked up at the lovely vixen, wondering why he hadn't seen it coming.

"Weren't expecting that were you?" She was leaning against the wall, arms lightly crossed, regarding him casually.

"What do you want?" He stood taller as the pain faded. Vampires felt pain, but not as strongly, and not as long. He would be fine in another minute.

"I wanted to meet the most powerful vampire in the city. Slayers and vampires told me that I could find him here. Then, I heard there was going to be a huge party to celebrate the Captain's birthday." She shrugged as the lie spilled from her lips. "I decided to crash the party and meet the Captain and was disappointed to find out that the most powerful vampire and the

Captain were not the same person. I started to ask your guests why the two weren't the same. Do you want to know what your guests told me?"

Vincent nodded, mildly curious. The pain was gone; he shifted, pretending to readjust himself into a more comfortable position. He was actually preparing himself to strike. She was quite a human, but he did not like being tricked.

Natalia pushed herself away from the wall, took two steps toward Vincent and laid a hand upon Anthony's shoulder. He did not stir. "They told me the Captain was an uncaring fool named Christopher Tyler, but the most powerful vampire in San Francisco was an older one named Vincent Grey, and that one day, he would rule the city."

She was looking in his eyes again, staring down into him. He wanted her between him and the wall again. A frustrated growl escaped his lips. He bared his teeth, letting her see their length and sharpness, hoping to get a reaction out of her. She reached out with her free hand and smoothed back his hair. A clump had fallen out of place when she kneed him. Her hand strayed to his cheek and stayed for a moment as she leaned in and kissed him lightly on the lips. His frustrated anger turned into pure bafflement. Natalia was just as surprised by her action.

Vincent grabbed her hand as he pushed her away and stood up, not bothering to pretend he was hurt. The baffled look was not gone from his face. "You're crazy."

"No. I just know what I want." She sobered and tried to take her hand back, unsure why she had kissed him. Vincent held on to her hand.

"What do you want?"

"A lot of things. But I'm not sure you're convinced I could be an asset." Her tongue was turning faster than her mind. Though she was looking for new allies, now was not the right time for that. And having a vampire ally while hunting a bloodsucker would probably be a bad idea.

"An asset to whom? Me?" He let her go and took a step forward. He had to be careful not to step on Anthony's feet. "Humans are assets in two ways: as food and as cannon fodder."

"Anthony, stand." Anthony did as bid, forcing Vincent back. "You forget, sir, that you were human once, and so was Anthony. I need you." The look on her face and the tone of voice revealed how she needed him, but he didn't think she noticed. "And I'm going to make you understand that you can use me. But for now, Anthony will walk me out. I'll release him when I'm safe and I'll make sure he comes back here."

Vincent wanted to stop her but couldn't. There were a lot of his people he would be willing to risk, but Anthony was not one of them. Anthony was too valuable. He balled his hands into fists and growled deep and long.

Natalia took Anthony's arm. "Was it that unpleasant to play with me?" Her voice was soft and seductive. The look in her eye was that of a lover saying hello, not a crazed fanatic ready to lead a prisoner out of his club. "By the way, love the name of the club."

Natalia said something to Anthony and they walked away. Vincent heard her. Though it sounded like Italian or Latin, he did not recognize the words. Vincent stood unmoving for several seconds unsure of how to proceed. If he alerted his security staff to the problem, she might kill Anthony. Vincent had no guarantee that she would let Anthony go as she said. He slammed his fist into the wall, rattling the mirror.

"Careful, sir, you might expose the cameras. Shall I follow?"

"Did you take care of 'Edwina'?"

"She had friends waiting for her outside. Kim took her and her friends to another club with a few of our other friends. We will take them to a few clubs. She and her friends will get into an argument. We will make sure they are separated and then when the sun comes up, she will find herself very far from civilization, alone, out in the open. She will not return."

Vincent nodded. When the girl was reported missing by her parents, though the trail would include the Red Thread, it would not end here, and would not end with his people. They were too experienced for that. He indicated Natalia and Anthony, who were almost to the door. "How much do you know of this situation?"

"I saw enough. I've sent Markus to L337. He'll be able to find some information about the lady."

"Good. Follow them and make sure she releases Anthony."

"Yes, sir." When Joseph left, he took almost the same path Natalia and Anthony had taken. Vincent watched until his bodyguard was out the door.

Ꮖ Ꮒ

Natalia walked Anthony out the door, down the steps, through the club and out the main entrance. As she passed each bouncer she spoke their name and one word. It would ensure that they let her pass and then remember her. She was sure that Vincent already knew how she had gotten past, so it was more for fun. Also, if they were punished for their folly, the bouncers would at least know why.

Once on the street Natalia led Anthony halfway down the block. There was a line of people waiting by the door of The Red Thread, and she did not want an audience. Once out of sight, she stopped and turned to her prisoner.

"Anthony?"

"…yes…"

"You're going to forget all about me. The next time I see you, you'll think it's the first time we've met. Thanks for all the information. In 30 seconds, you'll wake up feeling very happy." She kissed him on the cheek, said a word in Romanian, and walked into the alley behind them. She walked to door, opened it and closed it before the 30 seconds was up. She was in the back hallway of a coffee shop. People used this door a lot to get to the coffee shop from The Red Thread.

Natalia went into the woman's one stall bathroom and locked the door. Once the door was locked, she took off her shoes, stepped on the toilet seat and moved the ceiling tile out of the way. She grabbed the black plastic bag hiding there and threw it to the floor. She put the tile back, jumped down and changed. She also pulled her hair down from the twist and put it into a simple ponytail. Once done, she stuffed the high heels and fancy dress in the brown bag and threw it all into the garbage can. She bought the shoes and dress at a thrift store, knowing it would all end up here. She hated to throw everything away, but to get away clean, she had to.

Ready, she took another look at herself in the mirror, then looked around the room. Satisfied, she flushed, washed her hands and left the room. She nodded to the woman outside the bathroom left the cafe.

Natalia headed down the street. Her car was parked a few more blocks away. Halfway down the next block, at the head of an alley, she gasped as she felt herself being grabbed. In an instant, Natalia found herself pinned to the wall by a hand around her throat.

A large, strong male body pressed her into the wall. The man's free hand pulled her shirt away from her shoulder and his teeth sank into her shoulder, painfully. She cried out, but the hand at her throat moved to her mouth, stifling her cries. Pain and terror filled her thoughts but dissipated somewhat when the menacing figure pulled away from her shoulder and growled into her ear.

"Do you see how easy it would be for us to steal your life and change it or end it at our discretion?" His hand moved back to her throat.

"Yes." She tried to control her fear and failed. "Are you going to kill me?"

He pulled back, staring at her with his unflinching gaze. He took out a small napkin then slipped it under the shoulder of her shirt, pressing it against her bleeding wound. "If he asks me to. Are you going to kill him?"

Natalia stared at him for a moment, unsure of her intentions. She knew why she had been at the club tonight, but now wondered if she really wanted to go through with it. She placed her hand over her shirt and napkin to gain another moment of thought. She opened her mouth, not knowing what would come out. "No, I'm going to use him."

"I listen to Vincent. I protect him. If you hurt him in any way, I will not hesitate to end your life. Understand?"

Natalia tried to keep her heart calm and her mind steady, but it was hard. She finally placed the voice. She nodded as best she could, with his hand still wrapped around her neck.

"Good." He let her go.

"I know who you are."

He stopped mid stride, turned back and raised an eyebrow.

"I dreamt of you."

He smiled, turned and simply vanished. Though she recently saw the same thing with Tony Lam, it still unnerved her. Natalia cursed him for simply smiling at what she said. She walked the few blocks to her car and tried not to be upset. What had the smile meant, anyway? He gave her the same smile in her dreams.

She dreamt the dream about once a week since she returned to the area. She was lying in a large canopied bed. The fabric draped around the bed was deep crimson giving everything, including her skin, a blood red hue. The curtains parted, and a man handed her a goblet telling her it was time to rise. He called her child every time. The voice was his. She was sure of it.

Natalia shook her head, putting it all aside. She had another more important problem. She wanted Vincent, and her allies wanted him dead. She had the information Zechariah wanted, but didn't know if she wanted to give it to him. He would use the information to destroy The Red Thread while Vincent and his lot were in it. Natalia knew why Zechariah was going to destroy the club but didn't think it was necessary.

She had been trying to come to terms with her new path since she started about seven years ago, shortly after Charlie tried to change her. In that time, she learned a great deal about herself and the world around her. Natalia also trained in many different areas. Through it all she had come to one definite conclusion. She was not a Slayer; probably never would be. She tried hard to be one, because of her history with vampires and werewolves, but the fact remained: Slayers were just as monstrous as the creatures they hunted. Humans were no less gruesome.

She also learned that no one was truly innocent. Everyone had their good and evil sides; it was just a matter of perspective. Natalia sighed as she adjusted the napkin at her shoulder, cursing the vampire for the bite wound. Before she arrived home, she threw the napkin out the window. She knew what Vincent's money was invested in and wouldn't put it past him or his men to bug her. They wanted information on her; they would have to try harder.

Natalia parked and went inside her house, happy she didn't have to talk to Zechariah until tomorrow when he called. It would give her a chance to gather her mind and figure out what she wanted. Right now, she wanted a dangerous thing. She wanted Vincent. She wanted more than the light kiss she had planted on his cool, full lips. At least Slayers couldn't read minds.

5

Vincent woke from his dream with a frustrated howl. His hands were balled into fists, with the sheet entwined in his fingers. He loosened his grip and smoothed out his red silk sheet, checking for damage. Assured it was not torn, he threw the sheet back and rose from his bed.

The curtains were drawn back revealing the protected deck. Joseph was placing a laptop and a manila folder on the wrought iron table. Vincent walked out to the deck and accepted the folder Joseph handed him. He glanced at the papers inside; quickly scanning the small amount of information Markus and Joseph had gathered on Natalia. He put the folder aside, feigning disinterest to stare out the window toward the ocean. He had lived in many different places with many different views. The ocean was his favorite.

"Are they gathered?" His voice was mellow.

"They are awaiting you downstairs. Breakfast is in the sitting room. How long will you be?"

Vincent stretched, regarding the night sky. "As long as I wish. Dismiss breakfast. I'll eat later."

Joseph smiled and left. Vincent heard the door snick closed, staying where he was for many long moments. Eventually he turned, took a quick look at his finances, went inside and readied himself. Showered and shaved he stood before his closet, trying to figure out what to wear. He liked to dress well. Nothing in his closet looked old, although he did have clothing from most of the decades he lived in. He also had his Italian suits, but those were not right for the occasion. He examined his clothing looking mostly at his suits. He preferred suits when he was conducting business, but the business at hand would be dirty. If he wore a suit, it might be ruined, and he'd probably have to toss it. The vampire didn't like to waste.

Vincent went to another closet and pulled out a pair of black corduroys. Easy to clean, comfortable and went well with his microfiber plum shirt. He slipped on the shirt intrigued by how far polyester had come since its inception in the 70's. He pulled on some socks and his hiking shoes. Better traction for the job at hand.

Once dressed, he took a final look in the mirror and left the room. He was halfway down the stairs before his dream came flooding back. She had been pressed between a wall and him again. But this time, neither had resisted. He paused; hand on railing, halfway down a step. His eyes closed as the dream swept over him.

Vincent could almost feel her against him. A groan escaped him. Their encounter had left him wanting. He had enough willing women to keep him satisfied, but it had been a long time since he had felt a need this profound. He took a deep breath to try to steady his thoughts. He shook his head and continued down the steps. At least this evening's business would help alleviate his frustrations.

At the bottom of the steps, he opened the door by entering the code into the keypad. He stepped out and followed the maze of boxes to the only other door in the room. He, Joseph, and Mierka had created the maze and were the only ones who knew how to get in or out. Only the three of them came to this room, anyway. The storage room led to the large second floor bathroom, which was connected to the actual master bedroom. The master bedroom in turn led to another room, which he used as a sitting room. No one was allowed into the sitting room without Vincent's permission.

Vincent closed the door tightly behind him and continued to the main staircase. A very wealthy San Franciscan built the house in the late 1800's. Vincent acquired it in the early 1900's and made repairs and renovations to most of the house and restored the grand marble staircase. He enjoyed walking down a large sweeping marble staircase. It made for a grand entrance. Reaching ground level, he turned right, walked a few steps and turned right again, walking next to and then under the staircase.

There were five rooms on the ground floor. There were two meeting rooms, a state-of-the-art kitchen, a substantial library/sitting room and a ballroom. The large meeting room was connected to the ballroom/training room by a sliding wall. The dividing wall was often opened for parties. There was also a good-sized pantry and a bathroom. Vincent was headed for the cellar stairs, which were across from the kitchen. He opened the door, looked around, then stepped inside.

The stairs were well built, with reinforced walls on both sides. They were soundproof, as was the door. At the bottom of the stairs was another locked door. A monitor above him showed him the next room was empty. Vincent punched in a code and the metal door before him slid open. He stepped into the closet-sized chamber, and the door closed behind him. He checked the next monitor as the large fans above played with his hair. All was normal in the hallway on the other side of the door. He typed in his code into yet another keypad, and the second metal door slid open.

The smell of the place hit him like a brick the second the door started to open. Vincent turned his head slightly, thankful he didn't have to breathe. The smell was hard down here: this was a place of death and decay. He saw the crossbow point before he saw Mierka. Vincent smiled at her once the door was fully opened. The petite blond looked at his face carefully before moving the crossbow. He leaned in and kissed her cheek.

"Good evening my dear. I trust you are well?" When Joseph had approached him about bringing her into the family, Vincent agreed with no questions. She was incredible. She had been a spy in the French Revolution. The humans never suspected she was a spy or that she was vampire.

"I'm well. They're waiting for you in the main room. Have been since this morning." One of Mierka's assets was her poker face. No matter the situation, she always looked slightly amused.

"Good."

Vincent smiled then walked past her to the row of dungeons. There were ten rooms, most 10x10. The largest was a 300 sq. ft. room. There were two guards in front of its door. They greeted him as one held the door for him. Inside were three more guards, a thin Latino man holding a scroll, Joseph, and his three vigilant door bouncers from The Red Thread.

The human bouncer was chained to the wall, as was the vampire. All the chains in the room were strong enough to hold very old vampires. The mage with the scroll was standing in front of the third bouncer, Jordan, chanting quietly. Jordan was a demon, an urban wendigo, and needed additional security, hence the mage. The creature was grumbling, licking its arm. There was a nasty burn in its flesh. It growled at Vincent as it licked its wound. Twenty-four hours ago, it had sworn undying loyalty. Now, it would probably eat Vincent if it had the chance.

Vincent stood regarding the three for a few moments, not saying a word. Aaron, the human, was obviously scared; he was shaking, his eyes wide with fear. Aaron had been working for him for nearly a year, and had been told the rules every day and repeated the oath, every day. The human apparently did not take the rules and oath seriously.

Keith, the vampire, had been working for Vincent for almost five years. He understood the rules. He had seen three of Vincent's people lose their lives for not following the rules. He knew what to expect and seemed resigned to his death.

Jordan was still growling at him.

Vincent paced in front of them, feeling the fear and hate rolling off the three. It gave him pleasure to keep them waiting. Finally, he turned to them and spoke. His voice was mild, as if addressing a group of businessmen at a luncheon.

"The three of you have worked well for me and followed my rules as I have laid them out. The services you have rendered are not as easy as they may seem. You have had to deal with creatures you are not used to seeing. You have been quiet about it all and have proven yourselves over and over."

He paused, looked hard at each of them, his anger and disappointment coming through. "Last night, a mere human was able to waltz into my club uninvited. She hypnotized all of you into thinking she wasn't even there. I'm not surprised she tricked you Aaron, you're still young and susceptible to beautiful women. I am surprised she could trick you Keith; I thought your mind was stronger than that. And then there is Jordan." He walked over to the urban wendigo and regarded the creature from two feet away. He leaned in closer. Jordan kept licking his wound. "I didn't know you were a weak-minded fool."

Jordan's hand shot out. The magic field it was trapped in zapped its fingers before it could touch Vincent. Vincent smiled.

"I told you I could control you."

Vincent straightened as Jordan started beating against the magic field. The mage, a strong one, chanted louder. Jordan screamed in rage and pain for a few minutes before he finally stopped and fell to the ground. Smoke rose from various places and the smell of burnt fur and skin made Aaron gag. The vampires and other guards were unaffected. Vincent stood two feet away and smiled mildly. He noticed that Aaron was starting to understand the severity of the situation. The knowledge made the old vampire smile wider.

"I have to admit," Vincent's voice was rather composed, "the woman has affected me deeply. It was a joy playing with her, and I look forward to playing with her again."

A gasp of hope escaped the frightened Aaron. Vincent cocked his head to look at the human. Aaron was quieting; becoming still. A look of pure hope was indeed spreading from his green eyes to his tanned face. A few more words and he would be completely convinced everything would be okay. A hard need worked its way from the pit of Vincent's stomach throughout his body, making him tingle. Vincent loved the look of desperate hope on a human's face. It had been a long time since he had seen it. He decided to play it.

Vincent strolled over to Joseph and held out his hand for the key. Joseph looked his friend dead in the eye and understood. He reached into his pocket and handed Vincent the keys to the shackles, making as much noise as possible. Vincent took them, hid his glee and turned. He looked toward Keith first, who had known Vincent too long and knew the truth.

His grim demeanor was ever present.

Aaron was shaking again, but this time he was trying not to grin. His eyes were obviously glued to the keys. Vincent could smell the blood rushing through the human's over excited heart. It would taste so sweet. He jingled the keys, shifting through them and stopping at the one to the shackles. He ran his finger over the rounded teeth, wondering how many times the key had been used. Looking directly at Aaron, Vincent raised his arms and unlocked the shackles. Once released, Aaron fell at Vincent's feet and kissed his shoes.

"Thank you, sir! I swear on my life I will never disappoint you again!" The relief in Aaron's voice made Vincent lick his lips. He reached down and caressed Aaron's head, like a master to his loyal dog.

"Rise."

Aaron stood. He was shaking and drooling from relief. He started to say something then stopped. Started again, failed again, and fell to his knees.

"Sir, I can't tell you...I will never...just let me prove to you...." He looked up at Vincent, his face completely open.

Vincent reached his arm out and helped Aaron up again. He embraced the human, and a shocked Aaron awkwardly embraced him back. Vincent pulled back and looked the human in the face.

"Aaron, son, did you really believe that I would allow you more than one mistake?"

Vincent watched as reality hit the human. His happy grin slowly fell into an open-mouthed scream. Aaron tried to escape, but Vincent had him in a vice grip. One hand was holding Aaron's shoulder; the other was on his opposite arm. Aaron struggled anyway and, in his fear, succeeded in pulling his arm out of the socket. His fearful scream turned into a howl of pain. Vincent slowly pulled the man toward him, embracing him again. This time, though, he ripped Aaron's shirt off his shoulder, opened his mouth wide, revealed his fangs and bit into the human's shoulder. He drank deep and long, tasting the sweet saltiness as the hot blood filled his mouth, throat and his stomach. He drank his fill then let the man fall.

Two guards came forward and pulled Aaron away. The human was not dead yet, neither was he drained. He would be taken to another cell, left to heal, then fed on by whomever Vincent felt like feeding him to. All the vampires who lived under his roof were well fed, but Vincent enjoyed scaring stupid humans. It was fun to watch them.

Vincent wiped his bloody mouth with the back of his hand as Aaron was dragged away. He hated drinking from men. Fresh blood was an aphrodisiac to him; drinking from willing women was just more fun. Filled and yet highly unsatisfied, he turned to the mage.

"Banish him."

Jordan screamed, started beating on the magic field again. The mage simply started another chant. One minute after he started, smoke rose from Jordan's feet. Two minutes and there was so much smoke that Vincent could no longer see Jordan's legs. Four minutes and the smoke was so thick only Jordan's head was visible. With a howl of pain, the smoke and Jordan disappeared. The mage staggered back and almost fell. One of the guards caught him and helped him to his feet.

There was a small silence. Vincent regarded the mage. "Your service is no longer needed, Carlos. You may leave for the day."

"With respect, Vincent, I believe my debt is paid. I've been chanting for hours. It could have killed me." Carlos stood his ground even as the large vampire approached him.

"As could I." Vincent stood very close to Carlos, letting his size intimidate rather than his voice. "But I agree. Orlando will take you to my meeting room. I'll join you when I'm done." He looked to Orlando. "Take care of his needs."

Vincent turned his back on the mage but waited until Carlos and his guard left. The easy ones were done.

Keith was staring at him. "What are you going to do to me, sire?"

Vincent sighed. "I was impressed with you the first time I saw you. It was your first day at The Red Thread, remember? You handled the situation so well. While most of your co-workers ran, you remembered your training and used it. I saw so much potential." Vincent was now holding Keith's head in his hands, gently, like a father with his son. "I really believed you were stronger than this. You have been tested time and time again, and with each test you proved your loyalty. Do you know how many vampires I've created in my three hundred years on this earth? Eight."

He let go of Keith and started pacing again. "I remember each time, each person and know what each person is doing now. Two of them fell to Slayers. Three, like me, are living quietly and richly. One is helping my sire rule her city. Then there is you. You are the youngest, so maybe the comparison is unfair, but you showed so much promise. That is why, even though I prefer changing women, I changed you myself. I wanted to guide you and show you how things should be done, yet you decide to do as you please."

Vincent stopped pacing and stood with arms crossed in front of the boy. "I know where you've been sleeping."

Keith's expression finally strayed. Through all Vincent's ranting, he had looked slightly bored; as if he knew everything that was to happen. Now, he showed fear. Joseph came to Vincent's side; the other two guards flanked them. They no longer had their crossbows but were slowly changing.

"Please Vincent, don't feed me to them."

"They are here for my protection."

The creatures that only appeared human, were now standing taller than

Vincent. At over nine feet tall, they had to hunch in order not to hit their heads on the ceiling. Their clothing ripped, revealing hairy but matted arms and legs. Their most impressive features were their fangs and foot-long claws. Vincent had made a deal with the werewolves of the area. Work for him and he would house them and help to feed their more dangerous appetites. Vincent felt it was better to work with the supernatural population rather than hunt them down. Wars killed humans, which he needed, and brought Slayers, which he didn't.

"Your protection?" Keith was pale to begin with, but now he turned white as a ghost. "What are you going to do to me?"

A secret smirk blossomed on Vincent's face. He shrugged. "I forget."

Keith gave him a blank stare, and then his eyes grew very wide indeed. The shriek he let loose was louder and longer than any noise either of the other bouncers had uttered. Vincent smiled mildly as Joseph stepped forward to unlock the shackles. Keith kicked at him, and a Blitzkrieg stepped forward to hold the young vampire against the wall. There was no fighting after that. Fully fed, Keith could have struggled, but he was a day without blood, and the Blitzkrieg was well fed and happy. It was a new moon; she was in full control. Keith did not stand a chance.

Vincent stepped back and allowed Rebecca to hold onto Keith, then led the way to the last cell in the dungeon. This was where most of the stench came from. The door was already open; another guard opened it after the mage had been led upstairs. As the entourage walked closer, Keith started to struggle. The wolf had one arm around his torso, pinning Keith's arms, and the other was holding his head to her chest. Rebecca was being very careful. Vincent had warned that Keith's premature death would not be treated kindly.

They entered the room with Vincent in front, the Blitzkrieg holding Keith, and Joseph at the rear. The other Blitzkrieg stayed outside. The room was small with a large hole in its center. There was not much space to maneuver.

Vincent moved to the wall opposite the door and leaned against it, relaxing. Joseph stayed by the door and Rebecca brought Keith to one side. She let him go and he fell to his knees.

"Vincent. Please have mercy."

Vincent remained in the same position observing Keith. "As I said earlier, I know where you've been sleeping." He used the wall to push himself into a standing position and started to pace. There was four feet between the wall and the hole. "I know how you've been paying your bills, too. I told you when I changed you that your loyalty was of utmost importance, and you assured me I had it. But I don't, do I?"

Keith started to protest then simply hung his head. His voice was muted, but he did sound remorseful. "I was weak. Sire, forgive me."

Vincent walked around the hole, stopping at Keith's side. Rebecca moved one step away. Keith raised his head. Pink tears were running down his face. "Anything but this, please."

"If your only crime had been to let a human cloud your mind, I would have mercy. I would even consider letting you live, give you a second chance. You went to Edwin, drank his blood, used three children for your pleasure and took his money. Tell me, did it ever cross your mind that you were committing treason?"

"He has no power over me. I drank his blood for show. It did nothing."

"And the children?"

Keith closed his eyes. "I was caught up in the moment."

"Your excuse is that everyone else was doing it?" He shook his head and made a disapproving noise.

"I felt if I didn't-"

"Save your excuses. I don't care to hear your lies." Vincent squatted down, bringing him face to face with his child. "Why did he give you money?"

Keith hung his head again. "To buy women."

"No, Keith. What did you give him in return?"

Keith sank lower to the ground. His answer was barely a whisper. "The name of your favorite human at The Red Thread."

Vincent contained his anger. He needed one more piece of information. "Which is?"

Keith collapsed completely on the floor. He was weeping. "Markus."

The bellow started deep in Vincent's chest and bubbled then burst forth into a barbaric roar. Vincent grabbed Keith by the shirt and carried him across the room, slamming him full force against the far wall. "The fate that awaits you is too good for your betrayal."

He threw Keith at the far wall then followed, going around the hole. The Blitzkrieg had changed to human form and retreated to the door, giving Vincent space to move. He was on Keith in seconds. The younger vampire was still conscious. Vincent was glad. He picked the man up and swung around, holding Keith over the hole by his shirt.

"Have fun," Vincent stated plainly. He let Keith go.

Keith screamed the whole twenty feet down. When he hit bottom, bones broke, and he screamed again. Then he really started to scream. Vincent stayed and listened until all he could hear were the echoes. It didn't take long.

Vincent had established the oubliette when he bought the place. It was an old well. He had enlarged the reservoir and smoothed out the walls. There was one way in, a twenty-foot drop from the dungeon. Though old vampires at full blood could survive the fall and jump out, Vincent never threw anyone in the pit who was at full blood. Keith had not been fed in long enough that the young vampire would not be able to escape by jumping out. Also, the walls were too smooth to climb. In the reservoir was his other Judas: the child he had not told Keith about. It took care of the remains and made sure no one was able to leave.

Vincent left the room, and the memories, behind. It was called an oubliette for a reason.

Rebecca closed and locked the door once he was out. Joseph followed behind him as he walked up the passage to the cellar steps. Mierka and two others were waiting for them by the door. As they approached, one went into the air chamber. By the time Vincent reached the door, it was open. Mierka was standing by it, waiting. Vincent stepped through, closed the door then opened the other. His thoughts were far from pleasant as he walked up the steps.

Vincent waited in the main hallway for everyone to emerge. He thanked the werewolves and released them for the night. Their brethren were already in the woods behind the house, hunting. The wolves were primarily daytime guards. It was rare for him to need their services at night. Mierka passed by them, not needing instructions. She was on monitor duty, and now that the traitors were dealt with, she would sit in the security room and watch the monitors.

With everyone gone, Vincent turned to Joseph. "I must speak with Carlos. Please see to Markus' safety."

Vincent turned on his heel and headed down the hallway. Joseph left instructions with Mierka and went to take care of business.

6

Carlos sat on the couch at the far end of the small meeting room, waiting for Vincent. It was a comfortable room with plenty to keep his eyes busy. Vincent kept historical artifacts, books and maps of the world from many centuries in this room. Were he not so tired, Carlos would be sifting through the maps, plotting his long overdue vacation. Instead he sat on the overstuffed leather couch and tried not to fall asleep.

The mage rose from his seat when Vincent entered, too tired to make sure his shirt was tucked into his jeans. Both men looked haggard, dirty, and ready to start the day over. The vampire looked the man up and down. He took in Carlos' small stature without really thinking about it. Vincent felt it was always best to know with whom he were dealing with. He always scrutinized those he was speaking with, including those he knew well. The small Latino man looked wearily at his boss with his dark eyes and ran a shaking hand through his dark already unruly hair. When Vincent indicated Carlos should take a seat at the desk, the mage sagged into the chair. Vincent went to the side bar to pour himself and Carlos some brandy. He handed the mage a glass as he sat on the edge of the maple desk.

Carlos took the glass willingly, swirling the dark liquid, warming it. He looked up at the vampire who loomed above him and raised the glass in a toast. They clinked glasses and Carlos downed his drink, while Vincent sipped at his.

A shudder gripped Carlos as liquid fire rushed down to his stomach. The tremor passed and he placed the glass on the desk. "You shouldn't have wasted your good brandy on me tonight."

Vincent swirled the liquid and took a sip. "Did you enjoy it?"

"Yes."

"Then it wasn't wasted." He stood and walked to the other side of the desk. "How long has your family been in my debt Carlos?"

"Five generations." There was a tinge of disbelief in his voice, of something said so often, it couldn't possibly be the truth.

"Five generations is a long time for a family to be in debt to a vampire. Yet here you are. You have proven yourself a worthy mage, and a worthy ally. I have always found that mages make good allies and have considered your family's debt to me quite an asset. I feel it would be a shame to lose you. You've paid off your debt in full, but I would like to retain you. That's why I'm offering you a permanent place on my payroll. My resources would be open to you and you would be able to improve your skills beyond your knowing. What do you say?"

Carlos looked at him in disbelief then bent forward and hung his head. After a moment of silence, he got up and walked to the window. This side of the house faced woods; there was nothing to look at but the reflection of the room. Carlos looked at Vincent's reflection and found it fitting that the vampire's reflection was distorted.

"I want out, Vincent. I never wanted to be a mage in the first place. My mother foisted the responsibility upon me. She told me the story when I was very young. I didn't really understand what was going on. When I had to come home every day from school and learn spells, instead of playing with my friends, I started to understand how serious this debt was."

Carlos turned, crossed his arms and sat on the window ledge, looking at a point somewhere between himself and the wall behind the vampire. "High school was worse. I wanted to join clubs, sports teams, anything, just to not have to practice. That was when my mother told me the whole story; of how much you've done for my family since the debt started. She said that we had the house because of you. She only had to work part time because of you."

He looked at Vincent. "I started to wonder why. I threw myself into magic just to be able to maybe repay you for what you did for us, not what you did for an ancestor. Then I started wondering if you were helping us to keep us in debt. So now I need to know. What will it take to get me out of your debt?"

Vincent leaned back, slowly swirling his glass. "You are out of debt. Your life is your own. You may do with it as you please."

Carlos doubted the sincerity behind the words. "How? How can my family possibly be out of your debt? And how do I know you won't kill me like you killed your three bouncers?"

Vincent kept swirling the glass taking small sips of the fine brandy. "They betrayed me, you did not. I repay betrayal with death and torture. I repay loyalty in a much different way." He stood, placed his glass on the desk and walked over to Carlos. "Do you really believe I would repay loyalty with disdain?"

"I don't understand why you helped us. We were in your debt."

Vincent turned to the window and watched the wind move through the trees. The glare from the lights in the room barely hindered his sight. He drew a deep breath, letting it out slowly. "It's obvious you never truly understood the loyalty of your family." Vincent turned, sat on the window's edge and looked toward the map over his desk. The map was so old it still showed where the world stopped, stating 'Hic Sunt Dracones'. He folded his arms, then regarded Carlos. "Do you not understand how easy it would have been for your family to end the debt without re-paying it?"

Carlos looked at Vincent with a blank expression on his face.

"Obviously not. Your ancestor was an only child. No family, no wife, no aunts, uncles, cousins. Just himself. After I helped him, he vowed to repay me, found a wife, had a child and passed on the debt. Each generation has had one child, just enough to keep the debt repayable."

Vincent paused and walked to his desk. He unlocked and opened a drawer. He pulled out a small lock box, opened it, pulled out an envelope, and put the box back. "It would have been very easy for your ancestors to end the debt. Any of them could have ended it without paying it back. All they would have had to do was not have children or kill themselves. But generation after generation, your family made sure there was someone to pass the debt on to. It showed me the amount of loyalty your family had. And as I said, I repay loyalty."

Vincent placed the envelope at the opposite edge of the desk. Carlos stepped forward and saw his name on the envelope. He picked it up and opened it. Inside was a folded bank statement. He could see his name on the exposed half. Hands shaking, he opened it and looked at the ending balance, then at Vincent, then at the ending balance. Carlos backed away from the desk, tried to sit in the chair, but missed and fell to the floor. Vincent chuckled as he rounded the desk and helped the mage to stand up.

"Why?"

"I repay loyalty." Vincent placed Carlos in a chair.

"I can't accept this, Vincent."

"Don't upset me Carlos. I don't like being denied."

Vincent's voice had a hard edge to it and Carlos heard it. He looked at the statement again, folded it and put it back in the envelope.

"All right. Thank you, Vincent. You don't know what this means." He stood and took the offered hand. The mage was almost to the door before the vampire spoke again.

"If you have children and one happens to take up the arts, send them my way."

Carlos looked back at Vincent. He was sitting on his large desk again. Could he really deny this man a promise? "I will, sir."

Vincent watched the mage leave, upset to lose Carlos. The money didn't matter, not when put against five generations of loyalty. Having a mage in his debt had been ideal. It would have been pleasant to have one on his payroll. He hoped he could find another one, but knew it was near impossible to find one that would work for a vampire in this city right now. Vincent sighed and sipped his brandy, waiting to hear from Joseph.

His friend called an hour later with the news. Markus was still human, but Edwin had been trying to seduce him to his side. Markus, happy with his current boss, kept denying the vampire. Joseph, wanting to keep the human safe, had placed him on Vincent's private jet. Markus was being sent to New York. It was safer for him there. Vincent's sire, Lorraine, ran the city and was always happy to shelter Vincent's friends, especially of the male variety. Although Vincent was glad Markus was safe, he was rather perturbed. He was losing two of his most loyal people on the same night. It left him with a bad taste in his mouth.

7

Richard hovered nervously just behind Vincent's right shoulder. The manager/maître d' of The Ocean's Edge was always fidgety. When Vincent was around, he was ten times worse. The man had heard the entertaining rumors regarding Vincent and his lot and believed them. Vincent smiled remembering the first time someone accused him of being a mobster. He enjoyed the rumor; it kept the truth hidden.

Vincent normally let his accountant take care of the paperwork. When he arrived unannounced, Richard nearly fainted. Vincent was in the neighborhood and had nothing better to do then pester his manager. Vincent enjoyed throwing Richard off balance. The surprise inspections kept Richard and the rest of the staff on their toes. The Ocean's Edge was a five-star restaurant, Vincent expected it to stay that way. It was one of the reasons he was here at midnight on a Monday. It was early for Vincent, late for Richard.

"Is there a problem, sir?" Even his voice was fidgety.

"Richard, you've worked for me for five years. Have there ever been any serious problems?"

"Well, no, not that I'm aware of."

Vincent continued reading the invoice he held in his hand. "Richard, if there was a problem, you wouldn't be working for me."

Richard wrung his hands, moved forward a bit, then stepped back. "Then, with all due respect sir, why are you here?"

Vincent put the papers he was holding down on the large oak desk and turned to Richard. The tall thin man always seemed smaller whenever he was being scrutinized. Richard ran a shaking hand through his blond tipped black hair. His wide eyes were showing off the bright violet contacts. Vincent had no idea what the man's real hair and eye color were. Richard knew his job, and the customers loved his flamboyant attitude, nothing else mattered.

"I'm here because although I do trust you to run the restaurant with grace and dignity, I know for a fact that you're terrible at keeping track of things. How many times have you forgotten to write something down?" Vincent turned back to the papers. "I trust you to run the restaurant well, but I have seen your past mistakes with the paperwork. Although I must admit, you're getting better."

It was Richard's job to keep track of deliveries: how much came in, what was used and what was needed. Due to his busy schedule, sometimes the man forgot to note a delivery. Vincent had one accountant just for The Ocean's Edge who stopped by once a week. Though Richard occasionally forgot to write something down, he knew exactly where all the paperwork was kept. That was why Vincent kept him.

Richard finally moved from behind Vincent's shoulder to a chair on the other side of the desk. "The past couple months I've been getting help from one of the servers." Vincent looked up and raised an eyebrow. He was waiting to hear more before reacting. "She started here a year ago. I checked her out at her previous job. They were sad to see her go. She's a great server; came with great recommendations. And she always takes the harder customers. They love her. She started helping me on the deliveries about three months ago. I've rearranged the deliveries to come on the same day so she can help me. She's smart, knows how to handle people and doesn't take crap from anyone."

Vincent was only half listening. He'd mostly stopped listening when Richard said that he had seen her at her previous job. Richard was a horrible bookkeeper, but he had a very good sense about people. Most of the staff had been working at the restaurant as long as Richard.

"What's her name?" It was an off-handed question, meant mostly to keep the human's mind off the paperwork and relax him.

"Natalie Dovenski."

Vincent nearly dropped the papers he was holding. "Say again?"

"Natalie Dovenski. Actually, she's still here if you want to meet her."

"Why haven't I met her yet?"

"She's been working days until recently."

"She works nights now?"

"Switched about six weeks ago."

He considered the timing. Natalia had shown up at The Red Thread about three weeks ago. "You said she's here now? I didn't see anyone when I came in."

"She runs on the beach after her shift. Likes the privacy."

Vincent leaned back in the leather chair and looked beyond Richard to the bank of television screens. There were three cameras that pointed toward the beach. He didn't see anyone on any of them. Richard looked in the same direction then got up and pointed at a screen showing part of the deck. There was a table with a bottle of water, a towel and a backpack on it. Its two chairs were still set on the floor rather than in the storage area, as they should be.

"She'll set everything right before she leaves. Always does."

Vincent stared at the screen showing her personal belongings. Natalie Dovenski was not a rare name, but neither was it common. He wondered if it was his mystery woman. He could watch in here until she was within view, then go outside to meet her if it was Natalia Dveski. But there was a problem. He and Richard were the only people in the restaurant. Joseph, his usual shadow, had a date with Mierka. They were off for a few hours, doing whatever it was they enjoyed doing. Vincent's eyes slowly moved toward Richard. Three was a crowd.

"Go home, Richard."

Richard started wringing his hands again, faster than before. "What? Why?"

"Because I said so." He stood. "As I mentioned before, the paperwork looks better than it ever has. I'm confident my accountant will tell me the same. Go home, Richard. Get some sleep. You look haggard."

Richard stood stock still for a moment, not wanting to believe him. Then, "Ok. See you next time." He was almost out the door before he turned back. "Shouldn't I stay and lock up?"

Vincent smirked. "No, go home. I'll take care of things."

"Thank you, sir." And he was gone.

Vincent stood looking at the blurry backpack on the screen for a moment, then left the office to lock up the restaurant. He walked around, making sure everything was in its place, turning off the lights as he went. Leaving the outside lights on, he went back to the office. There was still no sign of Natalie Dovenski, and her things were still on the deck.

Vincent sat in the large leather chair and stared at the screens. It had been three weeks since their first encounter. A week after their encounter, Joseph had handed him a large file filled with Natalia's history. She didn't have a lot of friends, but she interacted with a great deal of people. She visited Slayers and vampires and had killed about half of both groups she met. Natalia was hard to pinpoint. Vincent felt this was the perfect opportunity to speak with her away from the meddling eyes of, well, everyone.

Vincent got up, started pacing, but kept his eyes on the screen. He could try to convince himself that all he wanted was to talk to her, but he knew better. All he wanted to do was find a way to get her into his bed, which was pure and simple folly. If she were a Slayer, as her current actions suggested, he should not only stay away from her, he should kill her. When a vampire let his guard down around a Slayer, the vampire, even an old one, died.

Finally, annoyed she was taking so long, he pulled out his cell phone and brought up the app that controlled the cameras. He made sure that though the cameras still recorded, the screens in here were off. First shift would turn them on in the morning when they arrived. No one at the restaurant checked the recordings unless there was a reason. He put his phone away, turned the lights off and closed the door. He was at the table in half a minute.

Vincent peered down the beach, trying to see what the screens could not catch, but there was still no sign of her. He made himself comfortable, looked down the beach, and waited for her to arrive. A minute later he picked up her backpack. Inside the main pocket was clothing, a notebook with a pen in the spiral, and a hand towel wrapped around a sheathed knife. Frowning, Vincent unsheathed the knife. It was a hunting dagger, quite sharp, too. Vincent brought the blade to his nose and sniffed. He turned his head away; she probably cleaned the blade with garlic infused oil. Not a half bad idea.

Vincent moved the water bottle, placed her clothing on the table in a neat pile, laid the towel on top, then laid the blade out on that. Her notebook and pen he put to the side. He found her cell phone in the side pocket. The phone was in a case that also held her Clipper Card for the MUNI and her state ID. The picture showed Natalia. None of the information on the ID was the same as Joseph found. Vincent looked very carefully, trying to find any imperfection. As far as he could tell, it was either real, or a brilliant forgery.

Vincent laid the case on the table next to the notebook and emptied out the rest of the bag. The only other item was a 20 oz bottle of orange juice. He placed the emptied bag on the floor in front of the table, on top of her sandals and sat waiting for her to arrive. He could see movement on the beach. She would be here shortly. He was glad; he was tired of waiting.

ଓ ଞ

Natalia loved running on the hard-packed sand. She ran barefoot, preferring the feel of the gritty sand to the cushion of a running shoe. She also hated wet shoes, which happened a great deal when running this close to the water's edge. She liked to run because the feel of the wind against her body, the smell of the salt and seaweed, and the drumming of the surf against the sand helped her to forget her thoughts, and she had so much to forget.

She didn't know what to do anymore. For the past seven years she had desperately tried to be a Slayer in the hopes of being able to redeem herself in the name of her mother's memory. But now there was Vincent. Her first encounter with him had left her desiring more. Since their encounter, she had hoped to spot him here but regrettably had not. She had applied to The Ocean's Edge a year ago. Zechariah wanted a spy in the vampire's network. Since she had experience, and the vampire didn't know her face, she was the perfect candidate. It had been easy to get a job here; Richard was very susceptible to hypnosis.

Natalia had been instructed to keep an eye on Vincent's movements in the restaurant: how often did he eat there? How often did his people stop by? Anything that would help Zechariah and the others plot. It turned out that Vincent did not spend enough time at the restaurant, and there were too many human lives at risk. Most of the people who came to The Ocean's Edge were humans. Most of the members of The Red Thread were what Slayers called Hellspawn: vampires, mages, werewolves, demons and other such creatures.

It took a long time to convince the Slayers that The Red Thread was a better target. Zechariah, for some reason, was convinced The Ocean's Edge needed to be destroyed. Natalia thought perhaps Zechariah wanted to make the headlines instead of killing Hellspawn. She was finally able to convince Zechariah a few months ago to use The Red Thread. Now Zechariah knew what to do there. Natalia didn't know what he was planning. She could guess though, and the guesses weren't very pleasant.

Natalia was against any grand-scale plan that would eventually involve the local government. When confronted with reality, humans tended to lose their minds, but Zechariah seemed to want that. He thought it might bring about the end of all Hellspawn. Natalia knew all it would do was kill humans. She shook her head, trying to clear her mind. She was back at the restaurant. She didn't want Richard seeing her anxious face. Then she realized that the main lights were off. Only the lights on the deck were lit. She had the place to herself. She heaved a sigh of relief as she ran up the steps.

At the top of the steps, Natalia stopped dead. She was not alone, as she had thought. Sitting at her table with all her things laid out was the vampire who flitted through her dreams. He was sitting with one foot resting on the other knee, elbows on the armrests, hands tented in front of his face.

"Natalia." She wasn't wearing much; jogging shorts, a sport bra and her ever-present silver necklace. Her skin was shiny from sweat. He wanted her toned body pressed against his. His eyes showed his thoughts.

She stood with her hand on the railing, one foot on the deck, one on the step just below. He was well dressed in jeans and a black button up shirt. He was quite handsome. "Vincent."

He stayed where he was, staring at her. "I was rather intrigued to learn you had a job here. My investigation of you didn't turn that up. But at least now I know another name to look under. Tell me, does Natalie Dovenski have as interesting a past?"

Natalia slammed the door on her emotions and continued onto the deck. She strolled to the table and took her water bottle. She took a drink, screwed the top back on and took it with her to the railing. She rested her back on the banister and regarded Vincent. His face revealed less than hers did. "Natalie Dovenski doesn't know that things like you exist." She took another sip of water. "What do you want, Vampire?"

"Call me by my name. I like hearing it whispering through your lips." Still no emotion.

A muscle twitched in her jaw as she ground her teeth. "You could have put my things back."

"I want you to know how much I know about you." His blue eyes were locked with her dark ones. There seemed to be some humor there. He drummed his fingers together, waiting.

Natalia ground her teeth again, then shut her eyes tight, hiding the anger that clouded them. She opened her eyes and stared at him. "And why would I care?"

"It's a sad past, checkered with much horror. How old were you when you met your first monster?"

Her anger thickened. Was he making fun of her? "Ten."

"What kind of monster did you meet?" He was intrigued. He knew about the werewolf she met seven years ago. He did not know about the monster she met at the age of ten.

Her head reeled as if she'd been slapped. A tear slid down her cheek as she remembered her first real monster. Her voice was a whisper. She was surprised he heard. "Human."

Vincent was not expecting the haunted look. He had expected, wanted, her anger. Passionate anger, always easy to stoke, could be transformed into something far more pleasurable. He had come out here to play. He would have his way. But first, "He's not the one, though, is he? Not the one who made you a Slayer."

Her anger came back at the word. "I'm not a Slayer."

"You spend much of your time with them. The past seven years you've done nothing but train and study. The past year and a half you've spent much time with Zechariah Haynes." He drummed his fingers on the table. "How did you decide it was a good idea to join with the Slayer who locked you in a spiked closet?"

Her teeth clenched, followed by her whole body. She bared her teeth, turned and threw her water bottle at the opposite railing. It exploded against the wood. She nearly scremed. "WHO WAS I SUPPOSED TO TURN TO?"

A small fire started in Vincent's blood; a smile came to his eyes. His chances of burning in her were growing. He stood and walked to her. She stared him down, teeth still clenched, seething. She could see the wicked glee shining in his eyes. She braced herself for the next blow.

"Werewolves?" He pressed forward, forcing her back to the railing. She didn't realize what he was doing until her back hit the railing and he placed his hands on the banister, trapping her between his arms.

"Untrustworthy." Her heart was hammering in her chest. Why was he standing so close?

"Unless you are one. You spent a long time with Charles Bartholomew, why did you stop dating him?" His voice had grown softer; the fingers of his left hand were caressing her bare arm. He was rattling her with his knowledge. He knew too much, and why did his cool fingers feel so good on her overheated skin?

She pulled her arm away, clenched her fist; tightly crossed her arms. "None of your business."

"Tell me what you were doing with him for a year and a half."

He took another step and was pressing lightly against her. His fingers breezed up her arm, agonizingly slow. Her breath caught as his fingers skated across her collarbone then down her other arm. She closed her eyes and thought of Charlie; all the delicious things he used to do. She wondered what Vincent would be like in bed. Her mind screamed at her and she tried to break away from Vincent. He simply pressed forward and encircled her in his arms.

Her resolve was slipping; he could feel it, see it on her face. She was more out of breath now than after she ran up the steps. Her heart was beating so fast, he could smell her blood through her skin. "That bad? Or that good? What did he teach you Natalia?"

Natalia's thoughts were screaming at her. She could hear Zechariah in her mind spouting off about throwing her sinful ways to the roadside and picking up the fight on the side of good. Her resolve grew and she stood taller. Her heart and breath slowed. Natalia felt in control.

"To be mindful of creatures with sharp teeth."

Their eyes locked for a moment, as they dared each other to make the next move. A gleam came into the vampire's eyes as he saw the challenge in Natalia's eyes. He imagined most men would run away at that look. He was not that easily frightened.

Vincent smiled as he leaned in closer to whisper in her ear. One arm was wrapped lightly around her waist. The other hand brushed against her bare skin. "I enjoy having you trapped in my arms."

His words caused Natalia's emotions and thoughts to turn into gale force winds, which threatened to knock her out of his arms and over the side of the banister. A small whimper escaped her lips as she realized she liked the feel of his fingers on her skin; craved the feel of his body pressing against hers. His legs were between hers; she had no idea how that happened. She could feel his erection through his jeans. He was shifting

49

back and forth rubbing against her lightly. The friction was driving a wedge in her determination.

She was swaying slightly with the motion of his body. Her eyes closed slowly as his fingers brushed her jawline and neck, missing her necklace completely.

"Did you have fun with the werewolf, Natalia? Did you enjoy every moment he was touching you? Did you hunger for his touch when he was gone? Do you hunger for mine?"

Her whimper was louder this time. Her hand was tight on his wrist, trying to stop the maddening touch. Zechariah was screaming at her in her head, telling her to fight the temptation. Vincent's hand was not stopped by her grip.

"When was the last time you were with a man, Natalia? Did you take up the celibacy of the Slayer who ruins your life? Have you allowed yourself any pleasure in the past seven years?"

His hand, as if unhindered, slid down her chest between her breasts. As he explored further, she was forced to let go. Her hands went to his chest, gripping his soft rayon shirt in her fists. As his hand slipped between her legs, she tried to push him away. Half of her wanted to get away and the other half wanted to wrap her arms around him and give in. She hadn't been with anyone since Charlie. Hadn't wanted anyone since Charlie, except the man who now tempted her.

He felt her hands on his chest. She pulled at his shirt one second and pushed him away the next, as if trying to make up her mind. He wondered how strong she would be if she actually tried to stop him. His research revealed how much training, and what kind of training she had had. Vincent didn't think she could kill him, but it would be an interesting fight. He wasn't interested in fighting tonight though and continued his seduction.

He was rubbing her slightly through her nylon shorts; could feel her wetness through the thin fabric. There had been underwear in her backpack. He wondered if she were wearing any now. His smile widened as his need mounted. He leaned his head in to nibble on her ear. Without thinking she leaned her head to the side, allowing him better access to her neck. He growled softly in her ear, sending shivers down her spine. She switched from pushing him away to pulling him toward her. His arms slipped around her, tightly pressing her to him.

"Do you give in Natalia? Do you give yourself over to pleasure? When was the last time you did anything that felt good? That made your skin tingle with anticipation? That made your head swim and your thoughts fade? I am your temptation Natalia, your chance at pleasure. The devil on your shoulder, whispering dark notions in your ear. Wouldn't you love to know how I feel inside you?"

His words were thrashing through her whirlwind thoughts, destroying all resolve. His touch, icy to her burning flesh, singed her bare skin. She was grinding her teeth, pushing herself against him while trying to push him away. Finally, unable to think clearly, she threw back her head and howled her frustration. The din tore down the beach like a great beast in heat.

Her battle with her feelings was done. A different look of determination grabbed her features. Vincent watched the transformation, entranced. Her teeth were still clenched, but this time in hunger, not anger. The craving in her eyes matched his. She became the woman from the club: seductress, temptress, his match. Was she playing him? Vincent wasn't sure. Didn't care. Her hand went to his head, tangling in his short sleek blond hair. She pulled him toward her; he came willingly. Her kiss revealed the depth of her thirst. He crushed her to him, enjoying every moment of the deep, long kiss.

They parted, both breathless. Natalia looked intently into his eyes. "You have me Vincent. What would you like to do with me?"

He bent forward and growled in her ear. "I should just drain your blood and leave you for dead on the side of the road. It'll probably save me a lot of trouble."

She laughed devilishly. "You're chance for that has passed." She wrapped one arm around his neck, gripped his hair with the other then pulled herself up and wrapped her legs around his hips. She whispered into his ear. "What do you really want to do with me, Vincent?"

"If you don't know the answer to that, you're not as smart as you think you are."

He gripped her tightly, kissing her roughly. He seized her shorts and thong and pulled them down. She removed her legs from his hips, kicking off her garments. She heard his zipper and swung her legs around him again. Holding on tight, she moved herself up and down getting him wet. Vincent enjoyed the friction for as long as he could stand it, placed Natalia on the banister, and ripped off her sports bra. Natalia grabbed his black shirt and ripped it off, popping the buttons. The shirt fluttered to the wooden deck.

Natalia's head cleared long enough to wonder what she was doing. She looked into Vincent's face and saw nothing but a deep craving. He gave her a short, frustrated growl, and showed her his fangs. Fear exploded on her features, but Vincent smirked and retracted his fangs. He plunged his icy erection into her, instead of his teeth. He pushed further in, grunting with satisfaction as she seared him.

Natalia's nails dug into his back as his icy length pushed deeper and deeper. The contrast of heat and ice made her tighten around him and she let out a squeak. He gave a small laugh before pulling out and plunging back into her. Soon, she was moaning in rhythm with his movements.

Vincent dug his nails deep into Natalia's back causing her to arch. She threw her head back, elongating her neck. Her hands gripped the banister edge for better support and the arch deepened. Vincent stared at Natalia's olive skin, mesmerized by the curve of her neck and the pulsing jugular just visible under her skin. His mouth watered, and his pace quickened as he caressed her neck. He growled low as his fingers curled down. He raked his nails down her chest leaving a trail of welts. She moaned then cried out as pleasure mixed with pain. He grinned, loving the sound.

Drawing her closer, Vincent once again quickened his pace. Natalia's hands moved to his back as she gave the large man her own grin. Her long nails dug deep into the middle of his back. His impish grin only widened as she raked her nails across his skin. He felt it, but there was no pain. Laughing at her annoyed expression, he placed one hand at the base of her neck and the other at her lower back. He pulled her as close as he could, moving faster. Her fingers tangled in his soft blond hair, gripping hard as she pulled herself off the banister.

Natalia tightened around him again and his pace quickened for the last time. When her cries came faster, he pulled her head to face him and watched as a wave of ecstasy seized her features. A scream ripped through her throat, and she arched into him as shudder after shudder ripped through her body. Vincent's grunts turned into a satisfied growl that was almost a purr.

Natalia collapsed into Vincent still shuddering. Gripping her head, he brought her mouth to his and kissed her deeply. Already out of breath, she broke away quickly, gasping for air. A small moan escaped as a last shudder racked her body. Unable to hold herself up she rested her head on Vincent's shoulder. They stayed unmoving for a moment or two, while Natalia caught her breath.

Natalia pulled back from him unsure of what to do. Her legs were still wrapped around him, and his arms were still at her back. She looked into his face, trying to read him. It was impossible. He had an incredible poker face.

Vincent stared down into her eyes, wondering if he could feed from her. He was hungry, and he greatly enjoyed taking blood from willing women. Her breasts were brushing against his chest making him think about what else he could do to her. He was still in the controlling position. His mind changed from wanting her blood, to wanting her body. He let the desire show in his eyes and slight smile. Natalia saw the look and her breath caught, then came quicker.

"What happens now?"

Vincent's smile turned into a full hyena smile as he redirected his blood flow. Natalia gasped in excitement and surprise. His smile deepened at her reaction. His desire was under control; now he could have his fun.

He spent the next few hours bringing her near climax only to back off, leaving her screaming with frustration and begging for release.

છ ૪

Natalia was spent. Vincent was a hell of a lover. She shivered as a breeze cooled the sweat beading on her skin. Vincent nipped at the side of her neck. His cool breath did nothing to help her shivers.

Vincent was sitting on one of the chairs with Natalia in his lap, her chest to his chest. Her legs were hanging over the edge of the armrests. When they had moved there, Natalia didn't know. Her memory was unreliable. She moved away a little and looked at the ocean and sky, wondering how she was going to have the energy to go home.

Natalia turned back to look at Vincent and realized he was wearing a silver necklace with a red stone pendant. She reached out to it and caressed the stone. There was an edge of silver around the red pendant and a silver fleur-de-lis that was attached to the edges. There were what appeared to be tiny silver drops falling from the fleur-de-lis. Vincent's hand went to cover her hand and stop her movements. She looked into his eyes.

"I've seen this as a drawing. What does it mean?"

He looked steadily into her eyes. "That is not something you will learn today."

She opened her mouth to answer but was stopped by a familiar alarm. She turned her head to the left as she realized it was her phone alarm. She had an early breakfast meeting and had set the alarm a few days ago. It was five in the morning. The sun would be up in less than an hour and her appointment was in two hours. Natalia needed to get ready. She tried to get off Vincent, but he held her to him.

"I didn't say you could leave." He growled.

"I want to turn off my alarm. And sunrise is sooner than you think."

Vincent let Natalia go. She grabbed her phone and turned off the alarm. Natalia searched for her clothing but could only find her shorts and panties. Vincent was up and searching for his own clothing. His were all together in a pile on the deck. His cell rang as he picked up his pants. He answered as he sat to slip on his jeans.

"Yes, I'm ready to be picked up." He paused. "Yes, at the restaurant." His voice went from casual to business. "Just get here."

He hung up, stood to finish putting on his pants, then sat back down to watch Natalia, who was throwing her things in her backpack. What was he going to do with her? He wanted to take her home. He would be revived after some sleep and some blood, and he would want her again. Ever since their first meeting he woke with her on his mind. Now that he knew what she was capable of, he was more determined to get her in his bed, permanently. Vincent drummed his fingers on the table, watching as she slipped on her jean shorts. They were not as revealing as the workout shorts, but more appropriate as street wear.

As Natalia dressed she drank the orange juice, wishing she hadn't destroyed her water bottle. She felt lightheaded and after that workout, needed to quench her thirst. She drank the juice slowly, pausing to pull on a dark green shirt. She caught Vincent watching her and stared back. "What?"

"I'm considering your statement from the club."

"That I could be an asset, that you can use me, or both?" She took an unladylike swig of the orange juice.

"That I could use you. You're coming home with me."

Natalia stood up and carefully walked over to Vincent's clothing. She picked up his shirt and walked over to him. "I have an appointment I can't break." She frowned. "Shouldn't you be going inside somewhere?"

"There will be a car here well before the Morning Star notices me." He paused to pull on his shirt. "What's so important about this meeting?"

Natalia stepped away, and calmly walked to her bag on the other side of the table. She stuffed her workout clothing into the bag and zipped up the pouch. She slipped on her sandals and drank the last of the orange juice, putting the bottle back in the side pocket. "I'm meeting someone who may have information I want."

Vincent reached over and grasped her wrist. He let her feel his strength. "Is it more important than your pleasure?"

"Vincent, please, just let me go." Hesitation broke through and reflected in her eyes.

He pulled her to him. "You don't have a choice, I'm taking you with me."

"Vincent, if you take me against my will and make me break this appointment, I'll find a way to expose you to the sun." She no longer sounded hesitant.

He pulled her onto his lap. She didn't resist. Under normal circumstances, she wouldn't have the strength. Now, she was low on energy. She had run three miles and had sex with Vincent for at least four hours. In her current condition, she wouldn't be able to pull away from a human.

"Then I will lock you in a room and take you out when I'm ready for you." He sounded serious.

Natalia adjusted herself to straddle and face Vincent. Her voice was seductive, but her eyes were hard. "If you do, I'll find a way out and I'll go to your room while you're asleep and I'll expose you to the sun, even if it means hacking through a concrete wall with my fists. I'll eventually take you up on the offer, but this meeting is very important to me. Let. Me. Go."

He saw her determination shining through. If he took her now, he would never be able to enjoy her again. He wanted this one. Wanted her as often as he could have her. Since he wanted her willing, he nodded as hunger crept into his mind. "I will, but before I do, may I take your blood?"

Uncertainty crept into her eyes. "If I say no?"

"I only take from the willing."

"Will it hurt?" Her voice revealed curiosity, not fear.

"You've been bitten before. You know the answer."

"I meant, is there a way for it not to hurt?"

"I will be piercing your skin with my fangs, Natalia. How would it not hurt?"

She shook her head. "I don't know. I guess I'm just nervous."

He gripped her chin in his hand, looked into her eyes. "Yes or no. May I take your blood?"

Natalia looked deep into the vampire's eyes and knew he would listen to her word on this. She was starting to understand him better. She felt trust grow as they stared at each other. Natalia nodded. "Yes."

"Stand to the side of the chair and face me."

She did as instructed.

"Give me your arm."

She held her arm out to him, palm up. Vincent grasped her arm at the wrist and elbow and moved her arm closer to his mouth. He bent over her arm and elongated his fangs. The back of his neck was exposed. He was in a vulnerable position and both knew it. In that moment, Vincent started to trust Natalia, as well. He caressed her soft skin with his lips, then again with his fangs. He bit her quickly and sighed as her blood washed over his tongue. He retracted his fangs, placed his lips on her arm and started to suck.

Natalia grunted as he bit. His fangs pierced her flesh close to the elbow. She stopped herself from pulling her arm away. She trusted Tony more when he took her blood. For Tony, it was payment; for Vincent, it was something more and that made Natalia nervous. Natalia held her arm still and felt when he withdrew his fangs. He sucked at her arm, her blood, and the pain did not diminish. Natalia waited for the vampire to be done, wondering if she made the right decision. She knew it would always be this way, would always hurt.

The thought made her understand she would probably allow this to happen again. She wasn't yet sure how she felt about that. A vision of her mother on the day Donald killed her came to Natalia's mind. Did Marina give her blood to the vampire willingly as Natalia had done with Vincent? Natalia didn't know. She looked at Vincent as he took her life's blood and wondered at her decision.

Vincent took a few swallows of her blood, then pulled his head away. He quickly reached into his pants pocket to grab a clean handkerchief. He placed it over her wound and allowed her to take her arm back. He licked her blood off his lips as he watched her turn her back. She shoved the image of her mother out of her mind and took a deep breath.

"Do you regret what you did?"

Natalia's heart was pounding, but she turned back to Vincent. She held the handkerchief to her arm. A soft frown creased her brow. "No."

"Then why the worry?"

"I don't..." She stopped for a moment, then shook her head. She didn't want to lie about it, but she barely knew Vincent. "There's a lot about my past you don't know, Vincent. Giving you my blood of my own free will brought up a lot of things I didn't want to think about."

"Is this the first time you've given blood to a vampire of your own free will?"

"No, this is the second."

He nodded. "How many times has a vampire fed from you?"

She gave a short, humorless laugh. "Other than the time your man took my blood as a warning?"

They stared at each other for a moment before Vincent answered. "Yes."

"Three times that I know of."

It was his turn to frown. He held out his hand to her. She took it and willingly sat in his lap when he pulled her closer. "Donald took your blood, yes?"

She gave him a startled look. She didn't know he knew about Donald. She wondered how much Vincent knew about her. That was a discussion for another day. "Yes."

"Who else?" He guessed from the police reports that Donald took her blood. She never stated it explicitly, but then, no one could really tell the police about vampire attacks and be believed.

She smiled and wondered if Vincent would know the name. "Tony Lam."

"Oh? Did it have something to do with his disappearance?"

"I found him right around the same time Slayers did. We ran from a bar. I gave him a contact out of the area and blood for getting us someplace safe."

"Where is he now?"

"If he wanted you to know, you would know."

Vincent nodded and let the subject go. "That was two."

She sighed. "I don't know who else. It was after I found out how crazy this world really was. I freed a werewolf when I was trapped in a Slayer's house. Charlie was human and in a cage. He asked for my help. I freed him. He turned Blitzkreig and killed the Slayer. I used alcohol to bury the memory. Woke up one day with a vampire bite on my wrist. I knew then that I had to change my ways or lose myself completely."

He gazed at her, intrigued. He did not know this story. "One day, you will tell me all your stories."

56

Natalia was surprised by the amount of interest in his eyes. He wanted to know more about her. She smiled. "Yes. Will you tell me yours?"

"I have been alive a long time, Natalia. I don't remember everything." Some he simply did not want to remember.

"Will you tell me what you can remember?"

"Yes."

They stared at each other for a moment, thinking their own thoughts. Natalia sighed and finally removed herself from Vincent's lap. She gathered her things and looked to Vincent.

"What happens now, Vincent?"

"Meet me." His voice, low and seductive, swept over her skin.

She closed her eyes. "When?"

"When do you work again?"

"Friday afternoon. It's a double. I'll be here until close."

"I'll have dinner here on Friday. We'll talk of our future." His phone rang. He let it.

"Yes."

Natalia turned and walked away, leaving Vincent to answer his phone. She walked to the end of the deck where a set of stairs led to the parking lot. She heard the car before she saw it. There was a short limousine idling at the bottom of the steps, with the back door hanging open. A woman was leaning against the car, ready to close the door for Vincent. Convenient for Vincent, inconvenient for Natalia. She nodded to the driver as she maneuvered around the car. Natalia was almost around it when she was whipped back around. Her bag banged against the trunk of the car as Vincent trapped her against the side.

"I thought we were done." Her voice mirrored excitement and a tinge of anger.

"Come with me. Someone will drive you to your appointment later."

Her hand was in his hair, massaging the back of his neck. "Vincent, do you have a car a waitress could afford?"

His hands were massaging her back under her backpack. With the door hanging open, it would be sinfully easy to throw her inside. "No, I don't suppose I do."

Natalia removed her hand from his neck, placed both hands on his chest and pushed him back. He did not resist, although she knew he could have. She had that determined look again.

"My appointment is at a church in Oakland. It would raise a lot of questions if I arrived in a limo, or a fancy sports car or whatever it is you own. I'll meet you here on Friday."

He grabbed her to him one final time, giving her a crushing kiss. When he let her go, they were both breathless. "Don't disappoint me."

"Have I yet?" She gave him a smile and slipped away.

He watched her cross the parking lot and climb the steps to the street two at a time. He shook his head and closed himself in the back of the car. The divider was already up; he settled back to relax but couldn't. She had riled him up.

Vincent had not expected her to be so willing. He had thought, after reading the file Joseph compiled, that he would have to kill her. Vincent had learned through the years that although female Slayers were not as powerful, their righteousness and belief often ran deeper and stronger than in male Slayers, making them deadlier. Maybe she wasn't a Slayer.

If she wasn't a Slayer, what was she? He narrowed his eyes as he thought about her naked body against his, of her blood in his mouth. He didn't know what she was; just knew what he wanted her to be. He wanted her to be his lover. A smile crept across his face as his thoughts turned back to every movement her body had made. She seemed rather willing to be his.

8

Natalia brought herself back to reality as her cell phone went off. She shook her head and blushed as she pushed aside memories of Vincent. She licked her lips, grabbed her glass of orange juice and went back to the breakfast table. She sat down and glanced at her phone. She smiled as she sent a text to Bethany, and let her know dinner next week would be great. She absentmindedly placed the phone in her pocket and went back to her breakfast. She had to stop thinking of the vampire but couldn't. While she was with him, she didn't think of the pain or losing her mom, or the aggravation of not finding her mother's killer. She also didn't think of Zechariah and the sheer frustration she felt when around him and his group.

She set her spoon in the bowl of cereal and sighed. Natalia had to admit, the vampire and his people seemed like a better idea than the Slayers. Vincent and his people could have killed her by now, but they hadn't. With his resources, Vincent probably already knew more about her than she knew about him. He didn't use it to find her. She felt comforted by that. She sighed again. If she were with Vincent, she might be able to find Donald faster, but she might also find more trouble. She had a feeling she would use her knowledge to help the vampire and his people stay alive.

She had to wonder if that was such a terrible thing. Vincent and his people were trying to rid the Bay Area of vampires like Edwin. The sick monster changed anyone he wanted, regardless of age. Edwin and his lot should be dealt with. Vincent seemed to be more than happy to get rid of them.

Natalia knew she wasn't a Slayer, but she didn't know if she wanted to help vampires. She sighed and caught sight of the newest bite mark on her arm. It had hurt a great deal, but only briefly. She licked her lips again as more thoughts of Vincent flitted through her mind.

The doorbell rang and threw her out of her memories. Natalia frowned and got up. She made her way quickly to the door, looked through the peephole and inhaled sharply. Zechariah stood on her front steps, a mild smile on his face. She wasn't even aware he knew where she lived. Natalia took a deep breath. She knew where the weapons were, he didn't. And he was alone. As soon as she opened the door, six men moved into her sight behind Zechariah.

"Hello Zechariah. How can I help you? I hope this is quick. I have an appointment to keep." She kept an eye on the men behind him.

Zechariah grinned. "Did you enjoy what he did to you?"

"What?" Natalia wasn't sure he was talking about Vincent but didn't have a chance to respond further as the men rushed into the house. She tried to close the door, but there were too many. They grabbed her, searched her pockets and held her arms behind her.

"Let me go! What's the meaning of this?"

Natalia felt when someone took her cell phone from her pocket. She heard it thud to the ground and cringed when she heard it break. The phone crunched under a heavy shoe heel. She tried to pull away from her captors, but they held on. Finally, one forced her to look at Zechariah. He smiled mildly.

"Did you or did not you enjoy what he did to you?"

"What are you talking about?" She nearly yelled through clenched teeth.

"I heard what you and the vampire did at the restaurant."

Surprise made her answer truthfully. "You were there?"

He held her gaze. "Answer the question."

Her mind worked quickly. If she could convince Zechariah it was all a ploy, he might let her go. "I seduced him to make it easier to infiltrate his club. I did what I had to. I was going to tell you about it when we saw each other next. Let me go and we can talk."

He stared deep into her eyes for a moment, then stepped back and took her hand in his. He placed his hand over her bite wound. "You allowed him to take your blood."

"It was all part of the act."

"Did you enjoy it?"

She closed her eyes as a tear slipped down her cheek. He was being too kind. She knew he didn't believe her. She told him the truth anyway. "No. It hurt."

"But you knew this already." His hand went to the mark on her shoulder, the mark Donald left. "Why did you allow it when you knew it would hurt?"

She opened her eyes and gave him a frank look. "There are many things I have allowed that hurt me in order to stop monsters from destroying the people I love."

He gave her a smirk. "Who were you protecting this time? Bethany?"

The color drained from Natalia's face. As far as she remembered, she never once mentioned her best friend to Zechariah or any Slayer. "Why did you bring her up?"

He gave her an awful grin as her hands were tied behind her. Natalia pulled against the men holding her to no avail. As she struggled, they wrestled her to the ground and tied her hands behind her back. She tried to scream, but a cloth was placed against her nose and mouth. She tried not to breathe, but it was useless. The chloroform seeped into her air passages and she passed out.

☘ ☙

The rough movements of the vehicle woke Natalia, but she didn't immediately sit up. She could tell she was lying on someone's lap, and there was a hand on her shoulder. The hand did not feel confining; it felt comforting. She took deep breaths and opened her eyes to darkness. She was blindfolded. Fine. She tried to move her arms and realized they were tied in front of her. Her legs were bound as well, but as there wasn't pain in her feet, she assumed they had not tied her tightly.

Once she understood she was bound, Natalia tried to sit up. The hand on her shoulder stopped her gently and Dean spoke kindly. "If you just woke up, give yourself a few more minutes before you try to sit up. You might be dizzy."

She relaxed as she realized that though there were probably other people in the vehicle, no one else seemed to realize she was awake. Natalia settled down and listened to the voices. There seemed to be two other people talking. She recognized Zechariah but did not recognize the other person. His voice was gruff and none too pleasant. Unfortunately, the pair were not talking too loud and Natalia could not listen for long. Feeling enough was enough, she pulled away from Dean gently and sat up carefully.

Natalia breathed deep as her stomach turned. She wasn't sure it was from the chloroform they used or laying down for a long time. Either way, she stayed steady until it passed. As she sat there, Zechariah called from the front seat.

"Ah, you're awake. Did you enjoy your nap, Natalie? The trucks windows are tinted. No one will see in. And don't try to take off the blindfold. I will knock you out again."

She didn't say anything, as there wasn't anything to say. Natalia sat back and listened to the sound of the traffic and the low hum of the conversation, trying to figure out where they were going. She started counting, trying to discern how long they were driving. When they finally stopped, she figured they had been driving for around two hours. As she didn't know how long she had been out it was hard to know how far a drive it was from her home. Also, they could have driven around in circles for all she knew.

After the truck stopped, and the engine died, she heard two doors open and close. Hers opened a moment later.

"Don't move. I'm removing your blindfold and untying your legs." Zechariah's voice was pleasant, but she knew that tone and didn't trust it. Nevertheless, she let him remove the blindfold and watched as he removed the rope from her ankles. He then helped her climb out of the truck.

Natalia blinked hard as the sun shifted through the trees and nearly blinded her. She took a deep breath and smelled pine. They were in a coniferous forest. She looked around and confirmed that tall pine trees nearly surrounded them. She looked to Zechariah, then saw Dean behind him to the right. To Dean's left was a man she'd never seen before. He had a look on his face she didn't like. She stared him down until Zechariah stepped in front of her to gain her attention.

"Come now. I'll take you to your room."

"I want to know about Bethany." A quiet but insistent voice reminded her of Bethany through the entire ride.

"We'll talk inside."

She wanted to demand answers but realized that would be foolish. She didn't know anything. Demanding more knowledge might prove deadly to her or Bethany. Natalia nodded and allowed Zechariah to place his hand on her arm and lead her into a nearby cabin. It was made of log woods and looked well maintained. Dean hurried forward to open the door. Once inside, Zechariah stopped and allowed their eyes to adjust to the lower light.

The inside smelled of wood. The room they were in was dining room, living room and kitchen combined. She could see a staircase leading up and two doors upstairs and downstairs. In other circumstances, it would be cozy; a great place for a vacation. Natalia doubted greatly it would be a vacation for her.

Zechariah took her to a room on the main floor. The room was empty, and the floor was bare. If there were lights, there were no bulbs. The curtains were closed. Sunlight seeped in around the edges but gave very little light. There was a wooden post in the center of the room that looked out of place. The wood was a different color than the rest of the room. There were steel plates and thick bolts holding the post to the floor and ceiling. Zechariah took Natalia to the post and indicated she should sit with her back to it. She did as instructed and he untied her hands.

"Put them behind you, around the post." His kind but awful voice stated.

Natalia tried not to grimace and did as he asked. She could see the third man. He grinned at her with malice as Zechariah tied her hands behind her. She settled her back against the post and looked to Zechariah.

Before she could say anything, the third man laughed. "Easy pickin's now."

"Marshal, none of that." Zechariah turned to look at the man. "Go park the truck out of the way. You know the place."

Marshal gave Zechariah a guarded look but turned and walked out the door. Dean stood with his back against the wall near the door. Natalia saw Dean gesture to Marshal, who growled an unintelligible answer back. Natalia turned her attention to Zechariah.

"He seems a bit unsteady. Are you sure I'm safe around him?" She felt odd asking, but she knew Zechariah was celibate. He didn't believe in fornication, as he put it, and frowned when he knew a Slayer was in a relationship. From the way Marshal had looked at her and what he said a moment ago, Natalia knew Marshal did not believe like Zechariah.

"If he tries anything, I will stop him. The cabin is too small for secrets. For the moment, you will stay tied. I can't have you running away."

"If you have Bethany, I won't run."

The tone of her voice made Zechariah perk up. "She is important to you, isn't she? A lover perhaps?"

"No. A longtime friend. Let her go, Zechariah. She knows nothing of the creatures in the shadows. She's not like us." Her voice was soft, timid.

He looked at her mildly for a moment, the shook his head. "I'm sure time will tell."

Anger grew in Natalia, but she clamped it down as frustrated tears started to flow. "I want proof that you have her."

"I'll bring you some, if you're good."

She bared her teeth as he started to turn away. Her anger grew with each step he took away from her. Finally, her anger boiled over. "You bastard! If you harm her, I'll kill you!"

Zechariah continued to walk out of the room as Natalia let out a string of curses. The Slayers left the room and locked the door behind them.

In the dark room, Natalia allowed herself to cry silently as she thought of Bethany. They met in college, when Natalia was 15. Bethany took an instant liking to her. She treated Natalia like a younger sister, going so far as to buy her clothing and give her hand me downs.

When she was younger, Natalia threw herself into books to escape the horrors of her life. Bethany helped her to see the world in a different way, in a normal way. Natalia was not able to escape the shadows completely, but hoped Bethany would be spared the truth. Natalia would do everything she had to and keep Bethany safe, even if it meant doing nothing.

9

Vincent was trying to pretend to enjoy the exquisite wine he was sipping but was having trouble doing so. Natalia was nowhere to be seen. He was loath to ask about her, not wanting Richard to waste his time prattling on about her virtues or coming to the right conclusion about his favorite waitress and his boss. Therefore, he let it be.

He was sitting at his table on the private mezzanine. It overlooked the main floor of the restaurant but kept customers from staring at him. It also kept the human customers safe from his frustrations. Vincent worked with humans as he needed to and preferred to mingle with them only on certain occasions. This occasion, he wanted to deal with one human, and she was nowhere to be found.

Joseph and Mierka were seated at the table with him, pretending to enjoy the Five-Star cuisine. Vampires didn't need food, therefore rarely ate. Joseph, as always, was aware of the situation. At a table nearby sat his two top werewolves, Rebecca and Charlie, who were obviously enjoying the food. He didn't often take along the werewolves but wanted the extra protection. His people had reported more Slayers than usual in San Francisco; Edwin and his lot were attracting the wrong kind of attention.

Vincent could have taken someone else, but wanted to see Charlie's reaction to Natalia. He had not informed either the werewolf or the human that Charlie worked for him and didn't plan on it. Surprises like that amused the vampire.

Vincent sipped at his drink, trying to enjoy the full flavor of the old wine. It was a twenty-year-old red from a local vineyard. It was supposed to be good, but he couldn't care less. If it wasn't blood, he didn't enjoy it. He frowned into the glass wondering how to proceed. Richard was climbing the stairs to see to his boss and must have noticed the look. He was at the table in an instant.

"Something wrong with the wine, sir?" There was an anxious tone to his voice. He hated entertaining his boss even more than having the imposing man look through the paperwork.

"Not with the wine or food, Richard." Joseph answered. "We want to meet the waitress who helps with the books. Natalie, is it? Is she here tonight?"

Richard wrung his hands and looked nervously away. "Well actually, she was scheduled, but she didn't show up. I haven't been able to reach her at home or on her cell."

Joseph caught Vincent's look before it was tucked away and hidden. No one else saw the look, but Mierka did sense a change. She caught Rebecca's eye and saw the woman signal Charlie. Richard was handled while money was left on the table for the meals. The werewolves left, heading for the car. Their instructions were to be at the limo first. Charlie was at the car first and held the door open for Vincent and Joseph. Mierka went to the driver seat, Rebecca went to the front passenger and Charlie got in back. He sat by the door and tried to ignore the conversation.

"What do you think happened, sir?"

"She's toying with me. I should have guessed this would happen."

"Are you certain, sir?"

Vincent gave Joseph a steady look. "From the moment she entered my life, Natalia has been nothing but trouble. I refuse to allow her to play me any longer. Twice she has been within my grasp, and twice I let her go. Next time, I will take her, and I will not let go, even if it means squeezing the life out of her."

Charlie tried hard not to pay attention. He stared out the window, wishing he didn't know whom his boss was talking about. It was easier once the conversation turned to business.

⚃ ⚄

They were back at Vincent's estate before long. Everyone was left to their own devices. Rebecca, wanting to stretch her muscles, turned into a wolf and ran off. Vincent owned the hill the house was on and the one next to it. The two hills were filled by many farms run by humans. They willingly gave their blood to Vincent and the other seven vampires who lived under Vincent's protection. The werewolves could run the land as wolves but were warned on a regular basis that the humans had tranquillizer guns to take them down if they did something foolish. If for some reason the tranqs didn't take them down, the humans had shotguns with silver buckshot, and would use them if they were threatened.

Charlie went to his room and started pacing. Vincent had gone to the restaurant to meet Nat. The werewolf worried that she wasn't there. When Charlie knew her, she never once missed going to work for any reason. And she liked to tease. By now, Charlie heard about her visit to the club; most of Vincent's men had. He also accidentally saw the recording of Natalia and Vincent at the restaurant. He remembered how she had been with him. She loved to toy with her prey; and her prey loved to be toyed with. His body flushed as he thought about her.

He belonged to Rebecca now and she belonged to him, but Natalia was a part of his past, and he still cared about her. He pulled out his cell and called her home, almost amazed her number hadn't changed. When the machine picked up, he called her cell which was also the same as it had been when they were together. There was no answer on her cell either. He didn't want to leave a message, it didn't seem like a good idea. He called the restaurant next, demanding to speak with Richard.

"The Ocean's Edge. This is Richard, how may I help you?" He sounded frantic.

"This is Charlie, I work for Vincent. I need to know the last time Natalie was at work."

There was a pause. "Who did you say you were?"

"I was sitting at the table to the right of Vincent."

"Oh yes, sir. I know who you are." Another pause. Charlie was wondering if Richard was going to talk to him when he finally came back on. "The last time she worked was Monday."

"Has she called?"

"No."

"Has she ever missed work before?" He already knew the answer.

"No. Never even been late."

"I want you to call me if you hear from her." He rattled off his number and hung up. He drummed his fingers on the phone then decided. He had to find Vincent. Charlie paused with his hand on the doorknob, really considering his actions.

If he told Vincent he wanted to investigate Natalia's disappearance, then he'd have to tell the man how he knew her. He would have to tell her he had slept with her and would probably have to divulge any and all information he had about her. Charlie really didn't feel he had the right to do that. Everything she told him had been in confidence, and although Vincent might consider his silence a betrayal, talking would be a betrayal to Natalia. He already betrayed her once by trying to turn her into a werewolf.

Charlie set his phone down and took off his shirt, shoes and socks. He padded downstairs silently and went to the back door. Once outside he took off his jeans and underwear and concentrated. It was close enough to the new moon for him to retain most of his human intelligence, if he held onto just a few thoughts. He kept it simple: find Rebecca and tell her about Natalia. He repeated the phrase like a mantra for a few moments, then changed. The thought buzzing in his head, he sniffed the ground and went looking for his alpha.

It wasn't hard to find her; she was returning to the house. The scent of blood was all about her. She had probably caught and eaten a rabbit. They were rampant in these mountains but challenging to catch. He greeted her playfully, allowed her to show her dominance over him, then licked her jaw where she had missed a spot of blood. She let him up and instinct almost took over. The buzzing in his head stopped him from running off to find a hare of his own. He stopped and howled at his alpha. She stopped, and cocked her shaggy gray head at her mate, wondering at his game. He concentrated then turned back into a human. Charlie shifted uncomfortably on the rocky ground and waited.

He watched as Rebecca transformed and stood. She shook her head, stretched, and showed off her naked body. Another instinct took over and he stood to embrace her. She wrapped her arms around him.

"Hi, Charlie. What's up?" She moved against him as she kissed him, not allowing him to answer for a minute.

"I'd like your permission, as my alpha, to take care of something." He caressed her back, loving the feel of her muscles as she moved her arms to caress him.

"And you're not asking Vincent because?"

"I don't want to explain why I'm worried about her." He looked at his mate sheepishly. She knew of his relationship with Natalia, and knew he tried to change her.

"This is dangerous, Charlie. If he sees this as a betrayal, he might kill you." She held him tighter and he whimpered. She felt good against him. She was shorter than he was, which he preferred, and was able to rest her head on his chest. "I love you Charlie, I don't want to lose you because you're worried about an old girlfriend. Please talk to him."

He pulled away a little and lifted her head to look at her. "I'll tell him when I come back. I don't want him to tell me to stay out of it."

"But I still can." Her tone changed slightly, and she was no longer his mate, but his alpha.

"I know." He let her go and stepped back, wondering what she would tell him.

"If I order you to go to Vincent and explain?" Her voice was hard; it was a leader's voice.

"I'll do what you want, but please, let me do this. Let me tell him when I get back."

"She could just be teasing him."

"Not her style. She likes to look her man in the eye when she teases. She also wouldn't risk losing her job. She's too responsible."

She sighed. "I don't like this."

He grinned wide. She was letting him go. "I'll tell Vincent as soon as I get back."

"No, when you get back you'll talk to the both of us." She was his mate again. He kissed her deeply.

"Thank you."

"You're insane." She hugged him hard and kissed him. "Get out of here before I change my mind."

He grinned again and ran back to the house. He put on his jeans and ran up to his room to grab his phone, the rest of his clothing, his car keys and wallet. He was smiling as he left. He ran down to the garage and jumped into his car. It was a beat up, 15-year-old, four-door sedan. Vincent did not approve of the heap, but Charlie wasn't comfortable driving anything fancy, and only did so when driving his boss around.

It took an hour to drive into the city. It would have taken less time, but there were a lot of speed traps. He parked a few blocks from Natalia's house and walked past her place two times before walking up like he owned the place and going through the gate. Once the gate was closed, he squatted down and looked around. There was enough light coming from the street to see a couple days of newspapers piling up. No one hid in the front yard. He walked to the front door and picked up the newspapers along the way. At the top of the four steps he set down the papers and dug out his keys. He never gave her back the set she made for him, and he had never thought to get rid of them.

The key still fit in the lock, but the door opened without his having to unlock anything. He tensed, not liking the unlocked door and forgotten newspapers. Charlie knelt and opened the door slowly. The mail was making it hard for him to ease the door open.

"Crap." Charlie gave up the stealth and shoved the door open. He turned on the light as he walked in and then stopped. Something crunched under his boot. Backing up carefully, he looked down and became angry and scared. He had stepped on her already broken cell phone. He knelt and touched the broken pieces. Had she tried to call for help? Her phone was completely dead; he couldn't even turn it on.

Charlie stood and continued his search of the house. The kitchen was the only other room with anything out of place. Whoever took her came while she was eating breakfast. There was a bowl of congealed cereal sitting on the kitchen table. A hard piece of half eaten toast was next to it, along with a glass of orange juice. A breeze came through the open window and ruffled the paper napkin being held down by the butter stained knife.

Charlie stood clenching his fists, regulating his breathing. There was no use for his wolf form now. Calmed, he took out his cell and called Rebecca.

Half an hour later, he was in Vincent's limo, wondering, among other things, how the vampire had arrived so quickly.

Vincent was sitting back in the seat, both feet planted firmly on the limo's floor, hands entwined and resting on his legs. He was blocking the only door out. Charlie was seated across from him, feeling very antsy. Joseph was sitting to the side, a briefcase resting in front of his legs, watching him. Charlie got along with Joseph, and admired the vampire for his fighting skills. It was Joseph's fighting skills that the wolf was now afraid of.

"Why did you come here?" It was the first words Vincent had said to him.

"I was worried about Natalia." He tried hard not to reveal any emotion.

Vincent narrowed his eyes and stared Charlie down. "The more questions I have to ask, the angrier I get. The angrier I get, the more likely I am to kill you before hearing the whole story, despite what your wife made me promise."

Charlie ground his teeth: it wasn't too close to the full moon. He could easily control his emotions, but he was too worried about Natalia. He wanted her to be safe, wanted to find her. His anger parted as he realized the quicker he told Vincent the situation, the quicker his boss would use his resources to find her. To his credit, Vincent left someone back at her house to investigate, but they were only to assess the situation at the house and await further information.

"I was with her for a year and a half. I still care about her. When I heard earlier that she might be missing, I wanted to find out what happened."

"Why didn't you tell me you knew who she was before this?"

"I didn't know I did until yesterday. Joseph was telling me my schedule while watching the recordings from the restaurant. I saw who you were with and realized who she was. I was afraid to tell you I knew her." A bragging tone snuck into his voice and he had a mad twinkle in his eye. "And since you two seemed to be enjoying each other's company, I didn't think it was right to tell my boss that I had slept with his new girlfriend first." He gave Vincent a wolfish grin as a thought occurred to him. "Or did you already know?"

"Will you be apologizing for your current attitude?" His demeanor and tone did not waver from his original stoic position.

Charlie settled back in the seat and tried to relax. He breathed heavily, thankful that Vincent was giving him an opportunity to apologize. He had no idea where the attitude snuck in. Jealousy was probably a big factor, and he was riled up with worry. "Are you going to look for her?"

Vincent considered the question, mulling it around in his mind. He unfolded his hands, brought his right hand across his body and rested his left elbow on his wrist. His left hand went to his face to caress his chin. He placed his ankle on his opposite knee and his stoic expression broke. He stared out the window and thought things over.

Charlie's anger ebbed away as the time passed and Vincent stayed quiet.

It impressed him that the vampire was thinking things over. He waited patiently while Vincent decided.

"Answer my question first werewolf."

Understanding how little it would take for Joseph to simply reach over and tear his heart out, Charlie knelt on the floor of the limo and bowed his head. Vincent had considered the question, or at least looked like it, and that had to be enough for Charlie. It was Vincent's call; she had invaded the vampire's life. But Charlie couldn't give in completely.

"I'm sorry for my attitude and tone of voice, but I care about her, and if I had to do this again, I wouldn't change anything. If you feel I betrayed you, I'm ready for my punishment."

He felt a hand on his shoulder and looked up. It was Vincent's hand. He was leaning forward, reaching out to him. His eyes were not kind, but neither were they deadly. "Sit, wolf."

Vincent was degrading him; calling him his dog, reminding him of his place. Charlie sat back down and took it. There was no other choice.

"I'll see what Justin has to say, then I'll decide what to do about her and you." Vincent settled back in the seat and regarded Charlie. "What can you tell me about her?"

Charlie took a deep breath. "What do you want to know?"

"Everything."

Charlie's mouth dropped open. "Um, everything?"

"Don't be crude, Charlie." Vincent looked perturbed.

"We met when she saved my life." He continued the story from there, being as thorough as Vincent asked. He wanted to avoid telling him too much but had no choice but to tell Vincent Natalia's story as well. There was an uncomfortable moment when he told his boss about biting her to make Natalia his permanently.

"She kicked you out of her life for that?"

"She saw it as a betrayal."

Vincent nodded. "Was that the last time you saw her?"

"No. We said goodbye after she found out she wasn't a werewolf." He looked away from Vincent's steady gaze.

Vincent held his hand out to Joseph, who opened the briefcase and took out a thick manila folder. There were several rubber bands holding the folder closed. Though the information could easily be stored on a disk, it would not have made as big an impression as a thick folder. Vincent took the folder and threw it at Charlie. "I know more than what you told me, Charlie. I've done my homework."

"Then why put me through that?" He sounded rather perturbed as he caught the heavy folder.

"You came here without telling me. I couldn't let that go unpunished."

Vincent paused as Joseph took the folder away from Charlie. As the werewolf muttered under his breath, Vincent's thoughts strayed back to his encounter with Natalia. Vincent could almost feel her warm skin against his and could almost taste her blood on his tongue. The only part of their encounter she complained about was when he drank her blood. His need for her had grown in the past few days. He closed his eyes briefly. He pulled his cell phone out and phoned Justin. He said very little.

"Find her. She may be held by a Slayer named Zechariah Haynes." He closed the cell and watched as Charlie tried hard to hide his smile. "Take care werewolf, I'm not done with you yet." He reached over and pressed the talk button on the intercom. "Pull over."

Charlie felt the big car pull to the curb. The car shut off and the driver side door opened and closed. Seconds later, the back door opened. Vincent stepped out and Charlie followed suit. With no other word Vincent stepped back into the limo. Mierka smirked at Charlie as she closed the back door. She went back to the driver's door, smirked again, got in and drove off.

Charlie looked around. He was in the Embarcadero. The California St. Cable Car line was two blocks off; Charlie glanced at his watch, and at this hour would still be running. He shrugged and started toward the trolley, which took him to the Hyde St. Cable Car line. That one took him a few blocks from his car. He took his time driving home, mulling over the night's fiasco. He knew he was not out of the woods. He had betrayed Vincent, who didn't look kindly upon betrayers. Everyone who worked for Vincent knew of the oubliette. Charlie hoped he wouldn't end up there.

He arrived back at the house close to sunrise. Rebecca was waiting for him in their room.

"What happened?" She sounded like his alpha.

"She's been kidnapped. He thinks a Slayer has her."

"Is he going to look for her?"

"Justin is, yes."

"Good. I'm glad you're home." She sounded relieved.

"Vincent knew everything before I told him. Knows more than I do. Made me tell him anyway." He sounded defeated. She watched him undress, admiring his sleek toned form from the bed.

"I told him I gave you permission." No hint of regret.

He sagged. "Are you in trouble?"

"I spoke to him as soon as you left, so no."

He slipped into bed with her, spooning with her. "If I got you in trouble, I'll never forgive myself."

She giggled. "I'm a big girl, I can take care of myself."

He held her silently for a few moments, enjoying the feel of her. He took a deep breath and inhaled her scent. She smelled of woods and fields. He held her closer, then, "Is this bothering you?"

"What? That you care for a woman who saved your life more than once? Come on Charlie, we've talked about this. I'm not a jealous woman."

Rebecca turned and slipped her arms around his neck. She pressed softly against him, her hard nipples brushing against his chest. She pulled his head to hers and kissed him softly, then with more urgency. His strong arms pulled her even closer as he rolled onto his back, pulling her on top. She spread her legs, straddling him, then squeezed her legs and rose to a upright position.

"Besides," she shifted and guided him inside her, "I know how to make you mine."

She squeezed him and shifted slightly, moving exactly the way he liked. He groaned, reached up and tried to pull her to him. She resisted, grabbed his hands and squeezed again. He groaned even louder, then twisted and flipped her onto her back. She laughed out loud and wrapped her legs and arms around him. They held tightly to each other and moved in sync, touching, caressing and teasing each other until they each came, laughing and crying out.

They lay in each other's arms, still giggling and teasing. They knew how to enjoy each other and depending on the phase of the moon, were either rough or giggly with each other. Charlie kissed his mate deeply, feeling elated, having completely forgotten how much trouble he was in.

ᙢ ᙣ

Charlie was reminded some hours later when Joseph grabbed him from his bed and threw him in the dungeon. As the door closed behind him, Joseph informed Charlie that he was to be kept locked up for three days. He would be given food and water and would not be shackled. Since he left without Vincent's permission to pursue Vincent's woman, he would be confined. Knowing it could have been a lot worse, Charlie accepted his punishment and settled in his cell to outwait the three days.

10

atalia's head shot up at the tiny sound by the door. It was full dark out and therefore pitch black in the room. Natalia stayed silent for a moment, wondering if she had dreamt the noise. She calmed herself and slowed her breathing, which slowed her pounding heart. She closed her eyes and listened. For a moment, there was nothing, then she heard a slight scrape on the floor. She didn't say anything and kept calm. A moment later, another scrape sounded, and another. Natalia very carefully pulled her feet under her and stood up. She had tried the maneuver many times before and knew she could do it.

The movement was not done silently. If someone was in the room, they would hear it. That was the point, though. Natalia wasn't sure how long she had been here. No one cared to tell her. She was fed seemingly when they remembered her. She was nearly starving when someone, usually Dean or Zechariah, brought her food. Natalia didn't let them know how hungry she was, but ate the food and drank the water. She asked for proof of Bethany every time and every time was told it would happen when Natalia had proven her worth.

A small part of Natalia's mind was sure Bethany wasn't captured, but she couldn't act as if her friend wasn't captured. Natalia felt if she tried to escape, and they had Bethany, they would kill the woman. She also felt that if they didn't have Bethany, they would find a way to kill her friend. Natalia didn't want to be the cause of Bethany's death. Therefore, she didn't try and escape, but she did try to defend herself.

As soon as she had been left alone the first day, Natalia tried to stand using the post. It worked easily and she held onto the post with her arms and back as she raised her legs up. It kept the boredom away, her blood circulating and it felt like exercise. She was grateful to have thought of it when Marshal crept into the room the first time.

It was night that time as well. She woke when he tried to grab her legs. She kicked him hard in the face and stood quickly. She screamed. In moments, Zechariah arrived and threw Marshal out.

Now, as the scrape came again, Natalia prepared herself. If something touched her, she would scream and kick out. She waited in the dark, in the near silence, as the scrape advanced. When a hand touched her leg, she grabbed the post, pulled her legs up to her chest and kicked out. It took under a second to kick out. Her attacker yelled as she connected. Natalia did not hesitate any further. She screamed, long and loud. In moments, her door was thrown open and flashlights were trained in her direction.

"Marshal? What did I tell you! That is uncalled for. God does not condone what you are doing!" Zechariah sounded rather angry and it made Natalia's heart calm down. At least he was on her side in this situation.

"That bitch kicked me in the head!"

"Good! She may not be one of us, but no woman deserves what you were trying to do!" Dean yelled.

Natalia thanked God for Dean and waited as the men stepped forward. Zechariah moved forward but Dean stayed by the door. Natalia could see Zechariah now and the look on his face was anything but kind. She couldn't remember the Slayer this angry. She was filled with gratitude as Zechariah grabbed Marshal by the arm. As he hauled the man out of the room, Zechariah hurled instructions to Dean.

"Put back one of the lights then untie her. Let's see what he does when she can really defend herself."

With that stated Zechariah left with Marshal. Dean looked to Natalia. She gave him a brave smile, then sagged and allowed herself to sit back down. He rushed over.

"Are you all right?"

"I will be. I was terrified of what he might do."

"I can untie you now?"

She shook her head. "No. Do what Zechariah said. Put the light in first, then untie me. He probably thinks I'll try and attack you. I don't want him yelling at you."

"I really don't understand why he has you tied up."

"I won't be after you replace the light." She gave him another brave smile and he blushed, mumbled and left the room. Once he closed the door, a cold, calculating look took over her features. Now that she would be free of her ropes, and not afraid of every little noise, she could concentrate on other things.

CS BO

Once she was allowed to move around, Natalia did a number of exercises each day. She wasn't allowed outside the room, but she could walk, even jog around the room. She did squats and sit ups, anything that came to mind. She didn't hide what she was doing from anyone. If the door opened while she was jogging, she continued to jog. Dean brought her food on a more regular basis and talked to her. She rarely saw Zechariah and she never saw Marshal. After what seemed about a week, Dean took her on a walk outside.

"This is a nice surprise."

"Zechariah said you probably won't try and escape after I show you these."

He held out a manila envelope to Natalia. She took it with shaking hands. Natalia opened the envelope flap carefully and pulled out two polaroid photographs. One was of a woman in a bedroom on a bed. She looked to be asleep. The bedroom belonged to Bethany. Natalia had been in that room too many times to count. The next photograph was closer to the bed, showing the woman was blindfolded and gagged. Natalia frowned. It was a blurry picture, but it was Bethany's bedroom in her apartment in the city.

She sighed and handed the photos back to Dean. "He's right."

Natalia wasn't sure if the woman on the bed was indeed Bethany. The photograph was blurry, and the blindfold and gag hid most of the woman's face. It was her bedroom though. Even if the woman wasn't Bethany, they were still able to get into her room. Natalia took a deep breath as she stared off into the trees. She could easily overtake Dean, knock him out and run to her freedom, but Bethany might die. She hung her head.

She was done thinking about it. She would operate on the thought that they had Bethany. At the very least, they knew where Bethany lived and could get into her apartment. Natalia would do as the Slayers asked. It was the only safe route for Bethany.

Natalia turned to Dean. "He's right. I'd like to go for a walk though. It's nice out and I haven't seen the sun in ages.

Dean smiled as he put the photos in the envelope. He continued to smile as he led the way to a path. It wasn't a long walk, but Natalia enjoyed it. All too soon, she was back in her room. She sat down and waited, wondering what to do about her situation and Bethany's.

Σ Σ

Natalia wanted nothing more than to stand up on the table and scream a warning at all the oblivious customers of The Red Thread. If she did that, Zechariah would probably kill her in her seat. As she didn't have a way to save herself and Bethany, Natalia stayed silent. She listened to the others talk about what kind of monsters were going to die tonight.

She was sitting in the middle seat of a horseshoe booth at the back of The Red Thread, flanked by two Slayers on either side. Zechariah was to her right, with Marshal beside him. Miguel was to her left with Dean beside him. They were here to count the bodies. It was the middle of the week; there were fewer humans than usual, but there seemed to be more Hellspawn. The Slayers were betting on how many would die.

Zechariah and Miguel had been at The Red Thread the night Natalia met Vincent. At the time, Natalia was the willing distraction; they had been the scouts. That night, she even hypnotized the doorman into placing her name and Zechariah's on the guest list. Natalia was surprised their names were still on the quest list. She wondered if Vincent allowed their names to remain.

After meeting Vincent and his people, Natalia reread the journals that spoke of him. Then she slept with the vampire. Now, Natalia wanted to be with him. Alone in her room at the cabin, Natalia had time to think. Though Vincent had threatened to take her home against her will, he didn't. It was more than she could say for the Slayers. Miguel didn't even bat an eye when he saw her at the cabin and found out she had been captured. The Slayers wanted to win against all odds. Vincent seemed to want her on his side.

She sighed and stole a glance to Dean. He was the reason she was here tonight. She convinced him that the only way for her to truly be released from Vincent's grasp was to witness his death. Dean was easily convinced; she hadn't even used her hypnosis necklace. It took longer for them to convince the others.

It was eleven o'clock. She had one hour to try and figure out a way to get a message to Vincent. Two Slayers had come to The Red Thread earlier today to set bombs. Natalia didn't know how many; didn't even know where. She had no idea how to send the vampire a message. It had to be done where the Slayers couldn't see her, which meant she couldn't slip a note to the waitress or the bartender; too obvious. She could try and signal someone, but none of the vampires she had seen the first night were here, as far as she could tell. There was one last option: write a message on the bathroom mirror.

They arrived half an hour ago and she had downed her water and her diet soda; her bladder was screaming at her. Natalia thought of faking needing to use the bathroom but didn't want to risk it. She tapped Miguel on the shoulder, and asked him to move. Zechariah slapped his hand on her thigh.

"Where are you going?" His voice was nowhere near pleasant.

"I need to use the restroom, sir." Her voice was submissive, as was her expression. Her mind was an angry buzz.

"Go." He turned back to Marshal, ignoring her completely.

Miguel and Dean moved to let her pass. She went slowly but steadily to the hall leading to the bathroom, trying very hard not to look around. She stepped into the two stall bathroom. It was clean and empty. She sat on the toilet, taking care of business, trying to think of a way to leave a message. It wasn't until she was reaching for the toilet paper that it hit her.

She finished up, then washed her hands, observing the mirror the whole time. She usually had lipstick and blush with her, but all her make-up was at her house. Dean gave her some lip balm some time ago, to help her chapped lips. It was clear, but it might still work. She slipped her lip balm out of her pocket and regarded the green see-through plastic stick. It was half used. Hoping it was enough; she uncapped it and started writing. She had just finished the word bomb when the door opened.

The woman who walked in was shorter than Natalia by about four inches. She was stocky, but Natalia could tell it was muscle. Her dark brown hair was pulled back in a ponytail revealing a large hickey. She was wearing ripped jeans with a blue button up shirt. The shirt was open to reveal her cleavage. She was a good-looking woman, but the woman's appearance was not what held the human's attention. It was her necklace.

The woman wore a silver chain with a large red stone. The stone was set in silver backing and had silver markings on it. To a casual observer, the markings probably looked like a random design. Natalia knew better. She knew what Vincent's pendant looked like from pictures and seeing it around his neck. His had a fleur-de-lis that wrapped to the edge of the stone. This one had a paw prints behind a silver fleur-de-lis. Natalia had a vague idea what the design meant. Since the red stone was the exact color of the necklace Vincent wore, Natalia could surmise only one thing. The woman worked for Vincent.

Natalia took exactly three heartbeats to assess the woman. It took one second for her to decide what to do. Having no time to try to hypnotize her, Natalia used brute force. By the time the door swung shut Natalia had the woman up against the wall. One arm was pressed against her throat, hand closed in a fist. The other hand covered the woman's mouth.

"You work for Vincent." It wasn't a question.

There was a very familiar look in her oddly yellow eyes. A disquieting feeling stole across Natalia's mind and she shut it down. There was no room or time for doubt and fear. The woman very slowly nodded her head the best she could, giving Natalia a look that would have chilled most humans. Natalia plodded on, ignoring it.

"Tell Vincent that there are Slayers in his club. They've planted bombs. I don't know where. They'll go off at midnight. Get the people out, now." Natalia lowered her hand as she talked. The anger in the woman's eyes slowly changed to disbelief. By the time Natalia was done, she was being given an assessing look.

"How do I know you're telling the truth?" Her voice was all business. She sounded like a leader.

"You don't, but if I'm telling the truth and you don't listen to me, a lot of people are going to die, including you." Natalia looked the woman dead in the eye, while taking steps away from her. She had her hand on the door, trying to find the handle.

"Who are you?" The woman's voice demanded an answer.

Natalia was turned toward the door, ready to pull it open. She didn't want to give her name, but if Vincent knew it was her, it might make him listen to her message. It might also make him ignore it. She decided to take a chance. "Natalia."

She pulled the door open and cursed under her breath. Two large men were standing in front of the door, staring at her.

"Did you really think you could come to his club without our noticing?" The woman behind her had a mocking tone to her voice.

Natalia cursed under her breath again.

"It'll be best if you come quietly."

For who? Natalia thought. If she let Vincent's men take her without a fight, Zechariah would assume correctly that she wanted to be with the vampire. It would also forfeit her friend's life. She couldn't do anything right now though, as there was no room to maneuver. If they took her through the main room, she would be able to fight. The woman was pushing on her shoulder blade, indicating she should walk. Natalia did as ordered.

As they walked, Natalia observed the two men, wondering who to take out first. She had no weapon, which was probably best. She didn't want to kill any of Vincent's people. She watched as the two men walked and understood that her best bet was to not engage any of them. They led her through the main room and were halfway to the steps to the private area. They had already passed the Slayer table. Natalia did not bother to look at the Slayers, not wanting to alert Vincent's men too early. If she moved at the right moment, she might be able to keep the Slayers out of it. They had weapons and would use them.

Ten feet from the steps Natalia glanced around, and realized the club was emptying out. That made things worse. If the club were empty, Vincent's men wouldn't hesitate to use their vampiric abilities. Natalia's foot hit the first step and she calculated. The men were two steps in front of her and the woman was two steps behind. Five steps up, Natalia grabbed the banister and vaulted over the railing. She hit the ground running, trying to get to the door. Outside she could run, but slowly enough to be caught. If she were caught, she could let her captors take her back to Vincent without the Slayers seeing.

There was shouting behind her, but she hardly heard it. There was a deafening roar, and something hit her back. She tensed as claws penetrated her shirt and skin. She felt teeth on her neck and stopped struggling. The woman was a werewolf. The look in her eye had been that of barely suppressed rage. The raging beast had thankfully decided to pounce on her as a wolf, and had her snout around her neck, pressing softly, not breaking skin. It was wolf claws penetrating her skin and not foot long Blitzkrieg claws buried deep within her body. Natalia had time to wonder, as hands grabbed her arms and the snout let go and the claws pulled away, how the woman controlled herself so well. The thought was hurled from her mind as she was slammed against the side of the steps. Her vision sparkled, and she nearly passed out.

Through her tunnel vision Natalia made out the shapes of four Blitzkriegs forming a barrier between her and the Slayers. One of her guards picked her up and calmly walked up the steps as the werewolves faced off the Slayers. She went limp and passed out.

CZ ЮD

Natalia woke moments later, on her side, on a couch in a nicely furnished office. She hurriedly sat up and looked around, nearly blacking out again from the pain. She leaned over with her head between her knees, breathing slowly. When her vision cleared, she looked up carefully. The couch she was on was soft black leather, as were the two chairs in front of the desk. The chair behind it was deep red leather and looked to be of even better quality. One of the chairs in front of the desk was turned around, occupied by the lady wolf. Her arms and legs were crossed. Her jeans were even more torn up, but somehow, her shirt wasn't.

"Are you going to fight me?" Her voice was rather matter of fact.

"Is someone looking for the bombs?" Natalia's voice showed her worry.

The wolf cracked a smile. "We found them after they left this morning. Nothing's going to blow up."

Natalia visibly sagged with relief. After taking a few deep breaths, she looked at the woman, ready to defend herself if necessary. "You're a werewolf."

Rebecca nodded.

"You're wearing Vincent's symbol. Are you his Alpha?"

Rebecca nodded again. She watched with near pleasure as the human paled.

Natalia's face went white as she understood how lucky she had been in the bathroom. Rebecca was probably ordered not to harm her irrevocably. Natalia very carefully moved off the couch to kneel with her head bowed. "If I had understood what the symbol really meant, I would have found another way to approach you in the bathroom. I ask forgiveness for my transgression."

Rebecca looked at the human with utter surprise, and appraised her for a moment or two. The werewolf then rose to her feet and walked across the room to Natalia. "Look at me."

Natalia raised her head more than necessary to expose her neck to

Rebecca in a show of vulnerability and subservience. The human understood the importance of showing Vincent's Alpha she was not trying to take over any one's position.

The wolf gazed down into the human's eyes, assessing her. She stood there for a few moments, thinking about all Charlie had ever said about this human and everything Vincent's household had dug up on her. This was not a stupid woman. Rebecca knew that on instinct as well as fact. As she stared down at the human, Rebecca reached out and placed her hand on the woman's throat, not in a threatening manner, but to see what she would do.

Natalia closed her eyes at Rebecca's touch, willing herself not to fear the woman. She had no reason to. The thought made her open her eyes and she met Rebecca's intense gaze with a steady one.

"Is it fear or admiration that I see in your eyes?"

"A healthy dose of both."

Rebecca nodded and pulled her hand away. "Sit down. You can't be comfortable."

Natalia did as instructed as the wolf went back to the desk and pulled a First Aid kit off one of the chairs. "You're cleaning my wounds?"

"I was ordered to."

"Why you?"

Rebecca shook her head as she walked toward the couch. "The humans are terrified of you and vampires want to change you."

As the wolf sat beside her, the human gave her a steady look. "But why you? There are other werewolves here."

"I don't often question Vincent's orders. I know my place in his household and take pride in it. Now, take off your shirt so I can look at your wounds."

"I never asked your name." She started unbuttoning her shirt.

"Rebecca Bartholomew."

Natalia's hands paused at the last name. Her voice was tense with worry. "I once knew a male werewolf with that last name."

"I married him." She sounded proud.

Natalia looked over her shoulder at Rebecca. "Charlie's alive?"

Rebecca nodded once. "Are you surprised?"

"There was some trouble when we were together. Some people seemed to be hunting werewolves where he ran. The Marine Headlands. After we broke up, I kept an eye on the news for that area. I know there were wolves dying in that area every so often. I never saw Charlie's name, but I always worried he was dead."

"Nope. He's too tough for that." She snickered. "You're not still after my man, are you?"

Natalia shook her head as she continued to unbutton her shirt. "Charlie and I were done a long time ago. I think about him and worry about him.

Since I was the one who demanded he stay out of my life, I didn't know if I should get in touch with him."

"I trust Charlie not to do anything stupid with his ex around, but I don't know you well enough to trust you. If there's ever a problem, I'll blame you and we'll settle things like the warriors we are."

Natalia stopped again and turned to Rebecca, giving the woman a very steady look. "Even when I was dating Charlie, I knew I would step out of the picture if he found his wolf. We knew then and we know now that he and I weren't meant to be. It was fun while it lasted and there are no lingering feelings that I feel like exploring. He has his wolf." *And I have my vampire,* was her unspoken thought.

"Then we shouldn't have a problem."

"No, we shouldn't."

The women looked at each other for a moment before Rebecca indicated Natalia's back. "Turn around. Let me take care of your puncture wounds."

As Natalia turned around, and started slipping off her shirt, she decided to warn Rebecca. "I have other wounds on my back. You may want to cut the bandages rather than unwrapping it."

"Figured. I thought something else was going on when you passed out. I was careful not to hurt you too badly, and I can smell the blood." She hissed as Natalia's shirt finally came off. There was bloody gauze wrapped around the human's torso. Natalia's back was almost completely crimson.

Rebecca opened the First Aid kit and took out the scissors. It took a few moments to cut away the gauze. Natalia breathed deep as the wolf carefully pulled the gauze away from her bloodied back. "What happened?"

"I underestimated a Slayer."

"Seems you do that a lot."

Natalia hissed as the worst of the bandages were pulled off. "What do you mean?"

"Never mind. What did he do to you?"

"With all due respect, I don't feel like being interrogated, but I won't mind if it feels more like a conversation. Let's make a deal. I'll answer a question, then you answer a question."

Rebecca paused, a small bottle of peroxide in one hand, cotton balls in the other. Her mission had been to gather information, not give it. She knew that the easiest way to get a person to talk was to talk back. If she stuck to Vincent's rule of never elaborating, she could probably answer quite a few questions without divulging too much information. She soaked the cotton balls.

"Deal." She examined the claw marks. "I did some damage, but it looks like the whip marks are worse. I've got to disinfect your wounds. Brace yourself." She watched as Natalia took a few deep breaths, then used the cotton ball to clean the wounds. "Why did you come here with the Slayers?"

"I wanted to warn Vincent about the bombs. Where's Vincent?"

"He's on his way. Why did they whip you?"

There were so many answers to that one. Natalia went to the heart of it. "I allowed a vampire to feed off me. Why did you say I underestimate a lot?"

Rebecca remained silent for a moment while she tried to maneuver around the worst of the whip marks. The worse was a deep gash in the middle of the human's back. If she were hit there any more, a spinal disk would be exposed. "Charlie's told me stories, including the one of you in a spiked closet." She paused as Natalia nodded. "You have the ability to take out all the Slayers. Why are you still with them?"

Natalia sighed. The questions were getting harder. She gave a longer answer, as she wanted to hear the logic as well as think it. "They kidnapped my friend Bethany. Or they say they did. I'm not sure they actually have her, but I don't dare try anything, in case they do have her or can get to her." Once stated out loud, her logic felt sound. It would have to do. "Did your guys catch any of the Slayers?"

"One. You're not sure they have your friend?"

"No, but what can I really do. Did you kill any of the Slayers?" She breathed deep as Rebecca started to bandage her back. "Don't make that look too good. Zechariah sees this, he'll assume the worse."

"If I don't do this, you'll have serious damage. And no, we didn't kill any of the Slayers, although we did scratch them up a bit." There was glee in her voice. "You sound like you expect to see Zechariah again. You don't actually think Vincent will let you go?"

"If he can, Zechariah will kill Bethany if I don't return to him. I'm going to leave tonight with or without Vincent's knowledge or consent."

"You're going to have to stand so I can wrap you." Rebecca's voice revealed nothing. They both stood and stayed silent until Rebecca was done. "How are you going to explain the new gauze to Zechariah?"

"I...haven't thought that far ahead."

"Interesting for a woman who's probably plotted three ways out of here." The low male voice interrupted from the doorway.

11

Both women turned at the low voice. Vincent was leaning against the wall by the door, which was across from the end of the couch. He was dressed in a black tuxedo with a dark blue shirt, and matching handkerchief in his pocket. He looked dressed for an elegant evening out. He had been at the symphony with Mierka and some business partners. He did not enjoy being called away; his body language showed his feelings.

Natalia's breath caught, and her heart threatened to jump out of her chest. Rebecca, close enough to smell the changes, took a step back, an amused look on her face. She snorted, placed the First Aid kit on the desk, threw out the old bandages and headed for the door.

"Don't scratch her back; she's badly cut up." Her hand was on the doorknob.

"And you're leaving without my permission because?" He was looking at Natalia, who was still standing in her jeans and gauze shirt that covered her torso from breasts to hips. The look in her eye intrigued him. He had to try hard to remember his purpose here.

Rebecca snorted again and stepped out of the room. "Because three's a crowd."

The door snicked closed and Natalia and Vincent stood looking at each other silently for a few moments. Vincent finally broke the silence. "You say they have a friend of yours?"

Natalia slipped her shirt on, one arm at a time, trying to stop her mind. "You bugged your own office?"

"The quicker you answer my questions, the better it will be for you."

She turned her head slowly toward him, a devilish look in her eye. There was a hint of seduction in her hard voice. "How are you going to force me to talk?"

His jaw twitched as his resolve broke with her look and he started toward her. He closed the distance between them but turned away from her at the last moment. He started pacing, trying to stay in control. He was rather angry but had been filled in about her situation. Joseph relayed the conversation to him on his cell phone as he was approaching the club. When he learned Natalia was here his first thought had been to drain her of her blood. His second thought had been to throw her onto the floor and have her in every way he could make her beg for.

Finding out about her current condition put a stop to that. He enjoyed including pain with pleasure, but not this way. She was truly hurt; which also meant she could not match his pace. He kept crossing his office back and forth, trying to control his desire. She watched him, her face confirming her hunger.

"Just answer my questions, Natalia. Do they have a friend of yours?" He stopped pacing to face her.

"Maybe." She didn't sound happy. She wanted to play with him not converse with him. Needing to release her own frustrations, she started to walk around the edge of the room. "They showed me blurry pictures of a woman in Bethany's apartment. The woman's face was covered with blindfold and gag. I decided when I saw the pictures to take them at their word. I was terrified that any act of defiance would make them kill her. I...I can't allow that."

He watched her for a moment, then asked gently. "Do you know where they might be keeping her?"

She stopped by an open window and stared at him. She perched on the window edge. Her voice reflected her frustrations. She shook her head and looked out the window. "I don't even know where they're keeping me, Vincent."

The vampire continued to watch the human for a moment. "Why are you their captive?"

Natalia looked back to Vincent, a haggard yet amused look on her face. "The last time we saw each other, Zechariah was there. I didn't know it. He went to The Ocean's Edge to talk to me and heard us talking. He was thinking about killing you while we were talking, but I gave in to your seduction before he could gather enough nerve to face you." She gave him such a lecherous look that Vincent didn't think he could contain himself. She laughed and broke the image. "I think he got off on listening to us. You should have seen his face when he confronted and kidnapped me two days later. It was like he was thinking about breaking his celibacy rule." She sighed and shook her head. "I don't think that's what made him realize I wasn't on his side anymore, though."

"What did it?"

She gave him a frank look. "He was there all night. When I fed you my blood willingly? He heard that, too. While I was convincing him to let me come tonight, he told me that no untainted human would offer a vampire their blood. That I wasn't to be trusted because I was probably Hellspawn already."

Vincent watched her again, not saying a word, thinking of their encounter at The Ocean's Edge. Suddenly, sorrow crossed her features and stole her mirth. When she spoke again, her voice was dejected.

"Can you tell me something, Vincent?"

He stood stoically with his arms crossed. "Possibly."

She turned her head to look at him. She looked irritated, but her voice was pained. "How long has it been since I saw you last?"

"That's an odd question to ask."

She took a deep breath to contain her frustrations. "I've been kept in a dark room since I was kidnapped. I had no concept of time. I've only been outside twice, including tonight. In the beginning, I wasn't fed on a regular basis. Someone brought me food when Zechariah felt like it. It's been better lately; I've tricked one of them into believing I'm turning back to their ways. Dean brings me food on a more regular basis, but I still don't know how long it's been."

"Four weeks."

The two little words crashed into her, making her mind reel. She did her best to hide how much the news shocked her. She pulled herself away from the window. Natalia walked back to the couch in case she should lose her fight with sanity. Her teeth clenched, and her hands formed into fists as her anger took control.

"You have one of them." She was speaking through gnashing teeth.

He nodded.

She stood and faced him, her hands in fists. "I want to see him."

Vincent watched the beautiful creature before him as she gathered her anger and her pain. It would be foolish to let her see the Slayer, but his curiosity was getting the best of him. He wondered what she and the Slayer would do upon seeing each other. Natalia had no weapons; she could not kill him. The Slayer was to be tortured, interrogated, and used for blood. Vincent was always intrigued by what humans would do when able to confront their demons. Natalia liked to let her demons out for pleasure. What would she release upon a Slayer who mistreated her? Blood boiling, imagination piqued, he went to her and touched her cheek, peering down into her sparkling eyes.

"And what will you do to him?"

A familiar look came into her eyes. Her beast had been released. "Take me to him and you'll see."

"Yes." He slipped his hand behind her head, bared his fangs and brought her mouth to his, giving her a crushing kiss. She felt his fangs with her tongue and shuddered with excitement. She pulled back, not sure of the feeling. Vincent sensed her hesitation and let her pull away. He then took her arm and led her out the door.

Rebecca stood in front of a door halfway down the hall and tried to hide her feelings. She had underestimated the human and felt just a little unnerved. She was not used to seeing humans with that look in their eyes. It was the look of absolute animal hunger. The kind a cat gets when stalking its prey; the kind a werewolf gets when about to change into Blitzkrieg form. Rebecca now understood why Charlie tried to change Natalia. There was something inhuman about her.

Rebecca walked behind Vincent and Natalia, watching the subtle interaction between her boss and his woman. His hand was lightly holding her elbow, but she was leading, even though she probably had no idea where to go. Natalia kept looking back over her shoulder, giving Vincent smiles out of the corner of her eye. He mirrored her look, and the fingers of his free hand were drumming against his thigh.

At the end of the hall Vincent reached out his hand to enter the code on the keypad. Joseph had already warned the main guard that Vincent was on his way. Two guards stood on the other side of the door to ensure everything was as it should be. Another two still watched the Slayer. The guards gave Natalia a look but let the trio inside. The room was well lit, with no windows or furnishings.

When Vincent came in the room, the Slayer stopped praying, trying to ready himself for torture. He stood with head held high, rosary in his fist. His jeans and t-shirt had been ripped in the fight, but he wasn't bleeding. He looked dignified, ready for anything. He wondered at the guards' reaction to their leader walking in the room. Then they parted, and he saw Natalia. He saw the look on her face and was afraid. He started shaking, making his rosary clink softly in the silence.

Natalia shook with delight. "Marshal. What a surprise."

Dean told Natalia not that long ago that Marshal was the newest of Zechariah's groupies, and the cruelest. He joined about six months ago and took great pains to torture anything they chased. He thought to have his way with Natalia, but she showed him she could take care of herself. Once she was allowed the run of her bare room, he stayed away.

Zechariah had no problem with whipping her, hitting her and causing her pain in many other ways. He was disgusted with the idea of rape, which she was grateful for. She heard the two arguing about it once; heard Marshal confessing he felt rape was the only true way to break a strong woman's will. Now, Marshal was at her mercy. Vincent, Rebecca and the guards backed away from her, smelling her gleeful hatred.

"Tables have turned, haven't they?" She started walking around him, making him turn in slow circles.

"Zechariah will kill Bethany, and it'll be your fault." He was counting rosary beads.

She shook her head, still walking in slow circles. Her hands were crossed at her back. "Why would he, Marshal? I'll be returning to him soon. He'll never know the truth."

The only one in the room not giving her surprised looks was Vincent.

"He won't let you go. He's going to kill you, same as me. Don't try to delude yourself into believing you're anything more than a sack of blood; a Hellspawn's whore-"

The slap rocked his head back. "Anything he gets from me, I give him willingly." She stepped closer, her face a mask of hate. "Which is more than I can say for you."

His face grew ugly, contorted with hate and rage. He bared his teeth, clenched his fists. "You don't know what you're doing, woman. This vampire will be your death."

Natalia looked over at Vincent. He was standing next to Rebecca, in front of his four guards. There was enough space between his guards for Vincent to back between them if he had too. She gave him a smile. He was quite striking in his tuxedo.

"You're probably right." Her voice was calm, almost light. She turned her head back to Marshal and started walking again. "But at least I'm aware and prepared for it."

"You're a fool." Marshal's voice was becoming harder. "Turn back to God before you see the true face of the devil."

All mirth dropped from Natalia's attitude. She stopped walking and faced off with Marshal. Her hands became fists. "My first glimpse of the devil was when I was ten. I've seen him many times in many forms since. I have yet to see as much evidence of your God."

"Zechariah's right. The devil has already claimed you."

Natalia gave him a devilish smile; her eyes were glinting with delight. "You're right. He has."

Vincent watched as she turned gracefully and sauntered over to him. She walked as a queen in her own castle. Once standing before him she placed her hand on his chest.

"And he will again."

As she stared into the vampires eyes, her desires took over. She wanted to leave all this behind her and allow him to take her home. She forgot about Bethany for a moment, forgot where she was and allowed her desires to take over. Natalia ran her right hand up his left arm to the back of his neck to tangle in his hair. Her left hand went to his right arm and squeezed his triceps lightly.

Vincent allowed her to pull his head down for a kiss. His arms wrapped around her when the kiss grew deeper. Careful of her back, his arms had gone to her butt and shoulders. It was an awkward position, but he still managed to crush her to him.

Natalia pulled away, finally, when she heard Rebecca snickering. Laughing nervously herself, she took some steps back, trying to get some air. Vincent's eyes grew wide and he reached for her. By the time he yelled her name, Marshal turned her around and slammed the fist holding the rosary into her face. The force sent her stumbling back into Vincent's arms. The guards came into her field of vision, fanning out to square the Slayer in. Rebecca cracked her knuckles as Vincent set Natalia on her feet.

Natalia caught Vincent's gaze and held it for a long moment. He could have stopped it; any one of the vampires could have stopped the Slayer. Since they didn't, she had to wonder why. Vincent held her gaze, no guilt showing in his eyes.

"The next hit is yours, Natalia. Do as you will, but do not kill him."

Vincent's words eased her throbbing cheek and helped her to understand his game. He wanted to see what she would do. Natalia stood taller as their gaze stayed locked. Upon entering the room, she wanted to kill Marshal. By the time she kissed Vincent, she became more interested in forgetting about the Slayer.

Now, all she wanted was to beat Marshal; take some of her frustrations out on him, and Vincent was encouraging her to do so. She knew several ways of knocking the Slayer unconscious with one blow, but that wouldn't do. A fight would mess her up a bit. She had to get back to Zechariah to keep Bethany alive. It wouldn't do to go back to Zechariah looking pristine. If she and Marshal fought, she would look the part she wanted to portray.

Knowing she could take the Slayer out with one punch, Natalia faced off, then slapped him on the cheek, trying to look like she didn't know how to fight. She had never fought in front of him before, and he didn't know her training background. The slap didn't faze him at all. The guards made him nervous, though, so he didn't do anything.

"Your move, Slayer."

Vincent sounded amused. He knew what Natalia was doing but wasn't sure he agreed with her actions. She said several times that she was going back to Zechariah, and Vincent hadn't given it much thought. He joked about it but dismissed it out of hand. He wasn't letting her go. Natalia took another blow to the face, faked a punch and took another hit. As he watched the fight Vincent began to understand her and respect the depth of her loyalty and determination.

Blood was running from her nose and mouth. She allowed the Slayer one more swing, which got her in her eye. She rolled with the punch at the last moment, wanting her eye bruised, but not swollen shut. She didn't want limited vision. She turned back to Marshal, a slight smile on her face.

"You do realize, you've just made my story more believable, don't you?"

She slowly made a fist with her right hand as it dawned on Marshal exactly what he had done.

"You'll never escape. You're dead. He'll kill you." He sounded like he was trying to convince himself.

She thought about his statement, then nodded. "Maybe one day, but not tonight."

Natalia slammed her fist into his face, making him reel backward. She didn't let up after that. He started screaming after the third punch. She didn't kill him, but she returned all the blows he landed and then some. Vincent watched, waiting until she was done, eyes on her face the whole time. Her expression never once changed. It was cold and calculating, considering the man as a target, hitting him precisely, causing as much damage as possible without breaking any bones or causing irreparable damage.

Vincent allowed Natalia to stand over the broken Slayer for a few moments before walking to her. He tugged on her elbow and steered her to the door. He let her out, closed the door and gave instructions to his men to take the Slayer to his dungeon. He opened the door and was almost surprised to see Natalia leaning against the wall. He specifically left her alone to give her the opportunity to leave.

Rebecca, right behind him, wasn't surprised. She shook her head and walked past her boss, down the hall and into the security office, leaving the two to their own devices.

12

Vincent stood with his hand on the doorknob, regarding the haggard looking woman in front of him. She had wiped away some of the blood, but there were still small traces. Her eye was starting to puff up, as was her nose and lip.

"Natalia, what a surprise."

"We're not done."

"Shall we go to my office?"

She took the offered arm and they walked back to the cozy room in silence. He closed the door after letting her in, choosing to take a seat at his desk. After a moment's hesitation, she sat at one of the chairs, trying to get comfortable. She ended up perched on the edge of the seat.

"You expected me to run."

"You want something more."

"My friend's life might be at stake. Will you find out if she's safe and free her if necessary?"

"If she isn't captured?"

"Watch her until I'm free. Make sure they can't get to her."

He leaned forward and laid his laced hands on the desk. "What do you offer in return?"

She closed her eyes. "Zechariah has artifacts, books. Help Bethany; I'll bring them all to you."

"What would I want with artifacts, Natalia? I already have many."

She opened her eyes. "These are used by Slayers. If you have them, they can't be used against you and yours."

He nodded in slight agreement. "What else?"

"Myself."

He gave a slight laugh. "I expect payment to be one-sided Natalia. It's not really payment if you extract pleasure from it. Try again."

Natalia closed her eyes and took a deep breath. Sure of her decision, she opened her eyes and locked gazes with him. "Blood."

Vincent stood and walked around to Natalia. She looked up at him, then took his offered hand. He sat on the edge of the desk and indicated she should too. Her face was masking her emotions. Humor was shining in his eyes.

"How much blood do you offer me and when can I expect it?"

"Some now; as much as you want when Bethany is safe."

He gave her a sly smile. "Sounds like an ideal plan. Leaves me in control, Natalia. Are you sure you want this?"

"If it means Bethany's safety, yes."

He traced the line of her jaw with his cool fingers, helping to relieve her pains. "So much pain, Natalia, for what? A human? Is she worth it? Would she do this for you?"

"No, but I wouldn't expect her to." Natalia's determined look was back. "She doesn't know what the world is really like."

"Why do this for her then, if she doesn't know the truth?"

She sagged, letting her head rest in his hand. "She's the last tie to a normal life that I have. I wasn't ready to let her go until I realized she might die because of me."

"And now?" His hand was caressing her neck.

"I want her to live a normal life, and that's impossible with me in it. I want her freed and sent on her way. And I don't want her to know what really happened." She sat a little straighter, a little taller, looking him in the eye. "Will you do it then? Will you free her?"

"For your blood?"

She nodded.

"And the artifacts and books?"

She smiled and nodded.

"Then yes, I will." He leaned in as if to bite her neck. "But there is something else isn't there?"

"Yes." Pleasure and pain mingled in her voice.

"You're willing to give your blood to me now because it will help to convince him."

"Yes." More pain this time.

"But if it looked as if I forced myself upon you, he would be completely convinced."

"Yes." She answer held no emotions.

He looked in her eyes. "What do you expect of me, Natalia? You are in no condition to take me on. You're hurt, and you know what I enjoy."

"You don't want me at all?" She wasn't trying to be seductive. It was just a question.

He considered the question carefully. Before her fight, he had wanted, planned on having her. In her current state, he wasn't too sure. Vincent would have to be careful and he didn't want to be. He closed his eyes as the evenings events came back in a rush. The image of her walking in the hall; how she acted with the Slayer. She had complete control of the situation, even when Marshal was hitting her. He opened his blue eyes and peered into her dark brown ones. He could see the determination, and then, slowly, he saw her desire coming through.

Most of the women in his life started out as human, but the only woman he had ever taken after a fight was his sire, Lorraine. She never showed any signs of fighting; vampires hardly ever did. Vincent took a deep breath, letting it out slowly through his nose. He closed his eyes; he could smell Natalia's blood and sweat. It was coming off her in waves. The scent of blood was arousing, but he didn't want her like this.

"Natalia," he paused, caressed her cheek, leaned in and placed a light kiss on her lips.

Natalia pulled back slightly, surprised by the tenderness.

"There is much that I would like to do to you and have you do to me, but you are in no condition to match my desires. I don't deny I want you, but if I take you now, when you're already hurt, I'll hurt you further. We're not doing this today."

She stared into his eyes, wondering what he had wanted to do to her before she took the beating from Marshal. She also wondered about the kiss. It revealed far more about him than he probably wanted. Natalia reached up and placed her hand on his cheek, caressing his lips with her thumb. She wanted him, but knew he was right. She wouldn't be able to take him on his terms. She nodded as her eyes closed to hide her emotions.

"You're right. I can't match you tonight." She opened her eyes and gave him a brave look. "Take my blood then, but not from my arm. That'll look like I offered it willingly."

Vincent nodded. Natalia unbuttoned the top few buttons of her shirt to allow him access to her shoulder. She tipped her head back and to the side, stretching her neck. She closed her eyes, but not too tightly, as her right eye was tender. Vincent stood to step between her legs. He placed one hand at the back of her head, and gripped her by her hair. The other hand he placed between her shoulder blades to help keep her steady. She was willing, but he didn't want to risk her pulling away. He bared his fangs, leaned in close, and bit into her flesh.

Natalia gave a whimper as he started softly sucking. Her hands moved to his lapels and gripped hard as the pain set in. Growing light headed, she whimpered, and he pulled away. Vincent pulled the handkerchief out of his pocket and placed it over her still bleeding wound.

"I'm not satisfied." His eyes showed his sheer desire.

"Help me and you'll have me anytime you wish."

He nodded once. "Give me your friend's address. We can find out if she's been kidnapped tonight."

Natalia rattled it off from memory. She was confused when Vincent didn't write down the address, then remembered he probably had the room bugged. Someone else would write it down.

He moved away from her to retrieve the First Aid kit sitting on the other side of the desk. He didn't speak again until she was bandaged.

"Where were they keeping you?"

Still lightheaded, it took a moment for her to understand why he was asking. "In the mountains, north of here. The cabin smells of pine." She brought her hand to her now throbbing head. "Zechariah didn't blindfold me until we were in the car when we came here. The path to the car was too rocky to try it blind. I saw the odometer before he put the blindfold on and saw it again before I got out of the car. It's about 300 miles away. I'm not really sure other than north, which way we came from."

"How are you going to get back to him if you don't know where to go?"

"We're supposed to meet at a safe house in the city."

"Give me the address." She did. He tapped his fingers on his desk. "I don't want you to leave."

"If I don't my friend may die."

He took a moment and asked Natalia again, "Is she truly worth it?"

"I've known her since I was 15. She's been my only friend for most of my life. I can't risk her death." The pain on her face was more acute than when Marshal hit her.

"How do you expect to leave me?"

"Any way I can." Her determination was back.

"I'm not going to make this easy for you." His hand went to her wrist holding it lightly. His lips were close to hers. She leaned in and gave him a soft kiss.

"I didn't expect you to."

The intercom on his desk buzzed, and Vincent ground his teeth. He leaned forward to hit the button. Natalia was still trapped in his arms. "Why are you interrupting me, Joseph?"

"Anthony is outside your office door. He has some information you need to hear."

"Fine. Be there in a moment." Vincent looked at Natalia. "I'm not done with you yet. Stay where you are."

Vincent turned from her, walking quickly to the door. He threw open the door and stepped outside. He closed the door most of the way. Natalia tried to watch him but couldn't; the vampires were just out of sight. She removed the gauze from her shoulder and tossed it into the trash. The bite was no longer bleeding freely. She pulled her shirt back on as she strolled to the window to check things out.

The windows in the room opened out and were tall enough for her plan. The second floor of the club was an add on and wasn't the same dimensions as the first floor. It looked to be a seven-foot drop to the roof. No problem. The drop from that roof to the street was a little bit harrowing. That was probably about twenty feet. She could jump to the wood awning covering the entranceway, then to the street. Natalia nodded. It would have to do.

Natalia turned and strolled to the opposite wall. The door was close enough that she could hear the two vampires speaking. Anthony was reporting on something involving Edwin, but she couldn't hear what. She looked through the open door, and saw Vincent's ear. She stared at it for a few seconds, closed her eyes and breathed deep. She turned to face the window.

"Vincent? Don't take too long." And she ran.

Vincent didn't think about her statement until a second later when Rebecca yelled from the security room door. "She's going for the window!"

Vincent turned, bursting through the door in time to see Natalia jumping through the window. He was at the window in time to see her landing on the roof, rolling on impact.

"Get her back here now!" He yelled, pissed off, yet impressed.

Vincent watched as she ran to the edge of the roof, looked over the edge and ran a little to the left. She was right above the entrance. Natalia was over the edge before his men even ran out to the roof. Rebecca, in wolf form, reached the edge first. She sniffed the area and turned back as Anthony reached the edge. Joseph, he knew, would have gone for the street. Vincent pulled the window shut and latched it. Turning from the window, he pulled out his cell and called Mierka, who was waiting downstairs by the door.

"Don't let anyone follow too closely; I want everyone back here in five minutes."

"Yes, sir."

Vincent put the phone away and walked downstairs, thinking about her last words. He had assumed she was telling him not to take long talking with Anthony. Now he understood she was talking about finding her friend. He walked downstairs pacing the empty room until his people returned. Rebecca came in first, still in wolf form. She went upstairs, but came back a moment later fully dressed, buttoning up her shirt. She did not have much to report: a wolf cannot travel far in a big city without attracting the wrong kind of attention. Anthony came next, admitting that he had lost her rather quickly; but he did not track, he gathered information. Joseph came last. He took his time returning and was able to give a better report.

At first, she just wandered, as if to lose any potential trackers. Eventually she did head in the direction of the address she had given Vincent. Joseph was confident that she gave the correct address.

Anthony stood with his arms crossed, angry. He did not trust Natalia but didn't seem to know why. Vincent didn't think it necessary to tell Anthony about their first meeting. He was more comfortable having one of his people suspicious about the human. His emotions were too tied up and confused when it came to Natalia. Joseph, usually suspicious of everyone, was uncharacteristically silent about his boss' new woman; therefore, he let Anthony be suspicious.

"Why go after her Vincent? She's a Slayer." Anthony didn't bother hiding his emotions.

"No, she's not." There was dark humor in Rebecca's voice. "You should see what she did to the one we caught."

"That only proves how far she's willing to go to deceive you. You need to forget about her. She'll end up killing you."

"Interesting. The Slayer said that about me to her. I wonder which version will prove correct." Vincent was still pacing, letting the banter continue, only half listening. He was concentrating more on the problem at hand. It would be easy to send someone to Bethany's address and find out about her. He would assign some of his humans to watch her, to make sure the Slayers didn't kill her. Finding Natalia would be trickier. They didn't have much to go on.

He turned to his Alpha wolf. "Rebecca." The banter stopped cold. "I need you to go to the address Natalia gave us for the safe house. Go now. Take a homing device with you. Find a way to plant it on her before she's picked up. When you have a secure location, I'll have two more wolves come out to meet you. I'm hoping she won't be picked up until morning, but you never know."

Rebecca nodded, going back upstairs to retrieve a transmitter from the security office. She left quickly, hoping to get to the safe house before Natalia did to scope out the location. Anthony gave the werewolf a hard look as she left, once again stating his opinion by his look and body language.

"Anthony." Vincent's voice was no longer allowing discussion. He had made up his mind and his people would follow it. "I appreciate your concern, but now is not the time. I want her; I will have her. In order to have her, I must find and protect a human who knows nothing of this world. I need you and yours to find out more about Bethany. We have her address. Send humans to assess the situation."

Anthony, tight lipped, bowed and left. He would do the best job possible, regardless of his opinion. Vincent was his leader and had given him an order. That was all that mattered.

Alone with his two oldest friends, Vincent allowed himself to show some emotion. He sagged a bit, but that was all. "Am I making a mistake?"

"I saw her fight. She would be an asset, if she were one of us." Mierka was always looking for fellow warriors.

"The mistake was in letting her go."

Vincent nodded, but only half agreed with Joseph's statement. "I don't believe she would allow me to enjoy her if I let her friend die." He paused. "The Slayer. Is he still here?"

"No. He's on his way to your dungeon as you requested."

"Then let's lock up and leave. I want to ask him a few questions."

The trio started locking up, getting the remaining wait staff to clean up as necessary.

Once in the car, Vincent attempted to turn the talk to more pleasant topics. His tone was light, but his body language revealed his anxiety. He was waiting on phone calls. They reached the Golden Gate Bridge before Vincent's phone rang. It was Rebecca. She was talking quickly, as if talking to voicemail. It meant she couldn't answer questions for fear of being overheard and couldn't move to a quiet location for fear of losing the quarry.

"Hi! It's me! Just wanted to let you know I'm at The Hook Up. My friend is waiting for people to show up I think, but no one seems to be home. If anyone calls for me, tell them to come join me. I'm bored."

With that she hung up. Vincent frowned. The Hook Up was an Internet club, a rival to L337, but not a very good one. It was in a semi-residential area. When Natalia had rattled off the address of the safe house, he had thought it familiar. Now he knew why. Vincent called the next two werewolves on schedule and told them where to meet their Alpha, telling them to dress in clothing appropriate to the situation. He closed his phone and stared out the window at the ocean liner slowly making its way to the bay. He took a deep breath and expelled the air through clenched teeth. He could do nothing more but wait. Vincent hated waiting.

13

To the passerby, Natalia probably looked like a drowned rat. Luckily, at this hour, the only passersby were the people coming to The Hook Up. Rebecca could see Natalia huddled in the entryway of the apartment building safe house. The lady werewolf sat at a table in the front corner by the big picture window. It was tinted to keep the glare out, which also made it hard for people to look in. Looking out wasn't a problem.

Rebecca was drinking a bad cup of coffee, wishing the safe house were across the street from a good coffee shop. She had been in worse surveillance situations though and shut her mind to the chatter. She watched Natalia out of the corner of her eye, wondering how she was going to get the homing device on the woman. It was a small device, designed to look like a quarter. It was marred on one side, as if someone had scratched up the backside. Rebecca was now twirling it slowly between her fingers, considering her options.

She thought that maybe the safe house was empty because it wasn't actually the safe house. There was the possibility that The Hook Up was the actual meeting place. It was not a good idea, tactically, to have a safe house across the street from a twenty-four-hour establishment. Rebecca figured that someone here, either an employee or customer, was the point of contact. She wanted to figure out whom but didn't want to look too suspicious. She was already quite conspicuous sitting in an Internet café without a computer. The public computers were by the wall, which was not a convenient place to watch her quarry. Therefore, she sat and looked at her watch, as if waiting on tardy friends.

About 45 minutes after her call to Vincent, one of her men showed up. She had hoped it would be Charlie, but he wasn't on duty tonight and he was always hard to contact on his night off. She didn't blame him. Doug sat at the table and brought out two laptops. He cracked a joke about her not being a true computer geek, since she never carried around her laptop. The two sat joking, pretending to surf the net, messaging each other and Orlando, who was out in the van, about the situation.

Rebecca told both men her thoughts on the Internet cafe being the actual safe house. Doug and Orlando assessed the situation upon arrival and came to the same conclusion. Orlando offered to stay in the van, as Doug was inconspicuous, and he was not. People generally noticed a tall black man with one blind eye and scars running down the left side of his face. The three werewolves sat and communicated for a while, trying to decide what to do.

C３ ８０

Natalia sat on the plastic milk crate, which had conveniently been left in the entryway of the apartment building. Upon arrival, she tried the door; it was unlocked. She went upstairs to explore and found various bits of nothing: broken furniture, rats, dust, drug paraphernalia, lots of used condoms and left-over food. There were also a couple tattered bits of paper, which turned out to be condemned signs. Unsure if anyone was here, she staggered around, acting hurt and confused. She even managed to call out in a strangled voice.

As she explored, Natalia thought of the story she was going to tell Zechariah. Her face was colored with bruises and there was blood on her shirt from where Vincent fed off her, but she didn't know if it would be enough to convince the Slayer. She stood looking at herself in a dirty, half broken full-length mirror and knew her clothing didn't look convincing.

Natalia started ripping her shirt. She tore one sleeve almost completely off then grabbed the shirt on either side of the buttons and pulled, popping the buttons. She then unbuckled her belt and pulled hard at her jeans button and zipper, breaking both. She buckled her belt and then let her shirt hang open, grateful for the gauze hiding her breasts. Now she looked as if she had been assaulted. She nodded to herself and went outside to sit on the milk crate.

Natalia sat in a huddled position, trying to look miserable. Considering she had just left the safety of her lover's arms for an uncertain reunion with Zechariah, it wasn't hard to pretend. She shifted until she found a position that allowed her a view of the street. Before long, she saw a maroon minivan with tinted windows pull up and drop off a young man carrying a large backpack. She watched as he went into The Hook Up, trying not to smile. She cringed as her lip split. She didn't try to smile again.

Natalia sat huddled, wishing she could go to The Hook Up and get some food. She was hungry. The events of the evening had not allowed for nourishment, and the blood loss was adding to her already aching head. She started to breathe deep, trying hard to control the pounding. Part of the headache eased when, about 20 minutes later, Rebecca and the guy with the large backpack came out of The Hook Up. She watched as they climbed into the maroon minivan then watched it drive out of sight. Another similar van appeared at the nearby corner moments later.

A tall black man exited right before the van took off. He loitered at the corner for a moment before crossing the street and heading in her direction. She shivered, trying to look afraid. As he came closer, it was no longer hard to pretend. The mild smile on his face only served to intensify his odd features. There were three pink scars running down the left side of his face. The middle scar went from his eyebrow, through his milky white eye, to his jaw line. It looked like a dog, or a wolf, had clawed him.

Orlando saw his target huddled in the corner, trying to look dejected. She locked eyes with him and he saw her defiance immediately. He gave her a look full of pity, reached into his pocket and threw her a couple coins, not bothering to stop or say anything.

The change landed in her lap. She took the coins and looked at the quarters. One had scratches on the head. She wondered about it, but didn't know if there was any significance. She noticed the license plate on the maroon van. The tall, scarred man had gotten out of Rebecca's van: he worked for Vincent. She pocketed the change and went back to looking dejected.

Just before dawn, she was finally picked up. A familiar truck pulled up to the curb, and Zechariah, dressed as a priest, got out and came to her. He didn't say anything, just held his hand out to her. She took it, looked in his eyes and started to cry. The tears were real. She had no desire to return with him to the cabin. She wanted to be with her lover. Crying, she was placed in the truck. They blindfolded her at some point, but she didn't see where or notice when. She was lying on the back seat, sobbing. Zechariah and Dean were the only ones in the truck with her. Miguel might already be back at the cabin, or he might be elsewhere. She didn't know and didn't care.

At some point, Natalia was woken from her light sleep. Zechariah was shaking her. She no longer had the blindfold, but as they weren't near any signs of civilization, it didn't matter. Zechariah, concern lighting up his face, helped her out of the truck. Once she was on her feet, he smiled kindly to her.

"You look hurt, Natalie. What happened?"

Natalia opened her mouth to speak and stopped. She was about to say that Vincent harmed her, that the vampire took advantage of her but the words didn't want to come out. She stood there thinking of the first monster who ever hurt her. She had allowed George to sleep with her when she was fourteen to be able to hypnotize him into leaving her and her mother alone. Tears formed in her eyes. She thought of Donald who tried to rape her and tried to change her in the same instance and started to shake. How could she lie and say that Vincent, a vampire who wouldn't even take her blood without her permission had raped her? As tears rolled down her cheeks, she realized she couldn't. But she had to try, for her own safety, she had to try.

Natalia opened her mouth to speak again. "He…Vincent…"

"Go on." Glee was evident in Zechariah's voice and Natalia new she would have to lie.

"Stop it." Dean's usually quiet voice was forceful. Both looked to him. "Don't make her go through that again."

Natalia looked into Dean's eyes, but he was looking at Zechariah. She knew she wouldn't have to say anything more. Dean saw her bruises, saw her expression and had put the pieces together. She sobbed in gratitude and hid her face in her hands as Dean and Zechariah argued for a moment. She didn't listen to the words, but knew Dean convinced the older Slayer when she felt a hand on her shoulder. She looked up into Dean's kind eyes.

"We're done with that." He pointed to another truck, close by.

Miguel was standing by the other truck, clothing in his hands. They were off the road somewhere in the woods. It was dim under the trees, and everything smelled of pine. Natalia took a deep breath to calm herself and waited for Zechariah to speak again.

"I believe you're finally ready for the next step Natalie. I will no longer keep you as a captive if you are ready to let all your past trappings go. Are you prepared, Natalie?"

She tried hard to hide her anger. She had heard this type of speech from him before. Whenever he said her name over and over, it meant he was trying to convince her of something. If she didn't agree with him and do as he asked, he was going to beat her. Keeping her voice submissive, she asked, "Does this mean you'll release Bethany?"

"Not until we know you are true to your word, Natalie." His voice was so mild, as if he were trying to be her friend. It made her want to strangle him.

She took a ragged breath, trying not to scream. It was time to take the pretense up a notch. "I'm ready to follow the path of righteousness."

He took her in his arms, hugging her hard. He stepped back and took the clothing Miguel held in his arms. "Let's start with the trappings of your past. Take off your soiled clothing and put these on."

Zechariah placed the clothing on the floor of the truck and turned his back. Miguel and Dean also looked away, out of decency. She stripped, wincing as she accidentally pulled her arms back too far while trying to pull off the shirt. She was grateful the men were turned around; they couldn't see the new bandages. She hurriedly put on the new shirt then stripped off her jeans and underwear. Miguel had thought to include a fresh pair. There were even socks. She let the torn clothing fall to the ground. Something tickled her memory as the belt clinked against a rock, but nothing clear came, so she announced she was changed.

The three men turned back around, and Zechariah checked her out. She was still wearing jeans, but her shirt was a button up white shirt that she had left open at the throat. He came forward, reaching out his hands to button the top button. He stopped and shook his head. His hands fell to his side. "All of it, Natalie."

She shook her head. "I don't have anything else."

His hand went to her necklace, touched it lightly, then dropped to his side. "This is not a part of your new life Natalie. It is a trapping of your old life. You must leave it all behind, Natalie, or you will not be able to accept God into your heart."

Natalia touched her necklace. There was no way she was taking it off. It was an important part of her past and she was not letting it go. Zechariah saw her hesitation and anger stole across his mild features.

"Natalie. Don't disappoint me." He did not hide the annoyance in his voice. It was the same voice he used before whipping or beating her.

Not wanting to be beaten yet again, Natalia gritted her teeth. If only she knew what was going on with Bethany... but Vincent was taking care of that; she had to play along until the vampire could act. Natalia, her mother's face swimming before her, reached around her neck to the clasp. Sighing, she undid the clasp but didn't move her hands. The necklace had been around her neck since age ten. She still remembered the day her mom showed her how to make it and the songs she needed to sing to weave her will into the beads. She felt something unwinding in her head. Natalia suspected it might be the control she had over the people she hypnotized.

Remembering how she felt when her mother died and gave back her memories, Natalia reeled the feeling in and clamped a hard mental hand on her control. Understanding gripped her. It was not just the necklace, but her will that made the hypnosis work. She could keep control of those she hypnotized without the necklace, but probably still needed it to get someone under her control. Knowing she could later retrieve her mother's necklace that still lay in her jewelry box, Natalia made her decision. She opened her eyes, slipped off the necklace, and handed it to Zechariah.

The Slayer took it tentatively, not liking the odd, unidentifiable look on her face. Thinking it would help, he gathered the necklace in his fist and threw it as far as he could. The look seemed to intensify. Confused, Zechariah shook his head and bent down to grab her clothing. The belt clinked again, and Natalia remembered the coins. Her expression changed slightly, but not enough to arouse suspicion.

"There's some change in the pocket of those jeans."

Zechariah continued to ball up the clothing. Dean brought over a plastic bag. "All of this is from your past. You don't need any of it."

Natalia held her tongue, knowing she couldn't say anything more. Whatever the coins really were, she had lost them. She hoped they weren't as important as she felt they were.

Feeling a little lost, she watched as Zechariah took the bag to Miguel, who climbed into his truck and drove away. She got back into the truck with Dean and Zechariah, lying down in the back seat. She was tired and hungry and at this point didn't care where they were going. There was no way she could tell anyone anyway. Natalia closed her eyes and slept, letting the rough movements of the truck rock her to sleep. As she slept, she dreamt of Vincent, hoping he would find her quickly, praying Bethany would be spared the truth.

14

It was an hour past sundown, three weeks since Vincent told Natalia he would find and free her friend. Bethany was easy to find. The Slayers lied to Natalia; they never kidnapped Bethany. Vincent's people found out that the human unknowingly sublet her apartment to Slayers. They used the opportunity to take the fake pictures. Bethany was currently living with her mom in Monterey. The Slayers made the right decision not to kidnap the human. Her family was well-off. They would have spared no expense in finding the young woman.

Once they found Bethany safe, Vincent turned his efforts to finding his would be lover. It was harder than they thought. Although unable to track Natalia all the way to her location, they still had a starting point from the discarded tracking device. His men thought they would be able to find her with that, but there were no records of her location. In order to find the place, Vincent went fishing with Marshal.

The ghul enjoyed that. The Slayer did not. The fishing expedition ended with Marshal begging for his life, promising to tell Vincent everything, as long as they didn't let him fall into the oubliette.

The house Natalia was being kept in was in the middle of a forest, surrounded by redwoods and pines. The cabin was on land owned by a logging company, which had gone out of business a few years ago. Currently, it was unused land. Vincent and his people felt it was a bad idea to have a hidden cabin here, as anyone might buy the land at any time. But then, he never accused Slayers of being smart.

The cabin sat in the middle of a clearing. There was a fresh aroma to the air and the wolves inhaled it readily. It was a week to the full moon, and they were frisky. Vincent did not usually ask much of them this close to the full moon, but he didn't want to wait until after the full moon. Also, there were no innocent bystanders here, meaning the werewolves didn't have to hide their true forms.

He could have asked his vampires, but it was easier to kill a vampire than a werewolf. Even an old, fully fed vampire could be taken down with a stake in the heart coupled with a beheading. Though silver would kill a werewolf, it was harder to hit a prepared werewolf. Vincent enjoyed using the werewolves when fighting Slayers, too. No one died easily when a werewolf fought.

The wolves had been here last night to scout. They learned the layout, found out how many exits and how many people lived in the cabin. It was a large cabin with two floors. There was no garage; two trucks were parked behind the cabin. The scouts reported seeing three people walking around the house. This number included Natalia; she had apparently gained some freedom after her trip to The Red Thread.

Tonight, there was double the number expected. Vincent made his plans based on the smaller number but had no choice except to proceed. Most of the new people arrived two hours before Vincent and his men. There was no time to call for backup. Vincent knew what his people were capable of and stayed the course.

Rebecca gave the signal and the three werewolves advanced. With them were three vampires: Vincent, Joseph, who was standing by his master, and Mierka, who was somewhere in the woods, finding an alternate way into the house. As the werewolves advanced up the long driveway, they changed into wolf form and merged with the woods. They were quieter as wolves, and less conspicuous. Vincent and Joseph, after checking to make sure that the wolves were doing well, ran up the drive. The werewolves were there for stealth; the vampires were there for speed and strength.

CB EO

Natalia heard the wolf cry before the others did and bit down on her fork in order not to scream for joy. She didn't know for sure that the wolf meant Vincent, but there was an almost human quality to the howl, and the howl was decidedly familiar. Natalia began shutting down all her thoughts and emotions, not wanting to reveal anything. She was sitting at the kitchen table, having a somewhat pleasant meal with five Slayers. Zechariah had gathered them here to talk about the vampire situation.

Zechariah stayed true to his word. As long as she did as she was told and showed no defiance, she was allowed to roam the cabin freely. She was allowed outside if someone was with her and allowed to bathe and change her clothing on a regular basis. Miguel bought her three pairs of jeans and enough shirts, underwear and socks to have clean clothing every day as long as she did her laundry once a week. She had to wash her clothing in the sink and hang everything out to dry, but she didn't care. It was clean clothing.

Natalia was still locked in a room at night, but she could count the passage of time. Also, she had a bed and a table in the room. She wasn't forced to sleep on the floor. And as the door was locked, she didn't have to worry about anyone coming in uninvited. Zechariah and Dean were the only ones allowed to unlock her door. She was also being fed on a regular basis; one of her chores was to cook the daily meals. Someone else bought the food.

Although allowed out and about, she wasn't permitted to discuss too much with the Slayers. Today was the first day she had been allowed to hear the dinner conversation. The others were talking mostly about the vampire hunters. Natalia figured the others didn't care if she knew about this slowly growing group.

Vampire hunters consisted mostly of the relatives of the tortured and murdered children who were looking for justice or revenge or both. The Slayers, against better judgment, Natalia thought, decided to take along these humans on vampire hunts. These humans didn't have the abilities the Slayers did and died a lot quicker. The Slayers in the area didn't seem to care too much about them and used them almost as cannon fodder. The whole situation disgusted Natalia, who believed humans should be kept out of the shadows and protected.

The true Slayers at the table, Zechariah, Miguel, along with the newest member Agnes, weren't skating around the cannon fodder situation, as Leroy and Ryan were smart vampire hunters. These two men seemed to hold contempt for other vampire hunters, because the others weren't as helpful to the Slayers. The only other vampire hunter this group did not mind having around was Dean, who was currently out on an extended errand. The young man was a planner. He almost never went out on missions, just made the missions run smoothly. Leroy was good with guns and could quickly kill young vampires. Natalia doubted he had ever been up against a vampire as old as Vincent. Ryan was an ex-cop and had many useful connections.

Another howl ripped through the woods and this time, everyone heard. Zechariah's head snapped back and forth, trying to see everywhere at once. Agnes jumped up so violently, she knocked her chair over. Natalia noted how nervous the woman looked and knew she would have to watch that one. Nervous people with guns seemed to fire without thinking. Miguel ran for the weapons calling for Leroy to follow. Ryan ran to a window to try and peer into the darkness.

Agnes removed her coat. She had four guns strapped to her torso: one on each hip, one under each armpit. She grabbed one with her right hand, her weaker hand, leaving the other open for the .357 loaded with silver bullets Leroy was grabbing. Natalia got up, her hand going to a necklace that was no longer there and waited to be told what to do. Zechariah was the first to speak.

"Everyone calm down. We don't know that it's werewolves out there. We need to keep our heads."

Another howl ripped through the cabin; it was very close, as were the next two. Miguel and Leroy handed out the guns with silver bullets to Zechariah, Agnes and Ryan. They were the best with guns. Miguel held a rapier and a dagger. Leroy held a staff. To Natalia they gave a staff, which Zechariah had taught her to use, or so he believed.

The staff was just one of the many weapons she learned to use during her five years in Montana. It had been easy to hide her abilities when she first rejoined Zechariah. As time wore on, he believed she needed to be able to defend herself. The lessons with the staff taught her one thing: she was better at the staff than the Slayer was. After observing him in fights, Natalia knew she was able to use most weapons better than Zechariah.

She took the staff and watched as the others arrayed themselves around her, as if to protect her. She shifted slowly, getting into the right position to strike. She slowed her breathing, listening to the scratches on the walls and doors. From the sound of it, there were three wolves. Natalia tried hard not to react. If Vincent was here, that meant four Hellspawn against five Slayers. Not the greatest of odds.

The howling stopped and the silence that ensued was thrilling. Natalia, glad the Slayers couldn't see her face, gave an evil smile. Her eyes gleamed impishly as desire spread through her body. When the front door was ripped off the frame, she inhaled through clenched teeth, desperately trying to control her true feelings. When Vincent stepped through the door, she nearly lost control.

The front door was in direct line with the dining room, which, as far as Natalia knew, had never held any furniture. It was a large open space, good for weapons practice. Now it made a great space for actual fighting. Natalia's position lined her up perfectly with the door, and therefore Vincent. He was dressed in hiking boots, faded jeans that hugged his lower body well, a tight black cotton t-shirt and a dark green button up shirt. He locked eyes with her, as if holding her up. A small shudder ran through her as she saw her feelings mirrored in his eyes. She would be in his bed by morning.

The vampire stepped into the cabin, with Joseph close behind. Three wolves loped in after him, two going to the right, one going to the left with Joseph. One of the wolves had a scar running through its milky left eye. Since most of the Slayers had silver rounds in their guns, Vincent and his men were severely outnumbered. Natalia waited for a chance to warn him.

Vincent assessed the situation carefully. Natalia was armed but surrounded by Slayers. Mierka's instructions were to position herself upstairs, and take out two Slayers before anyone noticed, but she was not yet in position. If she were, one would already be down. He decided a diversion would be fun.

"Natalia. Come to me. Now."

Fire blazed in her eyes as she took an almost involuntary step forward. Her mind stopped her before Zechariah's words did.

"Remember what he did to you, Natalie! You don't belong to him!" He prattled on in the same vein for a moment, allowing Natalia to calm her breathing.

"You're right, Zechariah, I don't belong to him." She paused and the evil look came back into her eyes. "Besides, with your silver bullets you'd overtake his wolves quickly." She took another quick breath and spoke in a seductive voice. "And I can't allow that."

She jumped into the air. Natalia spun around and used the staff as a long bat. She knocked down Miguel and Leroy, who were standing behind her. She heard the wolves growl and attack. A shot rang out from upstairs, causing Natalia to glance up as she landed. She saw a head and rifle barrel peering over the edge of the second-floor railing. It was a strategic location as the railing was solid wood. Natalia focused her attention back to the fray, wondering who went down. Ryan lay on the ground as blood pooled by his head.

There were wolves facing off Zechariah and Agnes, who had their guns pointed at their respective wolf. The third wolf was trying to circle behind them. Nervous, Agnes shot at her wolf with a silver round. It jumped out of the way, but too late, and was hit in the side. Agnes turned her attention to the third wolf. No one was paying attention to Natalia, who crept up on the two Slayers.

Before she could reach them, she heard a shuffling behind her. Leroy, having been hit second with her staff, was apparently still aware. He was on his feet and swinging his staff at her. Natalia tried to bring up her staff but couldn't move quickly enough. From above, another shot rang out, too late. Leroy's staff connected with Natalia's right shoulder as he fell to the ground dead. There was enough momentum to push her to the ground.

She was quickly on her feet and looking toward Agnes and Zechariah. Agnes stared at her, then shot at Natalia. Natalia spun to the right as the bullet sped past her arm. She lost her footing and fell to the ground as another shot rang out from upstairs. Agnes fell, pulling the trigger one last time. The bullet went wild and lodged into a wall.

There was a moment of quiet as the fighters looked around. Joseph was the first to move and went to the wounded wolf. He picked up Orlando and took him closer to the front door. The wolf was still conscious and whimpering. There was a doctor in their van, waiting. Orlando would soon have help. Joseph placed Orlando on the floor, trying to make him comfortable, then turned to the two remaining wolves and Zechariah, who had yet to take a shot. Considering two angry wolves were growling at him, it was a smart move. The vampire went to the Slayer and took the gun without a fuss. He then turned the man around and held Zechariah's hands behind his back. Joseph stood watching Vincent wondering what his boss would do.

As Joseph was handling the wolves, Mierka climbed down the stairs and made sure all the other Slayers were dead. She shot all of them in the head, just to make sure. She then started cleaning up the mess. Rebecca and Charlie, now in human form, helped, despite their lack of clothing.

Vincent controlled himself well enough not to run to Natalia. He could see the pain in her eyes. The vampire took a good look at her and saw her shoulder didn't look right. He guessed it was dislocated.

"Natalia. You're hurt."

She nodded and closed her eyes. "Shoulder is dislocated. I need to adjust it."

He started to her. "Let me help."

"All right. This has happened before. I know what to do. Just listen to my instructions." She opened her eyes and found a clear spot on the floor. When she started to lay down, Vincent went to her.

"We have a doctor waiting outside."

She shook her head. "I'll see him later. Help me."

He helped her lay down, then followed her instructions as she moved her dislocated arm parallel to her body, then over her head. With her right hand near her left shoulder, Vincent helped her move it further to the left. Pain creased her features, but she only let out a hiss of breath when her shoulder popped back into place.

Natalia breathed deep for a moment. The pain was not gone, but it was a lot better. She wouldn't be able to use her arm for a while. When she looked to Vincent and nodded, he helped her sit up. He stared into her eyes for a moment, before he leaned in and gave her a deep kiss. He pulled away as the smell of her blood found its way into his senses. Vincent pulled away and stared into her eyes. Deep pride was shining in her beautifully dark eyes, as was pain.

"You're hurt." He tenderly touched her shoulder.

She gave a small smirk. "Not as much as before." She grabbed his shirt with her left hand and brought his lips closer. The kiss did not last long.

Vincent pulled away. He could smell her blood like a cloud around them, obscuring his thoughts. He let her go quicker than he wanted, knowing if he didn't, he would take her blood. She started to protest, so he repeated his previous words.

"You're hurt. I can smell your blood and though your wounds are superficial, you're not able to match me tonight."

"All right. We'll leave that for later." She placed her hand on his chest. "You're here. Bethany?"

"She's safe. We'll discuss that later." He wanted to tell her more but felt it best to tell her all when the Slayer still alive was out of ear shot.

Vincent watched as the look in her eyes changed. Where before there had been some turmoil, now there was acceptance. Then her determination came through and she started to stand. Vincent helped her up. Once on her feet, she stood tall and seemed unhurt. Other than holding her right arm folded in front of her torso, and the small amount of blood where the bullet grazed her, she hid her signs of injury. She somehow managed not to feel her pain in order to fight for him, to help him win. He cocked his head slightly and squinted, as if trying to peer into her thoughts. Even now, she was standing defiantly, trying to stare him down. He finally identified her look.

Every woman he ever loved as a vampire had had that look. It was a look that carried strength, loyalty, passion and a willingness to stand tall through anything that came along. Vincent growled and stepped toward her, meaning to throw her onto the ground, despite the carnage littering the floor. A hand on his elbow stayed his movement. Mierka looked up at him and shook her head, repeating his words.

"As you stated sir, she's hurt."

The words brought the world crashing in upon him. Closing his eyes, he took a deep breath, startling the remaining Slayer and Natalia. He opened his eyes, picked up Natalia and headed for the door.

Natalia started to protest, but stopped quickly, loving the feel of him, knowing she was safe. It rattled her calm for a moment, to think she was safe with a creature that could easily kill her, but her calm quickly returned. Though Vincent was a vampire, he was not a monster, despite what the Slayers might say. As least, he had not shown himself to be monstrous around her. As she stared at Vincent's face, she wondered what the future might reveal about her vampire lover.

As Vincent walked out the door, he looked down at the woman in his arms. She looked back at him with strength and determination. He could still see the defiance in her face, as well. He knew now why he had hesitated to kill her when he had the chance. It wasn't just about having her as a lover. His feelings were more complex, and Mierka's statement held true. She would be an asset if she were a vampire. Vincent planned on convincing the human that Mierka's idea was a sound one. He wanted Natalia around for as long as he could have her. He looked up, not wanting to run into anything.

Once Vincent was outside he slowed and stopped, waiting for Joseph. His bodyguard came out a moment later, his cell already to his ear. Joseph was ordering the doctor to bring up the van. Mierka came out soon after, with the now tied up Slayer. She was leading him like a dog. He was scowling but walked at her pace. It kept the rope from going taunt and tightening around his throat. She led him to a tree and tied him to it. The van arrived as she was finishing. Doctor Elving got out of the van carrying a little black bag. He killed the engine but left the lights on. He was by Vincent's side quickly, trying to check out the now sleeping woman in his boss' arms.

"How many wounded?" He was a good foot shorter than Vincent. He almost had to stand on tiptoe to check out Natalia.

"Her and Orlando."

Dr. Elving started to touch her wound. Natalia winced. "Who's worse?"

"The bullet's silver. Natalia had a dislocated shoulder, and a bullet graze. Tend to Orlando first."

The doctor stopped looking at the Natalia. "Is this one a wolf?"

"Human."

He nodded. "Set her down in the van. I'll look at her first, since she's here. And bring Orlando, I'll need to see his wounds."

Mierka hurried to the van to fold the seats down. The seats were flush with the floor, making a good flat surface. She moved out of the way to allow Vincent to carefully lay Natalia down, then went to retrieve the wounded wolf. Natalia was starting to wake up and was rather disoriented. She sat up violently, striking out at Vincent. He gently restrained her, calling her name to wake her up.

"Natalia. Natalia! You're safe. Calm down." His voice was peaceful, gentle, trying to lull her back to sleep. Her eyes focused on him and she took a deep breath, which turned into a grunt.

"I was dreaming. I thought Marshal was trying to..." She took a deep breath and looked around a little confused at being in a van. She saw movement out of the corner of her eye and turned her head to face him the man coming closer to her. "Who are you?"

"That's Dr. Elving. He's here to help." Vincent turned her head to face him. "Let him look at your wounds."

"If you don't mind, I want to see where the bullet grazed you and I want to look at your shoulder. Would it be easier to cut your shirt or remove it?"

Natalia looked at her shirt. It was a short-sleeved button-down shirt. "I can remove it, but I'll need help with the buttons and, well, removing it from my right arm."

Dr. Elving nodded and Vincent unbuttoned her shirt. Once the buttons were gone, he helped her slip the shirt off her left then right arm. She wasn't wearing a bra but used her shirt to hide her breasts. Vincent had a rather interested look in his face and she felt it wasn't the right time to seduce him, even though she very much wanted to.

Instead of seducing her lover, Natalia sat still, and allowed the doctor to check her out. He lightly touched her whip marks and decided they weren't a problem. Those wounds were older and were healing fine. He touched her shoulder lightly and found it was back in place. She would need a sling for a few weeks, and possibly a scan to make sure nothing was broken or torn. He turned his attention to the graze wound and started to clean the area of blood.

While Dr. Elving examined Natalia, Vincent tried hard to ignore the fact that Natalia was half naked. He took a deep breath to calm himself and instead became even more aroused. He could smell her blood. He pulled back, trying to get away from the scent. To distract himself, he looked down to see how much blood he was covered with. She wasn't bleeding much, but his hands were somehow covered. He stared at his hands, which were sticky with blood, flexed his fingers, and tried not to lick his hands clean.

He caught Joseph's eye. Joseph nodded. "I'll watch her."

Vincent turned and headed for the cabin, to wash his hands. Mierka was walking back to the van with Orlando in her arms. He had a rope tied around his snout as a muzzle. There was a rip in her sleeve. The wolf had tried to bite Mierka. If she wished, he would allow punishment, as long as it was not too harsh. She knew the risk of handling a wounded wolf. Vincent nodded his head at the decision and continued into the cabin.

15

Inside the cabin, Vincent could hear Charlie and Rebecca searching the house. There was a pile of books and two chests waiting by the door. Vincent went to the kitchen sink to wash his hands. He needed to get her blood off his skin. Natalia's scent crept into his nostrils and made it hard to think. Once his hands were clean, he turned to regard the wolves. Rebecca came out of a room holding more books. She was dressed in baggy borrowed clothing. The wolves had clothing in the van, but since they were cleaning and searching, it was a prudent idea to borrow clothes.

"Anything interesting?"

"We won't know until we look through it. We'll need a translator for the books. The ones I looked at weren't in English."

Vincent picked up a book, turning the pages carefully by the corners. He didn't want the brittle pages to crumble. He put the book down once he recognized the language. Although he could identify Russian, he could not read it. "What are we doing with the remains and the cabin?"

"We can't burn it; the woods will catch. Who owns the land?"

"A bankrupt logging company," he smiled as an idea occurred to him, "for the moment." Vincent took out his cell phone and dialed his lawyer.

As Rebecca and Charlie finished searching the house and gathering all the books and artifacts, Vincent placed many calls. By the time the wolves were done, Vincent's people were well on the way to purchasing the cabin and the land around it for five square miles. Despite the lateness of the hour, the logging company was happy to have a buyer for that land. Sometime later, still on the phone, the vampire left the cabin with his wolves, and arranged for some of his people to come and occupy the land.

They would take care of the bodies well before the land was his. Though he was certain he would be able to acquire the lands, they needed to be cleared if anyone came to check. He used code words with his people, knowing it was safer than talking about bodies on a cell phone.

Plans set, Vincent closed his phone and looked to Charlie. Rebecca was nowhere to be seen, but Charlie was obviously waiting for his attention.

"Charlie?"

He gave Vincent a quick glance, darting his eyes between the makeshift ambulance and the large imposing creature. "Will she be ok?"

Vincent followed the wolf's gaze, letting his eyes rest upon the van. Charlie caught the look on Vincent's face before he hid it. There was respect in the vampire's look. "She'll be fine."

Charlie started to follow Vincent as he went to the van but stopped. His place was by the cabin waiting for Rebecca and the second van, not following his boss like a lost puppy. Instead he watched as Vincent leaned into the van to see what was going on. The second van came up the drive and blocked his view.

Rebecca got out of the full-sized van, went around to the side and opened that door. She then went to the back and opened both of those doors. She pushed the four plain wooden coffins out of the back, knowing they would need the room for the books. The vampires had slept in the coffins on the ride up to protect them from the sun. It would be dark for the ride back and they wouldn't need the protection.

"Hurry up, lover boy. We have a lot to do." She playfully slapped his ass on the way by. "The quicker we get done, the quicker I can go to sleep."

Charlie followed Rebecca in and helped her load the books and chests into the back of the van. There was a dividing gate between the cargo area and the cab to keep everything in place. Halfway through, they realized not all of it would fit, even with the back packed from floor to ceiling. When they were done, there were no empty spots.

"We can fit more in if we put some books on the front seat, but one of us will have to ride with Vincent." There was humor in her voice.

Charlie gave his Alpha wife an annoyed look. "You're enjoying this way too much."

"I could be jealous. Do you want me to be the jealous wife?" Her arms were crossed, an amused look on her face.

He leaned against the closed doors of the van, running his hand through his shaggy hair. "You're going to drive me nuts, woman."

She slinked over to him, wrapped her arms around him, giggling the whole time. "Isn't that my job?" She gave him a light kiss. "You drive the van; I'll ride with the vampires."

"We're going to have to make more than one trip anyway. There are still over a hundred books in there. Why bother?"

She backed away, nodded her head in Vincent's direction. "It's what he would want."

Charlie grabbed her arm and pulled Rebecca toward him. "How about we ask what he wants instead of assuming to know what he wants?"

"Because it's fun to tease you."

His arms were wrapped tight around her and he was smiling. "Bitch."

She gave him a wolf's smile. "Call me that tonight when you're screwing my brains out."

He laughed, planted a kiss on her lips, and let her go. Grinning and shaking his head, he led Rebecca to the others. The doctor was still in the van, but he was now working on Orlando.

Natalia sat at the edge of the van, legs hanging off the edge. She was asleep, but there was a distressed look on her face. Vincent was leaning against the side of the van, an odd expression on his face. Joseph stood next to Vincent and spoke quietly to him. Mierka sat at the end of the van, her hand on Orlando's head caressing his muzzled snout. Charlie noticed the ripped sleeve quickly, not really surprised the wolf had taken a bite out of the vampire. Orlando, generally cantankerous, was even more so when injured. Charlie admired the control it took his friend to stay in wolf form. Orlando would be able to communicate in human form but changing shape would undoubtedly make more flesh rip where the bullet pierced him.

Rebecca took Mierka's place, kneeling in front of the wolf to stare into his good eye. She held out her hand to his snout, letting him sniff her. She untied the makeshift muzzle and allowed the panting wolf to sniff her again. After whining a bit, he licked her hand, happy to know her.

"What's the word doc?" Charlie was hanging at the end of the van, not really wanting to talk to the vampires.

"Bullet's out. Just cleaning the wound." He had a bottle of peroxide in his bloody gloved hands.

"How long before he can change back?" This was from Rebecca who was still staring at Orlando.

"He'll rip himself open no matter when he changes. If he changes later, he'll rip open the stitches. If you can get him to change now, that would be of great help to him and me."

Rebecca stepped back and stripped. Charlie watched, as did the doctor. Rebecca was nice to look at, being fit and tan. Charlie held his breath as she changed into a wolf. It was an amazing thing to watch, even if you could do it yourself. She changed quickly, though, not allowing him his pleasure. There was business at hand, no time for play.

Rebecca, now in wolf form, placed a paw on each side of Orlando's head, whining to him and licking his face. She barked a little at him, whined again and barked a bit more. Orlando simply whimpered, looking dejected. Rebecca repeated her series of barks and whines, trying to convince him to change. He finally barked affirmatively and tried to get out of the van. Rebecca backed out to transform. Once human, she slipped her arms under

Orlando's body and pulled him out of the van. There was not enough room for him to change while in the vehicle.

Charlie helped his mate with his friend, as she would not be able to support his weight when he transformed. It was more fun to hold onto Rebecca when she changed. Orlando let out a howl as his muscles stretched out and ripped. Blood oozed all over Charlie's shirt, as he held tight to keep the man from falling out of his arms. Rebecca was standing in front of them, spotting Charlie. Orlando, now fully human, reached out and grabbed his Alpha's arm, squeezing hard. There was a sharp look in his eye.

"Don't ever make me do that again."

She gave him a hard stare. "Learn to avoid bullets." She gave him a kinder look as she pried his hand off her arm. "You were going to have to change at some point anyway, Orlando. Now is better than when the stitches are already in."

They helped him to sit on the edge of the van, allowing the doctor to take over. Orlando glared at his Alpha the whole time. Rebecca simply glared back as she put her clothing on. Charlie stole a glance at the three vampires and Natalia. She was leaning against the back of the passenger seat, fast asleep. Mierka, Joseph and Vincent were having a heated discussion, and it was getting louder. They speaking in French; Charlie didn't know what the vampires were saying.

Eventually, Vincent broke away, holding his hands up to his guards. He came around the van, shooting dark glances in Joseph's direction.

"Charlie. You will take Natalia back to my estate tonight. Take the van with the books. The rest of us will follow tomorrow night."

"I can drive her back, no problem, sir, but why? There's plenty of time to get back before sunrise." Charlie almost never did anything without questioning Vincent, which sometimes amused his boss and sometimes angered him. This time, Vincent became angry, but answered truthfully.

"There is too much of her blood in the air."

Charlie's eyes opened wide, but Vincent's answer made him stop arguing. "I'll take her home tonight."

"She has an appointment with Bethany not this morning, but the next. It's at The Silver Spoon at ten in the morning. Make sure she gets there."

Vincent turned, leaving the wolf to do as ordered. He walked by Natalia, clenching his jaw. The smell of her blood was everywhere, making his mouth water for the taste of her, but to have her now was foolhardy. If he drank her blood, she would grow weaker. If he drank her blood, he would want her. Natalia could not take him on in her current condition. Joseph had suggested they stay, getting either Charlie or Rebecca to drive Natalia home.

Vincent decided Charlie should do the job as he had seen how Natalia's ex-lover reacted around her. Charlie was nervous, and that would never do.

He needed Charlie to have a clear head around Natalia as they would be around each other a great deal. If the wolf drove Natalia back, they would have plenty of time to talk.

Vincent, with Joseph standing very close, reached his hand out to Natalia's face, brushing a strand of hair out of her eyes. She was asleep but stirred when she felt his chilled hand on her skin. Her eyes opened, and she smiled.

"Hello, Vincent."

He knelt in front of her, his hand still on her face. "Charlie will take you to my home."

Her hand went to his. "And where will you be?"

"I'll see you when you're stronger."

She shook her head. "Then I want to go to my place. If I'm not sharing your bed, then I want to be in mine. I want to wake up tomorrow and take a shower in my bathroom, maybe go to the emergency room and get myself looked at."

The defiant look was in her eyes. Vincent shook his head. "I'll be home tomorrow evening."

"Well then, that's perfect. I'll go home tonight and see you tomorrow. And really," annoyance blossomed on her face, "I want to have sex with you Vincent, but I can't until this heals." She touched her right shoulder. "My arm isn't as strong. I want to be in bed with you right now, but that won't do. I need time to heal. Unless you have a healer on your staff?" She looked away from him as she questioned her own thoughts. "Can a healer take care of sore muscles?"

Though he knew the question was rhetorical, he answered anyway. "Yes, they can, but I don't have one on my staff at this moment."

She looked to Vincent. "Well then," she shrugged and winced at the pain in her right shoulder, "we'll just have to wait. I'm going home tonight."

His own annoyance started to rise. "And if I don't allow anyone to drive you home?"

Anger flashed on her face. She moved quicker than she should and placed her feet on Vincent's chest. She kicked out and he allowed her to knock him onto his back. Once he was out of the way, she stood and looked down at him. Defiance was her armor. She ignored the pain in her shoulder and took a deep breath.

"I have been trapped here for an unknown amount of time. If you think you can stop me from going home, you are tangling with the wrong woman. I'll walk if I have to."

As Vincent stared up at her in disbelief, Mierka laughed. Everyone looked to her as Vincent stood. He glared at Mierka.

"Natalia has a point, Vincent. She needs time to heal. And maybe you need time to get a healer." Mierka's smirk could be heard in her words.

Natalia looked to the woman. "Thank you."

Mierka nodded to her then went back to staring at Vincent.

"Fine." His teeth were clenched. Vincent turned back to Natalia. "Charlie will drive you home," he looked to Charlie, "but he will stop at my estates to drop off the van and use another car to drive you home. I want the books and artifacts unloaded tonight, not on a city street. You will stay with her and guard her until she comes to my estates."

Charlie nodded and headed to the van. Vincent turned back to Natalia. "I need to tell you about Bethany."

An odd look crossed her face. "What happened? You said she was safe."

Vincent took a deep breath. "She was always safe, Natalia It was as you suspected. They never kidnapped her. They were able to photograph her apartment as she was subletting. She's terribly worried about you."

Shock rocked Natalia back. She sat down and tried to make sense of his words. She felt this coming, but it still knocked the wind out of her. All the pain she endured to make sure Bethany was safe... She pushed the thought aside. It was useless to harbor ill will toward her friend. Natalia took a few deep breaths and closed her eyes. She calmed herself and finally looked to Vincent then beyond him to Zechariah.

"I had no way of contacting her. I took them at their word, as it was the safest bet. I don't know if I should be grateful or angry. I spent I don't know how long as a captive because I thought she was in danger." She hung her head. "I didn't think about asking for more proof than I was shown. I just..." she looked to Vincent, "I just wanted to make sure she was safe."

He saw the confusion and anger in her eyes and knelt to face her. Vincent placed a hand on her cheek. She leaned into him and looked into his eyes.

"All I want is to spend a few hours in bed with you and forget all that's happened. I can't even do that."

"That will come soon enough." Vincent nodded as he came to a decision. "I'll find a healer before I see you again. We may be apart longer than I thought, but I will find you a healer."

Natalia gave him a tired smile. He leaned in and gave her a gentle kiss. It slowly turned stronger and he forgot about her injuries. She did not protest as he wrapped his arms around her, stood and crushed her to him. The kiss grew hard, ravenous, and showed her the extent of his need. Her left hand went to his head and her fingers curled tight in his hair. She tugged fiercely, as he growled. As he inhaled to growl again, he smelled blood. Fresh blood. Her blood. He bared his teeth and fangs, pulling back a little to look into her eyes. There was no fear in her eyes and it aroused him further. Before he could bite, someone pulled him away by the collar of his shirt. Natalia protested loudly.

Furious to be ripped out of her arms, he turned to face his attacker, growling. Joseph looked at his boss mildly, knowing he could take Vincent on.

"What do you think you're doing?" The anger was evident in Vincent's tone. Everyone was staring at the two vampires, including the now sewn up Orlando.

"You bite her, you kill her."

"She can take it." He stepped up to Joseph, wanting to rip his friend's throat out.

Joseph placed his hands on Vincent's shoulders and turned the vampire around. The bandage Dr. Elving placed over her bullet wound was bright red with fresh blood. The wound was not large, about as wide as Vincent's middle finger. With that much blood oozing, he must have grabbed her arm by mistake when he kissed her. There was pain in her eyes as she touched her right shoulder carefully.

"She may not appear harmed, but she will rip herself apart to take you on. She is as obsessed as you are. Send her away. Now."

Vincent took a step toward her, then stopped. He could see a drop of blood forming at the edge of the bandage. Natalia closed her eyes briefly to hide her pain, but Vincent saw it in the line of her jaw as she clenched her teeth. It helped him decide her fate. "Get her cleaned up and get her out of here. Now."

Vincent turned, walking toward the Slayer, who was still tied to a tree. Zechariah had kept quiet the whole time, which truly amazed Vincent. He had never known Slayers to be quiet around his kind. Leaving the contemplation for another time, Vincent reached out, put his hand over the man's mouth, leaned in and took a deep drink from the man's jugular. The vampire's thirst was immeasurable. He pulled away, his craving unfulfilled, not caring that blood still oozed from the man's ripped throat. Zechariah's eyes rolled back in his head as he sagged and fell unconscious. Vincent glared at the Slayer, wishing he had something to chase, something to hunt and kill.

However, all the other Slayers were dead and this one was in no shape to run.

"Joseph!" He bellowed his friend's name, knowing Joseph was the only one who could take him on in a fight. If he couldn't relieve his frustrations for Natalia through Slayers, he would battle Joseph. He didn't truly want to fight, but he felt it was his only choice. Joseph and Vincent went around back to stay out of the way of the others. Halfway through the fight, they heard the van leave, and Vincent's blows became even fiercer.

Joseph allowed his master to win for a while, then started fighting back with the same intensity. Vincent might be his boss, but Joseph was the older vampire, and had been fighting for a far longer time. When he was helping Vincent's frustrations in private, Joseph used all his abilities; in public, the master won every time. At the end of the fight, neither vampire was bruised, and Vincent didn't feel any better. They went inside. Joseph went to find Mierka; Vincent went to pace the house, wondering how his woman was holding up.

Joseph found Mierka and Rebecca barricading the windows in one of the upstairs rooms. They had already blackened another room for Vincent and were working on Joseph's. Mierka smiled when her lover found them. Rebecca reported on the situation.

"We made Orlando comfortable in one of the rooms downstairs. Doc took the couch in Orlando's room to keep an eye on his patient. We've placed the bodies in the nearly empty room, where they probably kept Natalia. We tied Zechariah in there too, after the doc patched up his neck. He was still passed out from blood loss, but I gagged him to make sure he doesn't scream when he wakes up. I'll be going to sleep soon so that I can patrol during the day. If Orlando's up to it, he'll help me."

Joseph nodded and took over helping Mierka. "Go now, it's late."

Rebecca nodded, leaving quickly. She knew the look in his eyes and had seen it mirrored in Mierka's. Rebecca knew not to get in the way of vampires in heat.

Mierka and Joseph finished barricading the windows, saying little. The two met during the French Revolution. She had been an exceptional spy for the Revolutionaries. Vincent and Joseph allied themselves with the nobles; the vampires enjoyed fueling the ignorance of the wealthy and deepening the Revolution. The two friends never encouraged wars between humans and Hellspawn but took great pleasure in stoking the fires of human wars. It was easier to hide bodies during wars.

When Joseph met Mierka, he had been drawn in by her innocence. She was about five feet three inches with golden tresses and smiling green eyes. Her petite stature added to her youthful appearance. She had been posing as a maid for one of the particularly vain nobles. The man honestly believed he and his kind would win the war. Joseph first saw her at a wine tasting Jean-Louie held.

Intrigued by her large green eyes and golden tresses, he had flirted with her, asking the twit Jean-Louie about her. The man had been annoyed by the questions. The girl refused all his advances; Joseph was doing far better. She flirted back, shyly, acting as if she'd never been with a man. It only fueled Joseph's desires.

He left the wine tasting with the knowledge that he would have her and made a point of being at the next gathering the twit decided to have. He brought Vincent with him for his opinion. Vincent took one look at the seemingly young girl, laughed and stated that the woman was trouble. But Joseph flirted again, with the same results; she was rather receptive to his advances. He cornered her in an upstairs hallway, where she turned into a completely different creature. She matched his aggressiveness and then doubled it, exciting him to the point of needing her blood.

Joseph had lifted her up. He used the wall to support her and trailed kisses and nibbles down her neck to her chest. He gently bit her breast, drinking her sweet blood. He pulled away, retracting his fangs before she could see them. She smiled an absolutely evil smile and showed him her fangs, asking 'Isn't it polite to ask before you take another vampire's blood?' She took his blood then, but not as gently. When Joseph told Vincent, his boss laughed, not in the least bit surprised.

Over the generations, Joseph and Mierka had taken many lovers, but always came back to one another. Forever was a long time for a vampire, and relationships needed breaks, or one would end up staking the other. The pair seemed to understand that without needing to talk about it, and never begrudged one another for having sex with different partners. When Mierka brought up the situation with Vincent, Joseph seemed to be expecting it.

"He needs to be with a woman tonight."

They were hammering a thick, dark blanket to one of the window frames.

"There will be humans here when we wake in the evening. If there's a woman among them, she will be dead when Vincent sees her."

"He needs a woman, now."

"Will you go to him then?"

"I have before." She looked at her lover, her eyes reflecting the turmoil inside.

Joseph turned to her, taking her to him. "It would be dangerous to leave him alone. It's your choice, Mierka. I have never held anything against you; never will. Your mind is your own, as is your body. Do as you see fit."

She kissed him, loving how he felt against her, letting go reluctantly. They finished barricading the windows and she left, knowing Joseph could handle himself without her for one evening. Vincent was a dangerous creature when in the grips of obsession. He hid it well, but he was a man driven by his emotions: hate and love being the strongest. If left without true release, Vincent would rip apart a human in the evening. His humans trusted him to take care of them. If he killed one of them, the trust would be gone for a long time.

Mierka found Vincent pacing downstairs. She called his name softly, undressing as she approached. He watched, trying hard to control his reaction, but failed when she pressed herself against him and undid his pants. She knelt in front of him and devoured his flesh.

Barely able to control himself, he let her suck for a while, then pulled her up. His eyes were clouded with hunger. He turned her around, threw his arm in front of her mouth, grunting when she bit down and started sucking his blood. Nearly howling, Vincent threw his head back, bared his fangs, and threw his head down to her neck. He plunged his fangs deep into her flesh, and nearly ripped her jugular in half.

Vincent sucked her blood down for a moment, then pulled away roughly, ripping her skin even more. The savage beast growled, whipped Mierka around, gripped her head and attacked her lips. Mouths full of each other's blood, they kissed, letting their blood mix. They drank each other down as Vincent picked her up to take her upstairs. He had enough sense left in his addled mind to know it was safer to be in one of the darkened bedrooms. The closed room also helped to diminish the noise.

16

Natalia woke with a start from a dream that left her foggy and confused. Her bed was moving, and lights kept flashing. Her mouth was dry, her shoulder hurt, and her stomach was growling. The dream came back to her in bits and pieces as did her surroundings. Charlie sat in the driver seat, asking if she was all right. A piece of her dream floated into her memory and she bolted upright in the seat. The belt tightened around her and dug into her shoulder. She howled with pain, and startled Charlie. He pulled over to the side of the road and stopped.

He lifted the armrest, unbuckled his belt, then reached over to unbuckle hers. He knelt by her side, very concerned. "Hey, Nat. What's up? Are you ok?"

She was hunched over a little and cradled her arm. She talked through gritted teeth. "I need a phone. Need to call Vincent. Forgot something he needs to know about. Now."

"I don't have his number any more. I can call Rebecca or Joseph. What did you forget?" He reached for his cell.

"There was another Slayer with us. Name's Dean. He went looking for something, I don't know what. Don't know when he's coming back. Need to tell Vincent."

Charlie dialed Joseph's phone. He doubted Rebecca was still awake. Only she could patrol during the day. Joseph answered on the second ring.

"Is there a problem?" He didn't bother with a greeting.

"Natalia just woke up. She forgot about a Slayer named Dean. He's running an errand, and she doesn't know when he'll be back."

"Strengths and weaknesses?"

Charlie stared at Natalia, who seemed to be calming down. "Hold on a sec."

"Fine."

Charlie handed the phone to Natalia. "Here. Talk to Joseph. Be direct. He likes that."

"Is he the tall imposing, bald guy?"

Charlie nodded as she took the phone

"I've met him. Can we get some food? I think I'm hungry."

Charlie got behind the wheel and began driving again, trying to pay more attention to the road than to Natalia.

"Joseph, what can I tell you?"

"Dean's strengths and weaknesses."

"He's a good planner. Doesn't fight. He didn't go on raids but was connected by cell to Zechariah for last minute changes."

"What does he look like?"

"About five-feet six inches and overweight. He's Caucasian with black hair and brown eyes. He's about 19 with very bad skin. He's gullible, easily swayed. If a woman starts talking to him, she might be able to convince him not to do anything. That's all I know."

"Thank you." He hung up.

Natalia hung up and closed the phone. Charlie was pulling off toward a truck stop. She handed him the phone when he was completely stopped. "I don't want to go inside."

"I wouldn't let you. You shouldn't be moving your shoulder too much. What do you want?"

"Burger and water. Have them cut the burger into four pieces. It'll be easier to handle. Oh and chocolate shake if they have it."

"Sure, but are you ok?" His concern showed in his gentle voice.

"My shoulder was dislocated, a bullet grazed me. I've just been rescued from weeks away from my house and life, and I found out I could have escaped any time I wanted. How do you think I am?" She sounded perturbed, but her voice wavered.

"Dumb question. Will you be ok by yourself or should I wait a while?"

"Go ahead. I'll be fine."

Charlie gave her one last look, then left the van. She watched him run inside, then carefully slumped a little bit. She laid her head on the headrest and took deep breaths, trying to relax. Her shoulder hurt. The doctor had offered her prescription painkillers, but she refused. She didn't like to use any kind of drug. Natalia learned how to control her pain with breathing techniques, but sometimes it wasn't enough. She wished she had told Charlie to get her some over the counter pain relievers.

Sighing, Natalia tried her breathing techniques again, not wanting to give into temptation. A smile came to her face. She was pretty good at turning down temptation as long as it didn't involve Vincent. She smirked and looked toward Charlie and the diner. It had been the same when she was with Charlie. Natalia signed again. She hadn't had a chance to really say hello to him.

After all these years, when she woke up to his voice, the memories of him flooded her mind. They would be working together, possibility living together. It felt odd, but right, that after all this time, she would end up working near the werewolf who pulled her fully into the shadows. She remembered the first time they met. She was eighteen, and still innocent of the shadows. As she relaxed, she remembered going to Lucas Stevenson's house and meeting Charlie.

ଓ ଅ

Ten Years ago

"Hey, what's your name?"

Natalia looked up to see three young boys checking her out. They were prepubescent, probably no older than ten. This neighborhood was supposed to be a rough one, but the boys looked nicely dressed. It wasn't Sunday, therefore they weren't headed to church, just looked nice. She nodded to the one who spoke to her.

"Hello. My name's Natalie." Close enough to it, anyway. "What's yours?"

"Uh…" He seemed surprised that she answered. "Um… it's Letto."

"Short for Stiletto?"

He nodded once. "Yeah."

"Cool. How can I help you?"

"What are you doing here? People don't usually stop here and draw."

She had a sketch pad in front of her, and some drawing pencils, but only as a ruse. She was trying to draw, but art was not her strong suit. She was sitting in a neighborhood park, but Letto was right, no one came here to just sit. So far though, the only people who had bothered her were these boys. The park offered her a rather good view of Lucas Stevenson's home. It's why she chose to sit here.

Natalia looked to the three boys and all three met her eyes. There was no hostility, just a bit of curiosity. She felt that was a good sign, but still didn't want to give too much away.

"I'm trying to draw a house. I'm not very good at it, but a friend of mine really likes the house and I wanted to try it out."

Letto looked at her oddly. "Why would you do that?"

"Because I like him."

He frowned a bit. "That's weird."

"OK. Still going to do it."

"What house you drawing anyway?"

"The one with the really nice lawn, and all the trees."

He gave her an odd look. "Oh, no! You don't want to do that! That's bad voodoo. Lucas is crazy. You don't want his bad voodoo infecting you too!"

She looked at the boys in surprise as all three added to the description of Lucas Stevenson.

"He never comes out. When he does, the air doesn't smell right for a week!"

"Man never eats!"

"Man never sleeps!"

"He locks his trash cans."

"I've heard, if you visit him, no one ever sees you again!"

"That man is whacked and anyone who knows him is also whack!"

This went on for a few minutes. Natalia listened, nodding the entire time. Slowly, she reached up to her necklace and started twirling the silver beads. One by one, the boys were caught in the sparkling beads. She started to speak.

"Thank you for that information, boys. I have to be on my way, and so do you. You're going to leave first, and you're going to forget all about this conversation. If anyone asks what we talked about, you'll say I seemed like a fool. Now go."

The boys scattered. Natalia stood as she stopped twirling her necklace. She picked up the sketch pad and pencils and walked toward Lucas Stevenson's house. Enough was enough, she needed to know who he was.

A few months ago, she found her mother in bad shape. Marnia was dating a man named Donald who might or might not be a vampire. Natalia was trying to find out more information on whether or not vampires existed, and how to kill them if necessary. She felt Donald might be using her mother for blood, but wasn't sure how to tell and how to help her.

Lucas Stevenson had taken some books from a private church library that might have some information she needed. The librarian seemed to think he would return the books eventually, but Natalia didn't want to wait. She was here to confront him, and maybe find an ally, or at least someone she might talk to. It was rare to find someone willing to talk about the odd things that occurred in the world, the things the news failed to mention, or always seemed to report incorrectly.

Putting on a brave face, Natalia walked to his house. She set her sketch pad and pencils on his doorstep and knocked on his door. She didn't want anything in her hands. When no answer came, she knocked again. She was about to knock a third time when the door finally cracked open. An eye peered out at her. Even through the small crack of the opened door, she encountered the stench. It smelled a little like rotting meat and incense. The eye narrowed.

"What do you want?" The voice was not pleasant.

"I'm looking for Lucas Stevenson. He took some books from St. Benedict's." She tried to sound pleasant, but the stench was too much.

"What are you? Apprentice nun?" The door opened a little more and she saw part of a clean-shaven face.

"No, I just wanted-"

The door opened fully. "I recognize you. You've been reading my books."

The man standing before her was impeccably dressed. He sported a clean white shirt, a black tie, black dress pants and black shoes. He was the same height as her but thinner. Natalia reached for her necklace. Nicely dressed or not, he made her uncomfortable.

"Well, that's the point. They're not your books. They belong to St. Benedict's."

Lucas regarded her for a moment, frowned, then pulled her inside. He closed and locked the door behind them. The house was as spotless as the man. The stolen books were on a table by the door. She wondered if he had been about to return them. Other than the table, there was a couch and loveseat set, a recliner, and a television set half obscured by books.

"I know you." His voice changed. Natalia went back to twirling the necklace, trying to control him.

"You said; from the church." Her voice became melodious as she tried to clear her mind.

He shook his head. "Not just from the libraries. They told me about you. You're the one walking the edge."

She stopped twirling the necklace. "Walking the what?"

"You came to the right place. I can show you what you need to know. Then you'll make the right decision." He indicated the couch. "Will you stay and talk?"

He sounded normal again, and the desire to talk to someone about what she suspected was too tempting. Natalia took a seat at the end of the couch closest to the door. Lucas left the room and came back carrying an old book. Its leather binding looked frayed, showing years of use. He sat in the recliner, turned toward her, opened the book and started to read out loud.

"In the beginning, God created the heavens and the earth."

Natalia started off sitting on the edge of the couch, waiting expectantly for an answer. As the hour passed, she slowly leaned back further and further, disappointment seeping into her very being. If the answers were in the book, she would have found them the first time she read the Bible.

At the end of an hour, Natalia sat up and cleared her throat loudly. "Look, Lucas. If this is all you want to discuss, I'm going to go. I've heard this all before. The answers aren't there."

Lucas looked up from the ancient Bible, anger buzzing in his eyes. "You will sit and listen to the Word. The answers are in here, you just have to listen for them."

Natalia stood nervously. It was a mistake to seek him out. She needed to leave. "I appreciate your hospitality, but I think I'll…" she thought quickly, watching as he became angrier, "study the Bible on my own. Much better than someone reading it to you. More time to ponder the words and meaning. Bye."

They reached the door at the same time. He placed a gentle hand on her shoulder. "If you will not listen, will you at least look?"

His mood swings were dizzying. "Look at what?"

"What you'll become if you do not listen to the Word."

Natalia didn't answer but let him pull her along. If he had something trapped…. She had read about many different creatures in the past two months, but Donald was the only possible non-human she had ever encountered. She wanted to see something real, something concrete.

Lucas took her to the door at the end of the hall and stopped.

"This is the face of the devil." He took out a key, unlocked then opened the door.

There was a silver cage in the center of the otherwise empty room. In the cage was a naked man. Lucas became angry again. "Show her your true form BEAST!"

The man simply sat huddled in a corner trying not to move. Lucas grabbed her arm and led her to within inches of the cage. "I know how to make you change."

Lucas left, closing the door behind him. Natalia ran to the door, tried to open it. It was locked. Fear and uncertainty filled her. She should never have come here. "Fuck."

"Hey. Name's Charlie."

Natalia looked to the man in the cage. He still hadn't moved.

"You want to get out of here?"

"Yes." Her tone of voice mirrored her near panicked state.

"You help me, I help you."

Natalia took three deep breaths, wondering how much time they had as she fought back tears. "What do I do?"

"Get on top of the cage, grip those bars," he pointed them out, "and pull really hard."

Blood dotted his arms. Actually, Natalia realized, there were spots of blood all over him. Nodding she took a good look at the cage. The bars were spiked with little shards of metal, probably silver. Natalia looked at the man in the cage. Did Lucas think Charlie was a werewolf?

A door slammed at the other end of the hall. Natalia looked at Charlie then vaulted onto the cage using a gymnastics trick. She lightly touched the bars with her hands, managing to only scratch her palms. She landed on the top bars in a crouched position, grateful now for the spikes, which gripped her rubber-soled canvas sneakers. She stood, turned around, braced her feet on two bars shoulder width apart, and crouched down. Natalia grabbed the bars Charlie indicated and pulled up. Nothing happened. She could hear Lucas. He was almost to the door. No longer caring about the spikes she repositioned her feet, leaned forward, grabbed the bars and pulled hard.

Lucas opened the room door just as the bars pulled up. Natalia's bloodied hands could no longer grip the bars. She fell back against the top of the cage and screamed as the spikes bit into her back, butt and legs. She heard a masculine scream and tried to get up. There were strange growling noises and snarls coming from the door. Natalia wanted to know what was happening but couldn't get up without hurting herself more. After hearing more snarling, she finally braced herself, pivoting to sit across the bars rather than straddling them. She felt her jeans and skin rip.

Finally, in a better position, Natalia sat up, then rammed a bloodied hand into her mouth to stop the shriek. A deformed bipedal creature with boils and mangy, ragged fur had its snout buried in Lucas's torso. Its claws, about the length of her lower arm, were pierced deep into Lucas' chest and thigh. Natalia's other hand went to her mouth and she gave a strangled cry. The thing looked up at the noise. It stood up and changed as it approached, its matted hair receding quickly into its skin. It was Charlie by the time it reached her. He reached his hands toward her arms and pulled her hands out of her mouth. He sighed as he spoke.

"Welcome to Hell."

The words resonated in Natalia's head. He had spoken mildly: a statement, not a threat. A breathless, woeful phrase indicating his reluctance to induct her into this secret society. She sat there not speaking, trying to find her mind. Charlie saw the confusion on her face, sighed and spoke again.

"He captured me three weeks ago, been torturing me every day. If you want to feel sorry for him, that's your problem. I'm going home, getting some supplies and coming back to burn the place down. Don't be here when I get back." He let her go, turned and took two steps.

"WAIT!" Even to her ears, she sounded scared and desperate, but he did stop and turn around.

"What?"

She stammered trying to get the words out. Charlie cut her off with a soft voice.

"Look, just go home and forget about this OK? Pretend it's a bad dream. Whatever it takes, just get out of here." He turned and left. This time she did not stop him.

Natalia climbed off the cage and gingerly stepped to the floor. She hurt everywhere from puncture holes. She tried not to look at Lucas, but it was the first thing she looked at. There was a large ragged hole where his stomach had been. Intestines and organs protruded from the open wound. Some blood spurted from an open vein and Natalia fainted to the floor.

17
Present Day

Charlie came back to the van carrying two bags and a drink tray. The food smelled fantastic, but only because he was hungry too. He put the drink tray on the hood to unlock the door. Natalia was asleep again, so he had to maneuver to get everything inside. Once in, he gently shook Natalia awake. The smile on her face made his breath catch. He remembered that smile. He gave a low whistle and shook her again. She came awake this time, slowly.

Natalia turned her head, almost expecting to see her lover. Time warped when she saw Charlie grinning at her, and she almost reached out to him. She stopped when her shoulder flared. Her smile turned to a grimace and she exhaled hard. She breathed in slowly and smelled the food.

"Hey."

"Hey. You hungry?" The grin he wore was reflected in his voice.

She bit her tongue, trying to hide her reaction. It was one of their favorite jokes. She couldn't help it. She gave him a seductive smile. "Very."

He was sitting in his chair sideways, looking at her, his smile gone. "That's not nice."

She grabbed one of the bags with her good hand. "No, it's not. I'm sorry. It's just…" She paused to look into his eyes. "I don't know how to act around you anymore. I started thinking of how we met the first time, then I think fell asleep and remembered when we were dating. I saw you and for a second, thought we were still dating."

"I could live without the first and last memory of us."

They looked at each other for a moment before Natalia shook her head. "We're with the people we're supposed to be with Charlie, don't regret the bad. Just remember the good."

He made a non-committal grunt as he pulled a Styrofoam container out of the bag Natalia didn't grab. "I don't really know how to be around you either. I think that's why Vincent made me drive you. It's a long drive; we have a lot of time to talk, if you don't fall asleep again."

"I should be ok after food." She opened her container, revealing steak, eggs and American Fries. "This isn't mine."

Charlie took his food and handed hers over. The cook had cut her burger as ordered, which made it easier for Natalia to handle the food with one hand. They ate in silence, exchanging glances, but not wanting to say too much. Charlie finished her leftovers, as he used to when they were dating. Natalia leaned back in her seat, sipping on her chocolate shake. It was thick and rich, just the way she liked it. Once finished with the food, Charlie took the containers and bags out to the trash. After making sure she didn't need to use the restroom, he started the van and left the parking lot for the highway. It was fifteen minutes before either of them spoke.

"What happened to you anyway? How'd you end up with the Slayers?"

She slurped her shake, wondering where to start. She turned her head to look at him and knew she wanted to tell him the whole story. It always made her feel better to talk to him.

"About two months after you bit me, I went on a road trip to find Donald, my mother's killer. I was determined to find him and kill him. I found the route he used to take and drove it up and down, stopping at truck stops and restaurants; anywhere a trucker would stop. Along the way I met a Slayer. He told me about a training camp in North Dakota that was run by militants. Most of them didn't know about Hellspawn, but as long as I was willing to do as they said, I could be trained on any number of weapons. All I had to do was mention the Slayer's name and I'd be in. He gave me the information, but I wasn't sure I wanted to go. I kept looking for Donald…. It was a human that convinced me to get training."

She paused, took a few deep breaths, then took a pull at her shake. She had to admit; the shake was delicious. It was more dark chocolate than milk chocolate. She set the cup in the cup holder. "It was late at night at a truck stop. The place had a huge parking lot. I was going to my car for something. Guy came out of nowhere, put a knife to my neck, and demanded my wallet." She paused again. Charlie glanced over; her jaw was clenched tight. "A big trucker came out of the restaurant about that time and yelled. He thought I had forgotten my stuff in the restaurant; wanted to make sure I remembered it. The mugger let me go and ran off.

"I've taken some sort of martial arts my whole life. Gymnastics and yoga and all sorts of other classes, but a guy with a knife was able to get the better of me. I knew then that I had to get more training. If I couldn't take down a man, there was no way I could take down a vampire. And then there was you." She turned to look at him again and caught his sideways glance. "I didn't want to be afraid to be with the man I wanted to be with. I was furious with you too. I went to the camp with the vague idea that I needed to know how to defend myself. I worked harder there than I ever have before; learned things I had never thought about learning. It felt good to work and learn like that."

She giggled. "They wanted me to earn my keep. Get this: I told them I was good with computers. They had me watching government sites to make sure no one knew about the camp. Anytime the place was mentioned, I was to erase it. I figured it was better to redirect the government's searches rather than erase all knowledge. It was a great tool."

Charlie frowned and turned to her. "How so?"

"I made government watchdogs watch demons, vampires and other critters that were killing humans. They'd take care of the killers and the militia group stayed safe and out of the radar. They weren't out to hurt anyone, so I didn't see the harm in helping them. They were sad to see me go."

"What was the place like?"

"They ran the place like a military boot camp, but you could stay as long as you wanted. Three or four of the men who ran the place were ex-Marines. I'm not sure why they put the camp together and didn't care. They had no problem with me being there as long as I didn't ask too many questions and as long as I kept up. There were a lot of days I didn't think I'd make it; but I did. I learned everything I could. It took me five years, but it was worth it. I can take on any man or woman that faces me and I know I can take out a young vampire."

"So, how'd you end up with Zechariah?"

"When I felt I was ready, I came back to San Francisco, but I didn't know where to go. I needed something to keep me going in the camp. I decided to let it be anger. I took all the pain that all the men in my life had ever caused me and turned it into anger. When I came back, all I knew was anger. I was so clouded with it that I figured I was a Slayer. I tracked down Zechariah, who had come back to the area as well, and asked him to help me. He was very willing to take me into the fold."

She looked out the window at the passing trees. "I think part of me knew I wasn't supposed to be a Slayer; I never told Zechariah about my training. I just let him think I was a researcher. Every so often I would track a vampire on my own to practice and train. Every so often I would offer them their life in exchange for a fight. If they could kill me, they'd be free."

"A little dangerous, don't you think?" His voice told her what kind of fool he thought she was.

"I'm still here aren't I?" There was pride in her voice.

He huffed, then went back to concentrating on the road.

"Any other questions for me, Charlie?"

"Do you like him?" He tried to keep the emotions out of his voice and almost succeeded.

"Yep. Do you?"

"Mostly."

"How did you end up with him?"

"Are you done with your story?"

"Pretty much. I think you know how I met Vincent."

"I heard." He paused to concentrate on getting by a line of trucks meandering down the mountain road. They were almost off the mountains. He was glad. Mountain roads made him a bit nervous. Too many sheer drops.

"About a year after you left me, I was captured in a huge net. It was a straightforward trap. To this day, I can't believe I didn't see it, but it's harder for me to think clearly when in Blitzkrieg form. I tried to rip through it but couldn't. Then these guys dressed in black came up and shot me with a tranq. I don't remember the events fully; it was more like watching an old movie reel: fuzzy, grainy, no sounds, just visuals. I do remember thinking, 'fuck, we're being hunted again.' Then I passed out. I woke up some days later in a cage in a dungeon."

He laughed. "Because yeah, the bastard has a dungeon." He paused, took her shake from her and took a large sip. "Hey that's pretty good." He handed the cup back, ignoring the annoyed look on her face. "So, I woke up in a cage, in a dungeon. There were other cages. Most held wolves. Two others held humans. About two minutes after I woke up, a short woman walked in carrying robes. She handed me one without saying anything, then placed the others on the cages of the two other guys. They were still asleep."

He inhaled and let out a shaky breath. "She came back to my cage and leaned on it. She just stared at me for a minute or two. I couldn't say anything. The second I saw her I knew who she was."

"Your wolf."

"Yep. It was Rebecca." He paused as a memory inserted itself. "She looked really familiar, too, and not just because I had been dreaming about her." He grew quiet, and she let him. "I found out later she was Daniel's niece. Remember him?"

"Your boss at the security gig?"

"Yeah. She looks a lot like him, but more feminine. When he and I met through her, we nearly fell apart. For a while I wasn't sure if I was going to laugh with him or kill him. It seemed too much like a set up." He shook his head, clearing it of the useless animosity. "It wasn't of course, although he always said that wherever he ends up he usually runs into weres. I think he inadvertently seeks them out, so he can help them try and have a normal life. I probably wouldn't be alive if it wasn't for him."

He stopped talking for a moment, as he let the memories run through his head. Natalia, not sure of the look on his face, aimed his thoughts back to his story of meeting Rebecca. "So, what happened after you and Rebecca stared at each other?"

Charlie grinned as his favorite story came back to mind. "We stared at each other for a minute or two before she unlocked the cage." He grinned at her, huge. "We didn't introduce ourselves until after we were done."

Natalia laughed, feeling herself blush a little. It was odd to listen to him talk about another woman. "You didn't even know her name?"

"Didn't matter. I'd been dreaming about her for almost eight years. All I wanted was to be with her."

"Was it as good as you dreamt?" Her voice teased.

In the lights of a passing truck, she saw him blush. "Better. She didn't go away when we were done."

They both grinned. It was a friendly grin of two people finding their footing with each other. Natalia saw that grin and knew though it might take time, she and Charlie would be all right.

18

They were lost in their own thoughts for a while as the road passed under them.

Natalia broke the silence. "How was your first meeting with Vincent?"

"Well, Rebecca and I introduced ourselves and she told me she worked for a vampire that was interested in hiring more werewolves. She dressed, and I put on the robe and we went to meet him. I was introduced to Vincent, Joseph and Mierka. They make an imposing trio, especially to a guy in a robe. You know, the truth is, I wasn't really listening to what they were saying. I was looking at Rebecca, marveling at the fact that she was real. I interrupted them and told them that as long as she was around, I would follow her."

He laughed, remembering the look on Joseph's face. "Joseph wasn't happy about that; Mierka smirked, but she's always smirking. Rebecca laughed out loud and Vincent stared at me, not sure what to make of me. He let me stand there for a long time as he paced the room. Finally, he turned to me and asked if I'd be willing to give my own life for him. I told him that I didn't know him well enough to make that call. Then he asked me if I would give my life for Rebecca, and I said yes. He took a few more minutes then told me that if I wanted a job with him, I had it."

"He was ok with what you said?" Natalia sounded skeptical.

"I've worked for him since. It seems to be going well."

"Would you give your life for him now?"

He turned his head toward her and gave her a quizzical look. "I don't know. I've never been in the position to do so."

Natalia looked over at him, pausing slightly. "Were they the ones killing werewolves when we were together?"

"No. Vincent doesn't know who did it, although he has guesses. Since there's no proof, he doesn't want to start anything with the other vampires."

They rode in silence for a while, not knowing what else to say to each other. Natalia was starting to nod off when Charlie spoke up again.

"Were you happy to see me again?"

"Yeah, I was." Her voice was soft, sleepy. "I was glad to know you were alive."

"You think we can be friends?"

She laughed. "As long as we can keep our hands off each other."

"We've done pretty good so far." There was humor in his voice.

"True." She smiled, then looked through the front windshield. "How much farther?"

"To Vincent's estates, not that far. We'll have to grab a car before we head to the city. I think I want someone to look at your shoulder, too. There's a vampire at the house who used to be an army medic."

Natalia sighed. There wasn't much she could do but wait. She frowned as Bethany came to mind. "Vincent said I was supposed to meet Bethany soon, right?"

"You're supposed to meet her in two days at The Silver Spoon."

Natalia took a deep breath to steady her nerves. When she first saw Vincent, she assumed Bethany was either safe or dead. At the time, she hadn't wanted to think about either possibility. Vincent was there and that was all that mattered. Now, with her shoulder screaming and her stomach turning in knots from the pain, she found she could think of her human friend. She closed her eyes and a few tears slipped out from under her lids. Bethany had never been kidnapped. Natalia was grateful that her friend had been spared that horror. She turned her head to the side window, pretending to look out at the passing lights, and furrowed her brow.

"Where are we?"

"About an hour away from Vincent's Estates." He maneuvered onto an off ramp, slowing down as the speed limit changed.

"Doesn't feel like we've been on the road long enough."

"Vincent lives about an hour and a half outside of the city, in Marin County. We're almost there."

Natalia settled back in her seat and waited. Soon, they left the lights behind. About 30 minutes after leaving the highway, they arrived at a gate. Charlie reached up and pressed a button on what looked like a garage door opener. The gates swung open. Two men loomed out of nowhere and stood by until the van passed. It took another fifteen minutes to arrive at the house. It was too dark to see it all, but Natalia could tell it was a mansion. There was not much light, but the sand colored stone was illuminated nicely.

"How big is this place?"

"It's a big mansion. There are eight vampires, and about 20 humans who sleep in the house. Rebecca and I are the only werewolves who sleep in the house. The others live in the guest house."

"How much land?"

"You'll get a tour of the place soon enough. I'm not sure of the acreage. All I know is that there's enough room for us wolves to run around and not run into any of the ten farms he's got out here."

"What does he farm?"

"Humans. And sheep."

Natalia gave him a look. "For food?"

"Yep. Good cash crop and occasionally, the farmers herd the sheep out where we can get them. Doesn't happen much as that would kill the crop. Every two weeks, 20 humans from the farms cycle through the house."

"The vampires farm the humans; the humans farm the sheep and you chase fresh meat every once in a while."

"Yep." Charlie was parking the van in an underground garage. Natalia heard the large garage door close and watched the lights come on. Three men emerged from a door further down the garage. Charlie opened the driver door and yelled a hello to the approaching men. Natalia, stiff from sitting too long, opened her door and climbed out. The three newcomers were dressed similarly in jeans, t-shirts and work boots. They ignored her and went to the back doors to unload the cargo.

Charlie came to her as they started unloading. "Come on. I'm going to have Ben look at your shoulder. I also need to use the restroom." He gave her a fake frown as it looked like she was about to argue. "Don't give me that look. I'm taking you back to your place. I just need a pit stop, ok?"

Natalia gave a small laugh. "I'm sorry. Yes. Lead the way."

As he led the way upstairs, Natalia contemplated her situation. Due to the angel's voices in their head, some Slayers in the area probably already knew she was a vampire's woman. It wouldn't take long for most of the Slayers and Hellspawn to find out, and where would that leave her in her search for Donald? She hadn't heard a thing about him in years, but it was a big world, and he could be anywhere. Natalia came back to the present when Charlie opened the door to the kitchen.

"Oh, wow." The kitchen was half the size of her house. There was an island in the center, which held a double sink and a cutting board surface. There were two ovens and two refrigerators. There were countless cupboards and most of the countertops were marble. The glass front cupboards revealed china for any occasion. Most had the fleur-de-lis on them in the middle. Charlie led her to one of the stools and helped her to sit. She was entranced.

"Is the kitchen this big because of the humans that live in the house?"

"Yes. He also likes to have parties. You hungry again?" Charlie was opening the fridge.

"I need to use the restroom actually."

"Right. This way." He led her across the hall to the bathroom then went back to the kitchen.

The bathroom was large but standard. The room contained a toilet and a sink. There was a built-in linen closet and medicine cabinet, both of which were filled with items that would be found in any household. Natalia surmised it was for the humans. She used the restroom and left, going right back to the kitchen. Charlie was talking to a man with ebony skin. He was as tall as she and Charlie, but thinner. There was something about him that commanded respect.

As she walked to them, he turned to her and closed his eyes as he gave her a small bow. "M'lady."

"Natalia, this is Ben. He's going to look at your shoulder and arm."

"Nice to meet you."

"The pleasure is mine." He indicated she should sit on the stool.

She sat only after getting a glass of water. There was a tarp laid out on the counter, with bandages and tape and scissors, sitting on top. With Charlie's help, Natalia removed the shirt from her right arm. Once her shoulder was exposed, Charlie turned to leave muttering something about the bathroom. Natalia sat and sipped water while Ben checked out her wound and her shoulder. He patched up the graze quickly but complained a little.

"You're still bleeding a bit. Did you move your arm much?"

"Kind of hard not to in a moving van."

"Which means you moved your shoulder, too. If you can, I suggest going to a doctor for that."

"I thought about that, but what do I say about the graze? Someone is going to notice it's a bullet wound."

"We probably have someone you can go to. I'll ask and find you a name. Where are you staying tonight?"

"Charlie's taking me home once we're done."

"It may take some time to get a name. I can call you when I have something."

"Sure. No, wait." She cursed slightly under her breath. "You'll have to call Charlie. I don't currently have a cell phone." Her eyes went wide. "God, what about my bills?"

Charlie came back at that moment and nodded as he overheard her. "Oh, I took care of those for you. You'll have to get a new phone, but the bill is paid up."

"What? Charlie, that's... why didn't you tell me sooner?" There was a bit of shock on her face.

"We've had a lot of catching up to do. We would have gotten to it eventually. When we found out you were gone, I talked to Rebecca. We used Vincent's accountants to find your bills. I've been paying them for you." He smiled at the astonished look on her face. "Don't worry, you can pay me back."

She laughed and held out her good arm to him. Ben stopped checking her over long enough for Natalia to give Charlie a hug. "Thank you so much, Charlie. You don't know what this means to me."

He pulled back. "I've never been kidnapped, but there were plenty of times I didn't have a place to go. I figured you'd be living with Vincent once we freed you, but I had a feeling you didn't want to lose all your stuff, that you might also want to go home once we got you back." A sober look crossed his face. "A home is a good place to have."

Tears formed in her eyes. "It is. Thank you."

Charlie grinned and hid the look in his eyes by turning to Ben. "So, what's the word?"

"She needs to get her shoulder checked out. I'll call Anthony and find out if we have a doctor she can go to. Other than that, she needs to take it easy. If the bullet wound is still bleeding a lot in the morning, that's going to need to get checked out, too. It should be fine though, as long as she doesn't move. There's a sling in the medical room. I'm going to get it for her. Be easier on her shoulder."

Charlie nodded and turned back to Natalia. She was struggling with her shirt; he helped her put it on. "If you're hungry, there's plenty of food."

"Might not be a bad idea to grab something. What's the food situation at my house? Can we take something for tomorrow as well?"

"We probably should get some food to go. I'll grab peanut butter, bread, that type of stuff. Ben will be back quickly, I'm sure. Medical room isn't that far away."

"You really have a medical room here?"

"Lots of humans, vampires and werewolves living in one area. Safety first."

"Right."

They fell silent as Charlie rummaged around for some food to take. Ben came back within minutes and helped her into a sling. He gave her instructions which she promised to try and listen to. Once Charlie had what he wanted, he and Natalia left for the city.

They took Charlie's car. Both had a lot on their minds and were silent for the trip. There was no traffic, and they were unlocking Natalia's front door within an hour of leaving the estates.

Natalia looked to Charlie as they approached her front door. "I don't have keys."

"I have them." He grinned as he dropped a set of keys into her hand.

Natalia unlocked the door and went inside.

Once the front door was closed behind them, Charlie looked up into her eyes and saw tears. He stepped back and held up his hands. "None of that now. You'll get me going, too."

She laughed. "Charlie. God this is so strange, and really, taking care of my house? I never thought anyone would."

He looked into her eyes. There was nothing but sincerity in his words. "I love you, Nat. I'll always help take care of you."

She almost went to him, to embrace him, to cry in his arms, but stopped. Memories of the past surfaced and made her inhale sharply. "The last time we were here together…"

"It would be awesome if you didn't remind me of that." He sounded hurt.

She gave him a cold look, but if faded quickly. "You know what, I'm home. I haven't been here in weeks. I don't know if I care about anything else."

He grinned. "It's late. We should both sleep. I'll take the couch."

Her body sagged with relief. "I get to sleep in my own bed."

"Sheets are freshly washed. Rebecca and I came out here a couple days ago and took care of the sheets and the towels. She thought that would be a good touch."

Natalia stood with her mouth open for a moment then a happy look came into her eyes. "I have a feeling I'm going to be thanking you for a lot of things regarding my house, but I'm waiting for more surprises until tomorrow. I'm going to bed."

"I'll put the groceries away and make sure everything is secure. Goodnight, Nat."

"Goodnight, Charlie. Thanks for everything."

He gave a small bow and watched as she headed to her room. Once her door was closed, Charlie grabbed the bag of groceries he took from Vincent's and headed to the kitchen to put things away. Things were starting to look up.

In her bedroom, Natalia had the same thought as she snuggled into her clean, warm bed. As sleep found her, she slipped into dreams of Vincent and hoped they would not be separated for too long.

19

Natalia woke slowly, the sun streaming in around her curtains. She stretched leisurely. The memory of yesterday came floating back as pain hit her right shoulder. She winced and cursed herself for forgetting her dislocated shoulder was still healing. Natalia sighed and sat up. It was nice being in her own bed, in her own home, but there was probably a lot to do. She needed to check, well everything, and figure out how to salvage her life.

As she slipped to the edge of the bed, Natalia paused as relief flooded her. She was upset that she had not been able to confirm the Slayers kidnapped Bethany, but she was also grateful that her friend had been spared the horror. Natalia had no idea how they would have treated a human prisoner, or what they would have told her. Even though she had endured almost two months as the Slayers' prisoner, Natalia was overjoyed at finding out her friend was spared.

Unfortunately, Natalia also knew that she had to get Bethany out of her life. She couldn't have a human as a friend. She couldn't have someone in her life who didn't know there were monsters in this world. Natalia felt that soon, her world would be filled with creatures who understood the world. Her thoughts stopped cold. Her world would be filled with what Slayers and people who didn't understand, called monsters.

Natalia waited for her mind to recoil, to protest in some way, but there was only silence and peace. Natalia sat up straighter on her bed, comfortable with her decision. She would find a way to break off her friendship with Bethany, but that could wait. For the moment, she needed to get up and take care of all the emails that were probably piling up in her inbox. She slipped on her sling as a knock came.

"Come in, Charlie."

"Are you decent?" His voice was muffled through the door.

She laughed. "Wouldn't have invited you in if I wasn't."

The door opened. "Right."

"Good morning. What's up?"

"I received a call last night. Ben found us a clinic we could go to. It's in Oakland."

She nodded. "What time do we go?"

"When we're ready. They're expecting us whenever."

She shook her head. "I've never heard of that happening."

"Money buys a lot."

She looked to Charlie. "I've got a tidy little nest egg built up, Charlie. I couldn't get anyone to do that for me."

He gave her a serious look. "He has a lot of money. You saw his place in Marin. He has a place in Montana, too. I think it's just as big. He also has his own plane."

Natalia was silent for a moment as that all sunk in.

"He's been around a long time, Nat. He's smart and he knows what to do with money."

"All right." She let the thoughts go; there was too much to contemplate. "I need a shower and breakfast."

"I wasn't sure you drink coffee or not, so I brought decaf and regular grounds from Vincent's house. I can get breakfast started while you shower."

"Decaf and breakfast sounds good. Did you shower already?"

"Nope. I'll do that after. I have some clothing in the car but wanted to make sure you were up and knew the plan first."

"All right. Thanks."

Charlie nodded and left her alone. Natalia got up, grabbed some clean clothing and went to shower.

ભ જ

The shower felt like heaven. She used water so hot, it steamed up everything in the room within a minute. As she opened each container of her soap, shampoo and conditioner, the aroma wafted up and surrounded her senses. She lathered up, using more than she had in a long time. She had to be careful of her right arm, but she still enjoyed the over-long shower.

Once done, she used her thick towels to dry off. There was no blood when she wiped her right arm, which meant the bullet wound was healing well. Her shoulder still hurt to move, but it seemed a bit better. Natalia shook her head. She was probably only wanting it to feel better. It was too soon for the muscles to feel better.

Dressed, she headed to the kitchen. Charlie was standing by the stove, cooking.

"I don't think I've ever seen you cook."

"Rebecca's been teaching me."

"Nice."

"I do breakfast better than any other meal. Decaf is ready."

"Thanks." She grabbed a mug and poured herself a cup. "Do we have word on Vincent?"

"I talked to Rebecca while you were in the shower. They're going to head to New York. Vincent's sire lives there and kind of runs New York City. She's made alliances with a lot of non-humans too. I think she has healers."

"I feel a little silly, him getting a healer for me. I appreciate it, but this will heal in time."

Charlie snickered. "Weren't you the one to say you wanted to be healed quicker so you could sleep with him?"

She glared at him for a moment, before asking a different question. "Do you know when they'll be back?"

"When they have a healer. Not sure how long that'll take."

"I guess that gives me some time. Do you need to get back to the estates?"

"I'm your guard. I go where you go." He gave her a grin.

She laughed. "Why are you enjoying that so much?"

"Kind of fun. Also, I prefer not being around the vampires. I like them, but sometimes they make me nervous."

"And nervous werewolves are bad."

"Yep. Although we should probably head back to the estates before the full moon."

"When is that?"

"Six days."

"Keep reminding me."

"Yep." He turned away from the stove. "Food's ready."

She went to the stove and took the plate he offered. She ladled out some food and sat at the kitchen table. Charlie joined her a moment later. They talked of little things as they ate. Charlie went to shower as Natalia cleaned up and put things away in her own kitchen. She usually hated doing dishes, but today, it helped to remind her that she was home, and safe.

Cᴈ ᴇᴏ

Charlie drove Natalia to the doctor in Oakland a bit later. The staff and the doctor didn't ask the usual personal questions, other than her first name. Natalia didn't question it but asked about her shoulder. As far as the scan could show, she was fine. Nothing broken, and the doctor didn't find any indications of tears.

"You'll heal fine, as long as you keep the arm in a sling. I'm going to give you a better one. If you need anything, call and we'll take another look."

"Ok. Thanks, doc."

"Welcome. The nurse will get that sling."

He left and a moment later, the nurse came in with a better sling. Hers was fabric only; the new one was as well but felt sturdier. Natalia felt it would be better but took the fabric one to take back to Ben. Once set, the nurse left, as did Natalia. She knew if she called, she would get an appointment. Charlie confirmed it. As they were leaving, Charlie nudged her a bit.

"I know you've been through a lot, but you're more quiet than usual. Is that because of me or…?"

"No. I keep thinking about Bethany."

"Have you called her?"

"I did. She wanted to see me right away, but I told her I had a doctor's appointment and that I had to get all my affairs in order."

They were at his car, which was parked at the far end of the parking lot from the entrance of the doctor's office. Charlie waited for her to finish her thought.

"I had over a thousand emails in my inbox. I didn't think my inbox could hold that much. Most of it wasn't junk. My bosses freaked out, then got mad, then freaked out again. I have to call them when I get back to the house."

He unlocked the doors and waited until they were settled, and the car started before asking. "What about Bethany?"

"I can't have a human friend, or rather, I can't have a friend that can't take care of themselves anymore."

Tears started in her eyes and he could hear it in her voice. Charlie left the parking lot, not wanting to be in a parked car for too long. It invited too many questions. As he drove, he placed a caring hand on her knee. He wasn't trying to flirt with her, only to offer comfort, as he had many times before.

"I spent all that time thinking I was keeping her safe. I forgot about Bethany's parents. They're divorced now, but they still care about her so much. If she had been kidnapped, they would have done everything they could to find her. I forgot about that because I was too worried about her. It pisses me off."

He turned his head to look at her sharply. "Why?"

She sighed heavily. "Because all this time, while trying to save my friend, she was living it up." She shook her head. "Probably not really living it up, but she was fine. I didn't ask for good proof, I just assumed I had to take care of her."

"So maybe it's not that you have to have people who can take care of themselves, but you have to give people more credit for what they can do?"

She hid her head in her hands. "Yes. No. I don't know." She made a pained noise. "If I didn't know her, if I didn't have a human friend, they never would have been able to do this to me."

His hand moved to her shoulder. She was quiet the rest of the way home. After he parked, they stayed unmoving until she nodded. They left the car and went into the house. Charlie puttered around her garden as Natalia made calls to her bosses and tried to explain why she had been absent for almost two months.

CB EO

Natalia sat nervously in the corner booth at The Silver Spoon, waiting on Bethany. She'd come early on purpose. She used to work here and wanted to make sure people left her alone. She was in luck; she didn't recognize any of the staff or patrons, and no one seemed to recognize her. A few minutes later, Bethany walked in. Natalia sagged with relief. Bethany looked as beautiful as ever. Natalia stood and waved her over. Bethany rushed over and gave her friend a hug.

"Oh my god, Nat! I'm so happy to see you! Where have you been?"

Natalia hissed in breath as Bethany squeezed her shoulder hard. Bethany heard and backed away, to take a good look at her friend.

"You're hurt! I'm sorry!"

"I dislocated my shoulder. It's not that bad." She lied. "Let's sit down. Are you hungry?"

"Yeah, but I'm more worried about you than anything else." She sat in the booth and looked at Natalia. "Nat, you were gone like two months."

"Yeah."

"What happened? I thought you might have gone into rehab again until the detective showed up."

She nodded. After the sun went down last night, Natalia received a call from one of Vincent's men. He had posed as a detective to talk to Bethany and make sure she was in fact, all right. He had told Bethany nothing, as he didn't know what to tell her. Natalia sighed and told Bethany the same thing she told her bosses. It was the only lie that worked and explained her absence and her wounds.

"I fell in love with someone involved with a cult."

Bethany's jaw dropped. "Are you kidding? This happened because of a guy?"

"Bethany, please. It's been a long two months. I didn't know he was involved with a cult until it was too late. Then, when I tried to leave, he kidnapped me to try and recruit me."

"That is so messed up. How did you get free?"

"While I was there, someone else was trying to get free. She had a few friends helping her. When I found out, I asked for help. She agreed. In trying to get free, I wrenched my arm. My boyfriend, well, ex-boyfriend,

144

tried to stop me and wouldn't let go. I pulled too hard and, well," Natalia looked at her shoulder then back to Bethany. "And here I am."

"Wow."

"Yeah." Natalia could see the questions in Bethany's eyes and knew she had to stop her from asking any more questions. "Beth…"

But she had nothing to say, nothing to follow up with. Natalia was too tired to fight with Beth, to think up more lies. She didn't want to do it, but she reached up to her necklace. She had taken her mom's necklace out of her jewelry box and wove her will into it last night, just in case. She didn't want Bethany to be the first person to be hypnotized with it, but she had no other ideas.

"Bethany," she said in a melodious voice as she twirled the beads. "Bethany, you believe me. You have no reason to doubt me. You also know it would be best to stop being friends with me. My choice in boyfriends has never been good. It's best if you distance yourself from me."

She spoke softly, but Bethany heard her. She was caught in the light of the necklace.

"Bethany, did you understand what I said?"

Bethany nodded.

"Good. When you wake up, you're going to remember an appointment. You're going to say goodbye and rush out, head home. By the time you get home, you'll have forgotten about me. The next time you see my contact information in your phone, you won't remember who I am, and you'll delete me from your phone."

Natalia lowered her hand and grabbed her coffee cup. She said a word in Romanian and Bethany woke up. An odd look crossed the human's face.

"I can't believe that happened to you. I mean, I believe it, but I never thought I would know someone that experienced that." Another look crossed her face as if she were remembering something. She grabbed her cell phone and opened it. "Oh, my goodness! I totally forgot! Nat, I'm so sorry, but I forgot I have a doctor's appointment! I need to go! I'll call you later!"

Bethany hurried out of the booth and nearly fled from the restaurant. Natalia closed her eyes and tried not to cry. Her best friend was gone and would never call her again. It was possible the hypnosis wouldn't work, but if Bethany called her again, Natalia knew she would pretend she didn't know her. It hurt to have to push her best friend out of her life, but it was for the best. Bethany would stay out of her life and would therefore be safe from the shadows.

20

Natalia sat in the booth, gathering her thoughts. A soft touch on her hand made her look up. Charlie was sitting in the side Bethany just vacated. He had been sitting at the counter waiting for the meeting to end. He had been here the entire time.

"I'm sorry. I heard."

There was a lost look in her eyes. "I didn't know what else to say. I could have done all that without hypnotizing her, but I," she shook her head, "I didn't have it in me to make a scene."

"And really, would she have let you?"

Natalia looked into Charlie's eyes. "What do you mean?"

"You've been friends how long?"

"Years."

"She was there for you a lot, and you were there for her too, right?"

"Yeah."

"You really think you would have been able to convince her to stay away? Over the long run?"

Natalia thought about it for a moment, then sadly shook her head. "I don't know. Any time we had an argument or didn't talk for a while, I was the one to reach out."

He stared at her for a moment. "Look, Nat. I know this sucks, but you did the right thing."

"Doesn't make it hurt any less."

They looked at each other for a moment as the truth set in.

Finally, Charlie sighed. "Let's get you home. I'll call Rebecca and find out if they have an update."

"Sounds good." Natalia nodded and stood. She grabbed her wallet and pulled out a $20. Though they hadn't ordered, they had taken up space. She placed it on the table and left.

Charlie stood and followed Natalia out the restaurant. Out the door, they turned west on Union. It was a nice clear morning, with a soft breeze blowing off the ocean. It carried with it the smell of salt and seaweed. They were in Little Italy, and near enough to Chinatown that the breeze also carried an undertone of Asian and Italian cuisine. It was odd, but familiar and comforting.

After checking both ways for traffic, they crossed Columbus. At the corner, Charlie poked Natalia on the shoulder. He was to her left, near the businesses, to stay away from her hurt side.

She looked to him at the poke. "What's up?"

"You're really quiet. I mean, I know why, but you can always talk to me."

"This restaurant has too many memories."

He smiled. "I met you the second time because of The Silver Spoon."

She gave a slightly bitter laugh. "The memory isn't lost on me, oh observant one."

Charlie shrunk back into himself. Her tone of voice was not entirely kind. "Sorry."

She stopped and took a breath. Some tourists grumbled and walked around her and Charlie. "No, I'm sorry. I'm still wound up, Charlie. I was thinking about the fact that you were the one to show me the truth of the world. It seemed rather fitting that we should end up working for the same person."

"But…"

She was silent as they walked to the end of the block. They both looked left, then right. Charlie started to cross the street but stopped and looked back at Natalia. There was an odd expression on her face. As he watched, blood blossomed from her left thigh. She caught his gaze.

"Nat?"

"Charlie…"

"Nat!" He screamed her name and caught her as she fell.

From behind him, he heard the screech of tires stopping a fast-moving car. A car door opened near him.

"Get in!"

Charlie tore his eyes away from Natalia to see a small limo stopped behind him. There was a woman standing at the open back passenger door.

"Luxembourg. Get in!"

The password slowly penetrated his thoughts. Charlie picked Natalia up and ran to the limo.

ଓ ଞ

As soon as the shot was fired, Judith turned away from the silenced rifle and looked to Dean. "You made me miss."

She didn't try taking another shot, even though she could have. They were on top of the building across the street from Natalia. Judith could have taken another shot and killed either Natalia or the man she was with. Instead, she turned to Dean accusingly and stood up. Dean knew Judith didn't like him and didn't trust him. She felt any infraction needed corrective action, but at this moment, Dean was glad for that.

Judith was a Slayer and the angels had told her where to find Natalia. The angels didn't speak to Dean. He wasn't a Slayer and didn't know if he would ever be a Slayer. Judith turned to Dean fully and withdrew a pistol from her jacket.

"You made me miss. The vampire whore will live."

He tried not to visibly relax. Dean didn't want Natalia dead. He liked her and wanted to save her instead of killing her. Then he saw the gun. "Judith, you can try again another time."

"There won't be another time. The angels are warning me; my time is almost at an end. The whore needed to die today."

As she raised the gun to him, Dean lurched forward. He grabbed madly at the gun, hoping to get it out of her hands. By sheer miracle, he pulled it away from her. As he took a step back, they started at each other. She scowled, and Dean lurched forward again. He brought the stock of the gun down on Judith's head. He was taller than her and it worked. She grunted and fell to the roof. Without hesitating, Dean ran for the rooftop door. In a moment, he was on the third floor. He slipped into an apartment he and Judith had acquired an hour ago.

As he locked the door, he heard people on the steps in the hall, running up. He leaned on the door and prayed that no one would think to look in the apartments. Dean, terrified to be found by the people working for the vampire, ran to the second bedroom. He avoided the master bedroom. The apartment's actual tenant was in there. Judith didn't like leaving witnesses. Dean didn't like seeing bodies. As he hid out in the closet of the second bedroom, Dean wondered, not for the first time, if he had made a bad choice.

He had seen the carnage the vampires and werewolves caused freeing Natalia. He was on his way back to the cabin the night they arrived. He stayed back and watched and listened as the Slayers and his friends were easily killed. He couldn't fight; he didn't carry a weapon.

Dean looked down at the weapon he now carried and placed it on the ground next to him. He had probably doomed Judith. He could hear people above him on the roof. They were taking Judith. He shuddered. Dean knew what vampires were capable of and didn't want to think about it too much.

As the noise quieted above him, he hid his head and sobbed. He tried to get Judith to listen, to kill the werewolf Natalia was with first. Judith insisted on killing Natalia first. He wasn't sure why. They argued about it, and she seemed to change her mind. He saw who Judith was aiming at though and had to stop her. Natalia didn't deserve to die. She just needed to know the right path.

Dean sobbed as he realized he didn't even know what path he was to take. For the moment, he knew he had to give the vampire's people time to leave, and then he would need to escape. This room had the fire escape. He would use it to get out of the apartment and then the city. Maybe somewhere out there was something that would help him fight the vampires. He had researched a lot of artifacts for Zechariah. Maybe he could find one of them.

If nothing else, Dean knew he needed to learn how to fight. He couldn't count on anyone else to hit the right target, apparently. Sighing deeply, Dean waited until it was safe to leave.

⊂ℜ ℬ⊃

Charlie held Natalia as the woman wrapped gauze around Natalia's leg. When it looked to be tight, he understood the human was trying to make a tourniquet. Once the woman was done, Charlie laid Natalia on the floor of the limo and tried to make her as comfortable as possible. She was passed out, therefore he doubted it mattered much, but he still did it.

"Charlie, I'm Sandra." Sandra had a pleasant voice that did wonders to calm the werewolf, even as she wiped blood off her hands with baby wipes.

"Vincent ask you to follow us?"

"Joseph did. He didn't like the situation too much. There was something about a missing Slayer?" She threw the baby wipes into a plastic bag.

He remembered Natalia's phone call to Joseph as they drove to Vincent's estates. "Right. I don't know if he was the one to do this. Is Joseph back?"

She shook her head. "He'll be back tonight but sent instructions. We have people looking at the building the shot came from trying to find the Slayer."

He nodded then looked to Natalia. She was still out cold and there was blood seeping from the bandages. He looked up to Sandra. "Do you know if she'll be all right?"

"I'm no more than a field medic. I can dress wounds, and that type of thing, but I don't have training. We're taking the two of you to Vincent's estates."

"Natalia's place is closer. Or even that doctor we saw in Oakland."

"Though Vincent's Estates are further, Ben is there. It being daylight…" Her pleasant voice turned a bit sarcastic at the end.

Charlie blushed. "Right. I…" He looked to Natalia. "I forgot. I'm worried about her. What about Oakland?"

"Don't have that doctor's information and even if we did, it would take too much to have him take care of this. We'll have our people take care of her. What about you? Any damage?"

He shook his head.

"Let's just keep you calm then and get back to the estates. I've gone 34 years without a mishap with a werewolf and I would like to keep it that way."

Charlie gave her a kind smile. "I would like not to tear either of you apart. I'm doing what I can to keep my head about me. When we're on the estates, you might want someone to sedate me. I feel like I might explode at that point. I'm really not sure how I'm keeping calm."

Sandra gave a small smile. "Might be due to the fact that I have some magical energy and can cast a calming spell."

"You're a mage?"

"Um…" She frowned. "Not officially. I learned the calming spell when I was a kid. I've tried other things, and I even tried to get a mage to train me, but only a couple spells stuck. The calming spell, a sleep spell and a light spell."

It was Charlie's turn to frown. "Any ideas why you can't learn others?"

She sighed. "No. Mom and dad were raised on Vincent's estates. Dad died when I was two. Heart attack. She asked to leave, he had no reason to keep her. Vincent doesn't keep people who don't want to be there. Once we were on our own, Mom hooked up with this asshole who liked to beat her. I stumbled upon the calming spell and used it when he tried to hurt me. Didn't seem to work any other time. When she finally decided to come back to Vincent's estates, to keep her and me safe, I didn't use it too much. Then I started working with you werewolves and tried it out. It works when the full moon isn't out, and it only seems to work on one werewolf at a time. The sleep spell is an extension of the calming spell. I don't know why the light spell stuck."

Charlie nodded, but didn't know what to say. Sandra made small talk, mostly to keep him calm. Charlie was on the floor, sitting by Natalia, his hand on her good shoulder. Sandra was on the seat, trying to relax. Though she had been apprised of the situation before being sent on this mission, she really didn't expect anything to happen. Things usually happened at night, not in the middle of the morning. She was nervous but had done what she could. She knew Charlie would be fine until he was outside the car, and Natalia would not die on the way to the estates. It was all that mattered for the moment.

૭૪ ૪૦

The limo arrived back at Vincent's Estates an hour and a half later. There wasn't too much traffic, but the driver had to be careful. It wasn't a good idea to get pulled over with a bleeding passenger in the back seat. Though Natalia's bandages were red, they were no longer soaking through. Sandra applied bandages one more time before allowing Charlie to take her out of the car.

The limo parked in front of the entrance, and Charlie carried Natalia into the house and followed a human up the stairs to a spare bedroom. He laid her down on the bed and moved to the far wall as others came in to take care of her. The curtains were closed, and Ben was looking her over. They had to cut her clothing off to get to the wound.

Ben whistled at the blood. "At least the bullet went through the leg, but not through the bone. I can patch her up, but now she'll need a healer more than ever." He looked to Charlie. "You'll need to call Joseph and appraise him of the situation. Far as I know, people are still at the cabin."

"I thought they were supposed to leave for Lorraine's by now?"

Ben shook his head. "I don't know what happened, but since you're supposed to be watching her, you call him."

Charlie glared at Ben but left the room and grabbed his cell. He didn't even know if the vampire would be awake. He shook his head and called Rebecca. She would be patrolling but would take a call. She answered on the second ring.

"What's up?" She sounded happy to hear from him.

"I need to talk to Joseph."

Worry crept into her voice. "Why?"

"Everything went fine with Bethany, but Natalia was shot when we left the restaurant. Ben's looking her over now and says she's going to need a healer now more than ever."

"How bad was she shot?"

"In the thigh. Bullet went all the way through, and didn't hit bone, was Ben's preliminary diagnosis."

"Shit. All right. I'll go talk to him. I'll have him call you back."

"All right. See you soon?"

"I have no idea, but I really hope so." Her voice was hopeful as she said goodbye.

Charlie hung up and waited for Joseph to call. He went back to Natalia's room and looked inside the doorway. Ben and Sandra were working on cleaning her leg. He wasn't sure what they could really do about her leg though, when Ben turned to someone else in the room and asked them to fetch his medical bag. The human, just inside the room and out of the way, rushed out and nearly ran into Charlie. Charlie moved and decided it might be best not to be in this room, even though he still needed information.

"Ben. When you have more information on the wound, like how bad it is or whatever, let me know. I'm waiting on Joseph to call me back."

Ben nodded but didn't say anything. Charlie nodded more to himself than anyone else, and went to sit on the floor, back against the wall, right outside the bedroom doorway. The human came back with Ben's medical bag before Joseph called him. The old vampire sounded rather perturbed.

Charlie didn't blame him one bit.

"What is it?"

"Natalia's been shot."

"Give me details."

Charlie relayed what happened after meeting Bethany and told him what Ben told him. Halfway through the explanation someone tapped him on the shoulder. He stopped and looked to Ben.

"If that's Joseph, I have a better idea of what happened."

Charlie spoke into the phone. "Ben has an update. Here he is."

Ben took the phone and sighed. "She's lost a lot of blood. They did what they could with a tourniquet, but those aren't always great to use. Sandra did well. The bullet didn't hit the bone and missed the major blood vessels as well. She needs a doctor or a healer to look her over and get things taken care of. She may need surgery if we can't get her a healer."

He listened for a moment, said thank you and handed the phone back to Charlie. "He has a word or two for you."

Charlie took the phone and answered a few of Joseph's questions: no, he didn't see anyone, no he didn't hear the gunshot, and no, he didn't know if anyone found anything. He would find out for Joseph and give him a report when the vampire was back at the estates. They hung up and Charlie sighed heavily. Now that he had taken care of things, he felt the anger starting to unfold within him. He closed his eyes.

"Ben?"

"Kind of busy."

"I need to be sedated."

From inside the room, the human immediately appeared. "Come on. I can take care of you."

Charlie nodded gratefully and followed the young man down to the dungeon. After the young man locked him in a cell, Charlie started to think about all the ways he might have been able to save Natalia from being shot. As he thought about it, even if the thoughts were erratic and impossible, he grew angrier and angrier at himself. Within moments, hair started to sprout on his body. As soon as the transformation began, Charlie felt a pinprick on his neck. His hand went to the tranquilizer dart as he fell over. He was instantly asleep.

Once the werewolf was unconscious, the human put away the gun. He then went back upstairs to help Ben with the newest member of Vincent's household.

21

Vincent woke from a dream feeling completely unsatisfied. There was a knock on the door, but it was coming from the wrong direction. He came more fully awake and realized he was still at the cabin. Annoyance seized his features as the body next to him stirred. He had accepted Mierka's presence while here, to try and assuage his hunger for Natalia. It worked, but not as well as he had hoped.

He wanted to be at Lorraine's by now, but his plane had to go through a thorough inspection. As this never happened before, he felt that someone, Slayers, another vampire, or a human rival, had caused this to happen. He had people looking into it, and was rather displeased with the situation, but could do nothing about it.

They spent last night helping to clear some of the items out of the cabin. Things they weren't keeping. He could have driven to his estates, but with Natalia still healing, it wasn't a good idea. And now, for the second night in a row, with Natalia close but unattainable, he had taken Mierka to bed. He felt as Mierka sat up, slipped on a robe she had found in the bathroom earlier, and went to the door. She retrieved her rifle and held it at the ready as the door opened slowly. Vincent heard a whispered conversation and sat up, waiting for Mierka to let Joseph in. Instead, she turned back to Vincent and closed the door behind her.

Mierka stepped back to the bed, set the rifle against the nightstand and untied the robe. She let it slip off her shoulders and puddle to the ground. Vincent sucked in air as she climbed onto the bed and straddled him. She gave him a hard stare as she moved against him.

"Is there a problem, Vincent?" She was giving him a seductive smile.

"I enjoy having you as a partner, but I want another." He sounded slightly angry.

"I enjoy being with you as well Vincent. You needed someone who could take you on. I like that I'm one of the few that can." Her smile was seductive.

He halfheartedly tried to push her away. She felt delicious against his greedy body. "You don't belong to me. You should be with your man."

"Joseph has had me for many lifetimes. One or two nights away from him won't be detrimental to our relationship. And it's not like I haven't slept with you before." She stared into his light blue eyes. "But that's not what's bothering you is it?"

Vincent picked Mierka up off him and got out of the bed. He wandered over to the covered window, wishing to peer out of it. The blanket covering the window was securely nailed to the wooden frame, making it hard to pull the covering back. Unable to look out the window, he simply turned and leaned against the wall next to it. "You presume to know my mind, mistress?"

She was kneeling on the bed, naked. Her usual smirk was on her lips and reflected in her eyes. "You wanted to wake up with her in your bed, didn't you?"

Vincent growled and turned his head away from Mierka. She left the bed and came to him, running her hands over his chest.

"Mierka, leave me be." He didn't like being teased like this.

"Can't." She looked up into his eyes. There was some sadness there, which made Vincent frown.

"What did Joseph say?"

"There's been a complication with Natalia."

His jaw twitched, and he pushed away from her. "You didn't think to tell me this first?"

"I needed you calm, so that you would listen."

He turned and glared at her. "Tell me."

"We don't have all the details, but she was shot in the thigh. It missed the bone and the major arteries and veins, but she's lost a lot of blood."

His hands formed fists as he listened. "No other details?"

"They don't know who did it. Joseph sent a few people to follow Charlie and Natalia to make sure everything was all right, since we didn't find that other Slayer. Dean, was it?"

He took a breath and sighed heavily.

"You won't be able to touch her until she's healed. And now it's going to take longer." The tinge of sadness had turned to worry.

"We were headed to Lorraine's to find a healer. I'll call her before we leave and tell her it's more important now than we thought." He shook his head. "Leave me."

"No."

He turned to glare at her.

She stood with her feet apart and her arms folded. She gave him a cross look when he looked her up and down slowly. "Vincent, you may be able to lie to yourself, but you can't lie to me. I've known you far too long. I know how you are around women you desire. You don't think: you just act. You were ready to drink her blood two nights ago, even though doing so would have killed her." Her features softened as she stepped toward him. Her hand went to tangle in his hair. "You shouldn't be alone with your thoughts. It will drive you insane thinking of a woman you want to touch and can't."

Her body was pressed lightly against him, causing his skin to tingle. He placed his hands on her arms to push her away. He stepped around her and started to dress. "Mierka, you don't belong to me. Stop trying to tantalize me."

"Vincent, you know what would have happened if we hadn't spent the past two nights together."

"I do, but now I don't need you." He was pulling his shirt over his head, so his words were muffled.

"But do you want me?" She was leaning against the wall, her arms behind her, arching her back and accentuating her chest. His eyes slipped over her nakedness, appreciating the look of her.

Vincent was standing, pulling on his jeans. With his pants unbuttoned, he walked to her, and slipped his arms around her. "You are a desirable woman, Jacqueline.

She smiled when he used her real name.

"Truly unique, but you are Joseph's woman and I don't like sleeping with you when you are with him." He reached out to brush her hair out of her eyes and a smile came to his face. He pressed against her, peering down into her eyes. She had to look up to return the gaze. "But, if I am available the next time you two take a break, I would be more than happy to have a reminder of your talents."

Mierka gave him a false pout as he pulled away from her. "So, what am I supposed to do now?"

He growled at her, frustrated by her flirtatious nature. He threw her clothing at her. "Get thee to your man, temptress. Leave me be."

Mierka slipped on her panties, using the wall to brace herself. She pulled on her shirt as she walked toward him. "What will you do about the situation?"

"Gather my people downstairs. I will discuss my plans with everyone." He was sitting on the bed, tying his shoes.

Mierka, honestly worried, knelt in front of him. She placed her hand on his knee. "Vincent? Are you truly all right?"

He paused, giving her a blank look. "For the past two nights, I woke from a dream of her with the wrong woman's scent all about me. I'm told I can't have her until she is healed, which is far longer than I care to wait. You could exhaust me each night until she is healed, and I wouldn't be satisfied. I have felt like this before and understand the dangers. Since no woman but Natalia will gratify me, I will do what I have to." Vincent paused, a familiar look on his face. "There are humans downstairs, correct?"

"Yes." She sat on the bed to slip on her jeans, socks and shoes.

"Good. I'm rather hungry. Bring one up here."

"Yes, sir." Mierka left but was back within minutes with a human female. The woman was taller than Mierka and very muscular. Most of the humans on Vincent's land were. She looked at Vincent steadily with her hazel eyes but ran a hand through her short mousy brown hair.

Vincent regarded her over his tented fingers from the recliner he was sitting in. "Have you been fed on recently?"

"No, sir."

"Good." He stood slowly. "Angela, correct?"

"Yes." Her heart beat faster and her breath caught as the handsome vampire drew himself to full height.

He held out his hand. "Come to me, Angela."

She did so willingly and placed her hand in his. He pulled her closer to the chair and sat down. Once seated she positioned herself to the side of his chair and presented her bare arm. She pulled a sharp small knife from her pocket and cut herself. Vincent grabbed her arm and drank down her blood, staring into Mierka's eyes. Vincent's eyes glazed over then closed slowly as Angela's blood spilled down his throat. He gripped her arm tighter as he finished feeding. Taking one last draw, he opened his eyes and looked back at Mierka, as Angela stepped away and wrapped her arm.

Mierka understood the look Vincent gave her and smiled a lover's smile. Vincent stood from the chair as Angela left the two vampires alone.

"Thought you were done with me." Mierka walked to him but stopped two steps from him. He growled, grabbed her, and gave her a rough, blood laced kiss. Vincent fell back into the recliner, taking her with him. No other thought or word passed between them.

CB ED

An hour later, all were congregated downstairs in the living room. Vincent was pacing, gathering his thoughts. Angela was resting on the couch, eating a steak. One of the other humans had made it for her, knowing she needed the energy. Vincent finally spoke, breaking the slight tension the humans felt. Although they trusted him, he always made them nervous.

"I've received word from my lawyer. This land is now mine. We can do as we please. Angela, Jamie, Adrian, Leon, Peggy and Jill you will stay here to continue taking care of things. Find a good place for the bodies, then start tearing everything down. Anything that can be used for the farms can be taken. Everything else, give to a charity. Drive it there yourselves. Only let my people on this land. When the house is empty, tear it down, log by log. The rest of you will be returning home. Get ready, we leave within the hour." He turned and left the house, wanting a less closed in area. Joseph joined him in his brief walk outside.

"You're going to Lorraine's. The plane is ready then?"

"The plane is ready and waiting at the nearby airport. I already called Lorraine and told her about the current situation. I wanted her to send someone out now, but she doesn't have anyone yet."

"Who will be accompanying you?"

"If I may have her for a few more days, I would take Mierka."

"What does she say to this?"

"She was laughing when she told me to get your permission." There was humor in his voice. It was the first hint of emotion either man had shown. "Lorraine expects me to share her bed when I arrive. I need Mierka for her fighting skills, nothing more." He paused, watching his friend's expression. "I want you at the house to look after Natalia."

"You're worried for her."

"She's been shot. If something should happen, I want you there to change her."

"Do you think she'd agree?"

"Talk to her when you return, if you can. Make sure she's willing."

"If she's not?"

Vincent took a moment, trying to decide what to do. He knew Natalia would not appreciate being changed without explicit permission. If Natalia took a turn for the worse, though... "Try and get her permission. If she doesn't give consent, and is dying, do it anyway. I'll deal with her anger when I return."

"If you think this is wise..."

"I don't, but there's no other choice. I'm not done with her yet."

Joseph regarded Vincent, watching as determination took hold of the younger vampire's features. Joseph turned from his boss, to stare out toward the driveway and places beyond. He could see movement in the forest: creatures moving about on their nocturnal errands. "This may blow up in your face."

A shudder passed through Vincent. "It would be a great joy to take her on if she turned on me."

Joseph gave a short laugh, shaking his head. It was always impossible to deal with Vincent when he was in the grips of an obsession.

Vincent watched in silence as the shadows passed in front of the nearby trees. "It's time to leave this place. My plane is waiting, as is my sire."

Vincent turned, going back into the house. Joseph stayed for a moment, watching the creatures of the night. A stray thought flitted through his mind, something someone told him once, right before his change. A fortune teller stated he would never be a sire to a child. He thought it an odd turn of phrase, but while human, never had children. In all his many years as a vampire, he had never sired anyone, either.

The old vampire never met anyone he wanted to change, and now he was being asked to change Natalia. The first time he faced her, when she mentioned knowing him, dreaming of him, he walked away, knowing it was best. He had dreamt of her too. Of bringing her a goblet of blood and calling her child. It made no sense against what the fortune teller stated, but then, they didn't really see the future. At least, the fully human ones did not.

Joseph sighed heavily, an act he reserved for very rare occasions, and only grave ones. After years of dreaming of his possible child, he had finally met her. Joseph nodded once to himself then turned, went back inside and readied himself to leave. He would do everything he could to follow what Natalia wanted, not what his master wanted. It felt like the right thing to do.

Vincent's small group left the grounds shortly after, stopping only to drop Vincent and Mierka off at the nearby airport, where Vincent's plane was waiting. The vampire was tense with worry for Natalia. Though he had only known her a short time, he had spent a lot of resources to find her. He hoped Lorraine had a healer. If she did not, Vincent knew he would do everything he could to prevent Natalia's death, up to and including changing her against her will. He had just found her; he was not ready to let her go.

The first chapter of Inside the Grey House follows…

1

The jet landed on the private runway, barely causing a bump. Vincent and Mierka were off the plane within five minutes of landing and were being greeted by Lorraine's valet within seven. It was very close to sunrise, making the vampires grateful for Lorraine's private runway. She owned an incredible property in upstate New York, with space enough for a small airport. It was just large enough for Vincent's 16-seater jet. Human servants led Vincent and Mierka to separate bedrooms, gave them blood, and told them Lorraine would meet them in the evening.

The next evening Vincent woke craving blood, his head still swimming in his dream. He narrowed his eyes and snarled. Lorraine had a habit of drinking his blood while he slept. She had apparently crept in sometime during the day and taken her fill. She told him once she did it because she was his sire and could do as she pleased to his body. Grumbling to himself about his beloved sire, Vincent threw back the bedcovers and got out of bed, the dream cobwebs making his vision a little fuzzy.

He groaned a bit as the image of Natalia floated before him then ran away into the darkness. The dream, like all his dream of the human, was simple. This one started with the fight at the cabin: she was surrounded by the Slayers but was able to take down all of them with her staff before anyone else could move. She and Mierka, with the help of the werewolves, killed all the Slayers in seconds. When she was done proving herself as a fighter, she came to him, wrapped her arms around him and kissed him deeply. The dream dissolved into the night, and left Vincent with the image of himself taking advantage of all of Natalia's many abilities.

As he stood and looked toward the closets for clothing, he wished briefly that he had not ordered his people to destroy the cabin: it would be lovely to take Natalia back there and give her memories she would cherish instead of loath. Vincent shook his head trying to clear it, but he was learning it was difficult to remove her from his mind.

Vincent walked slowly to the clothes he saw hanging on the closest door. He wondered if he should have brought Natalia with him instead of ordering Charlie to take her home. If he had brought her to New York, she would not have been shot. If she were here, she would be healed in less the 24 hours. As it was, it would be more than 24 hours, and he probably wouldn't be able to be with her for longer than that.

Vincent's jaw twitched as he forced himself to stop thinking of Natalia. He would see her soon. He did not need her here as a distraction and Lorraine was expecting him. Vincent closed his eyes and took a very deep breath, letting it out slowly. Once his mind was clear, he turned his attention to the set of clothing hanging on the outside of one of the closet doors, waiting for him. He examined the jeans and button up shirt, smiling. They were his clothing, left over from his last trip.

Not wanting to waste any time with cleaning up, he slipped on the clothing and hurried out of the room. If Lorraine were anywhere, she would be in her study. She always started out the night looking over complaints and potential problems. There was generally a group of people waiting to talk to her each night. As Vincent descended the stairs, he noticed three people sitting on the couch outside Lorraine's study. Not bothering to acknowledge their presence, he strolled past them, barging into his sire's study. One started to protest but was stopped by the slamming of the study door.

Lorraine was on the phone, pacing back and forth, speaking rapidly to the person on the other end. She was dressed in a blue silk robe and nothing else. She was a shapely woman and stood five feet four inches. She had been turned at 25 but looked to be about twenty because of her small stature. "Is there any way you can get her here sooner…? Is there someone who can come sooner…? How experienced is she…? And you don't need her…? When can she be here…?" She looked toward Vincent. "But no one today…? That'll have to do. Just get her here as soon as you can. Thank you. You will be well compensated."

Lorraine hung up the phone, sat in her chair and looked toward Vincent, who was leaning against the door. "All my healers went down to North Carolina for a ritual. They can't spare anyone until this afternoon. Lilly will be here at sunrise. It's the best I can do."

Vincent stared at her fuming. "You said you had someone here."

Lorraine leaned back in her chair, placed her feet on the desk and her hands behind her head. The robe slid open revealing every inch of her pale petite body. Vincent felt himself reacting, knowing what she was capable of despite her size. "I told you I <u>thought</u> I could have someone here. And I really thought I could Vincent, love. I've been trying since you called."

Vincent's eyes traced the line of her body from the crook of her elbow down her torso to her tight thighs. She had shaved recently. Catching the ogle, Lorraine slowly drew her hand down her body to her thigh, showing off her manicured nails. The blood red polish was a sharp contrast to her ghostly white skin. Transfixed, Vincent's eyes stayed on her hand as it traveled back up her thigh. He shook his head to clear it then realized the trail of red he was hallucinating was actually her blood. Her fingers were digging hard enough into her skin to pierce the flesh and draw blood. He was by her side in an instant, kneeling by her thigh, waiting for permission. He was highly agitated, and very hungry. He wanted, no, needed blood.

Lorraine caressed his soft blond hair with one hand, then wrapped her fingers in his hair, and pulled his head back. The other hand went to her thigh. She dipped her middle finger into her blood then touched her finger to his lips, and traced his flesh with her finger. She healed herself, to stop the blood flow. Her thigh was still streaked with blood. She lowered her feet to the floor, and turned to the side as she did so. She placed her feet to each side of him, and scoot forward to trap him between her legs. Even though on his knees, as tall as he was, his head reached her breasts.

Vincent allowed her actions, as his nostrils filled with the smell of her blood. He enjoyed playing the submissive with her. It had always been the same between them. He could over power her, take what he wanted and leave her whimpering for more, but had no desire to do so. Since their first encounter, she held the dominant position. After nearly three hundred years, neither felt the need to change roles. The massive vampire allowed the diminutive woman to do as she pleased, as his wants and desires grew.

Lorraine leaned forward and brought his head toward her lips. She licked his lips clean, then dipped her tongue into his mouth, and ran her tongue against his. He took in a shaky breath and let it out in a growl. She heard his craving in the rumble and threw her head back to laugh. It had been a long time since she brought him to this level. She had had to drain a good deal of his blood in order to get him to this point, but it was worth it. And she wasn't even trying. She smiled as she bent forward to kiss him.

Vincent placed his hands on her thighs, feeling the tackiness of the blood on his left hand. The kiss grew more intense as she bared her teeth and bit his tongue. As the blood flowed into their mouths, his hands moved to her back to pull her out of the chair. He stood and set her on the desk. Her arms went around his neck to tighten the gap between them. She continued to suck on his bleeding tongue. He plunged one hand into her red tresses and pulled her head away from his. He healed the wound and glowered at her.

"Haven't you taken enough?" He could feel his control slipping. If she didn't satisfy at least one desire soon, he could become ornery.

"Vincent, love. You forget your place." There was a hard edge to her teasing tone.

"And you, lady sire, forget my nature." He was caressing the line of her breast, loving the feel of her soft skin, wishing she were warm. He closed his eyes, tried to pull away; realized she wasn't letting him.

She caught the look in his eye, not really surprised. They had been in this situation before, he always tried to run; she never let him. "Vincent? Why pull away? Let your desires loose upon me. At least I can take it."

"You're not whom I wish to be with." He reached around to pry her hands loose.

"She's quite the human, to keep my favorite from my bed." She moved her hands from his head to the waistline of his pants.

He ground his teeth, trying to control himself. He covered her hands with his, stopping her questing fingers. "Sire, release me."

"No." Her tone was once again hard.

"Lorraine-" He tried to pull her hands free. She wouldn't allow it.

She pulled him forward, snaking one hand up his chest to his head. Tangling her hand in his hair, she pulled his ear to her mouth. "You have a whole night here before you can leave Vincent, and I have a present for you. Something we haven't done in a long, long time. Do you wish to see it, or do you wish to spend the rest of the night hiding in your room, sulking because you can't have your human?"

Vincent pulled back a little, not wanting to give her a chance to bite his neck. His mind was turning in circles. There were many things they hadn't done in a long time. Ravenous and now rather curious, he picked Lorraine off the desk and set her on her feet. Reaching around her he set her robe to rights and tied it shut.

"All right, love. Show me what you have. But make it quick, I'm hungry and you haven't offered me dinner yet."

"I will." Her voice was slightly melodious. She turned and headed for the door, leaving him to stare at her back. He was right behind her as she opened the door. She was accosted as soon as she stepped out the door.

"Lorraine. You were supposed to speak with me next. This," the smaller man gave Vincent a sideways glare, "whelp had the audacity to step in front of me and take my place."

"Vincent is my child and is older than you by decades, Morton. Take your complaints to Max. He'll listen to your prattling; I'm bored with it.

The rest of you, please return tomorrow; I have other things to take care of tonight."

"Lorraine. There are things we must discuss." This was coming from an older vampire, one Vincent recognized.

Her voice was kinder when talking to this one. "Rowland, please, I know your grievances. I can address them tomorrow. Vincent is here for one night, and as I told you when he called, I will have my fun with him. It's been a long time since I've seen him, and I don't want to argue about it. Go about your duties and I'll see you again tomorrow night after he leaves."

Rowland seemed to shrink back into himself, unhappy with the situation. All Lorraine's children were aware Vincent was her favorite. All who lived near her were happier when he wasn't around. Rowland gave Vincent a nasty look but bowed to his sire and left. Morton stayed glaring, and the third vampire left without a word. Lorraine gave Morton a tempting look as she took Vincent's hand and led him away to her dungeon. Morton glared after them until he was led to the door by two of Lorraine's humans.

ABOUT THE AUTHOR

Cat Stark was raised in California and now lives in Illinois with her fiancé. She has finished 19 novels and has more than 30 unfinished works in progress. She has published a novel and a short story collection. The Elven Prince and Enter the Maze can both be found on Amazon. Book two of The Grey House Trilogy should be released within a year.

Find her here:

catstark.com
@catstarkwriter
facebook.com/catstarkwriter/

Made in the USA
Middletown, DE
18 September 2024

60548811R00104